FINDING ME

By: Angeline Larson

Published: ALH Books 2025
Cover Design: Angeline Larson 2025

ISBN: 979-8-9985287-0-5 (paperback)
        979-8-9985287-1-2 (hardcover)

To my mother – you deserve a better dedication than the one I gave you before. You've taught me to be brave, independent and fierce. None of my books would have become a reality if not for your faith in me and continued support.

Disclaimer

The content in this book is meant for mature audiences only and it delves into some serious subject matter that might be a bit too much for some to handle.

This book, and the events that transpire in it, are a pure work of fiction and are not intended to represent anyone's personal struggles or experiences. The characters and events in this book are not based on any actual persons or events. Any errors in medical terminology or processes are not intentional and grace is requested for such mistakes.

Please understand that the author is not making any statements regarding mental health or therapy. Depression, grief and physical harm to one's body are serious matters and help should be sought if anyone is experiencing thoughts of self-harm.

Readers, if you identify with the struggles the main character faces in this book and have engaged in some of the same destructive behavior please seek out assistance. No one is ever truly alone. All it takes is a single phone call....

National Suicide Prevention Hotline 1-800-273-8255(TALK)

or dial 988

Note to the Reader

This is one book from a connected series. The books do not have to be read in a particular order, and the reader does not have to read the other books to understand the events in each book.

However, please understand that not every book will visit each connected scene in detail if that scene was a focal point in another book. Each book is told form a different perspective, and the scenes have different levels of impact on the characters. That is why some scenes may seem like they are being overlooked or shortened. This was done intentionally.

Please be advised that each book may contain subjects that are of an emotional nature, include foul language, have descriptions of sexual contact, discuss substance abuse, and make references to or include descriptions of harmful acts. This book is recommended for mature audiences.

Each character is their own person, with their own perspective, and these books act as a telling of the interconnections that these characters have throughout their lives. These are flawed characters, with issues that may or may not be resolved. These are stories about life and the people who do their best to navigate it.

This particular book is Stacey's story and takes place after many of the events in the other books. It is not necessary to read the other books to understand and enjoy Stacey's story. Caution – Stacey is not the hero in this story.

And now,

Finding Me.

THE START, OR THE END

The weight on my chest is crushing me and I can't breathe. I throw the covers off of me and desperately rush to the bathroom, gulping in huge lungfuls of air as I stumble through the unfamiliar room. Despite being in the later part of a panic attack I manage to be cognizant enough to close the door before I turn on the bright fluorescent lights. My eyes blink rapidly through the blinding lights and I lean over the sink, thinking I'm about to vomit.

I don't.

Quickly, I turn on the sink and splash my face with handfuls of ice-cold water. The chilly feeling brings me back to the present and out of the panic my dreams had brought forth. It had been many years since I had woken in such a state, and I give myself a mental high five for my quick response. In the past I would have resorted to other means of coping.

My gaze wanders over to the scars on my inner thighs. The fluorescent lights of this hotel bathroom are not very flattering to begin with, but they somehow manage to accentuate the scars I had placed on my body during my adolescence. It is then I remember that I am still very naked. I look around until I find the plush white towels of hotel bathrooms and somehow manage to fit my middle-

1

aged fluffy body into the poor excuse for a body towel. It still baffled me why hotels had never picked up on the oversize towel trend that beaches seemed to have a handle on.

Once I feel I've positioned the towel sufficiently I turn back to the sink that is still on and cup my hands under the water once again. Intending to drink some water it takes me a moment before I see the complimentary cups sitting on the counter beside a small coffee maker. Dropping the water in my cupped hand, I reach out and remove the plastic wrap from the paper cup. I fill it with water, turn off the sink and sit on the edge of the bathtub. I gulp down the water and practice the breathing techniques I had learned all those years ago, when I had finally sought help for the panic attacks.

I was too young then to know what they were or why I was experiencing them. Too young to ask for help before resorting to harmful methods of coping. I trace the lines of my scars and tilt my head slightly in thought. Is it wrong that I find the scars beautiful?

It probably is.

I shouldn't find beauty in the physical representation of the pain of my childhood. There is something twisted inside me that I sometimes miss the feeling of creating new scars. My first therapist told me I cut myself because I was hurting. My second therapist said I had an addiction that I felt needed to be quenched. Maybe they were both right. I hadn't really listened to either one of them. It wasn't because of them I stopped doing it. And I didn't stop for me either.

I stopped for him. I stopped because he had asked me to.

Maybe that is the reason I now I find myself in my current predicament. I had been doing things for others for so long that I didn't even know what I wanted anymore.

Deep in thought, I stand and quietly open the bathroom door a crack. Careful to not let out too much light I peek out into the room on the other side of the door. It's dark but the shades are open and the lights from the parking lot provide enough glow for me to see the figure sleeping on the bed.

There were way too many pillows on that bed, and they were all flat.

How often do hotels change out their pillows anyway?

Shaking my head, I clear my thoughts of pillows and focus instead on the sleeping form. He snores slightly and then turns his body, a response to the noise he had just released. I smile slightly at this because he doesn't think he snores. He does.

Like my scars, is it also wrong that I find beauty in this? He is not mine and I am not his. At least, not like how I should be. I look down at my left hand and the solid band that encompasses my finger. Out of habit I begin to use my thumb to twirl it. I had noticed this practice a few years ago but it took me longer to discover that I only did it when I was having doubts or desires that I shouldn't have. One of those desires is now quietly snoring in a hotel bed that I had just escaped from due to a dream induced panic attack.

In the beginning, I had removed the ring, foolishly thinking that if I kept it hidden, I too could hide from reality before me.

After closing the bathroom door, I turn back to the sink and look deeply at the reflection staring back at me. I don't recognize this face. I know it's me but at the same time it doesn't feel like me.

I think I have been slowly disappearing over the years. It happened gradually and by the time the metamorphosis had been complete it was too late to turn back the clock. I touch the lines on my face, my cheeks, and the skin that had begun to loosen in my thirties. I don't even want to think about the extra pounds that had managed to desperately cling to my body despite the many diets I had gone on.

This face, this body, this life was not mine.

But it was.

And I hated it.

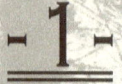

<u>Five Months Earlier...</u>

"Mrs. McNill, you can't go in there. Mrs. McNill, please let me announce your visit," the stodgy receptionist tries to get out of her chair and hurry to block my entrance, but she was too busy dusting the powder off her hands from the donut she had been eating to worry about silly things like phone cords and office supplies. She becomes tangled in the mess and has to unwrap before she can reach me.

"Really Gladys. We go through this every time. Don't you know me better by now," I say and pull down the handle on the office door, letting myself in despite the cries coming from behind me. The office occupant knows it's me before I even say a word.

"Hello again Mrs. McNill," the disembodied voice says from behind the massive leather desk chair.

Every time I see that stupid chair I can't help but snicker. It really is a ridiculous chair and not at all complimentary to the rest of the décor in the office. Pastels do not go well with poop leather. That is what I have so lovingly named the chair – the poop chair. My host does not care for the name but it doesn't matter because I like it.

"Mrs. McNill?" I laugh. The chair isn't the only ridiculous thing in this room today. "I've seen you naked," I say and not so gently plop down in the chair across from the desk and the hideously famous poop chair.

The poop chair swivels around, and I am met with a scowling

face that is clearly not pleased with my presence. I should probably apologize for busting in but I don't. Instead, I smirk and lean forward to grab a carrot slice off the plate that sits on the desk. I knew she was at lunch right now and wasn't seeing any clients. It wasn't like I interrupted a session or anything. I wasn't a heathen after all.

"You really should consider redecorating," I say as I munch on the carrot that isn't mine. A set of eyes narrow at me before a hand reaches forward and tears the carrot from my grasp.

"Somebody is hangry," I say and hold up my hands.

"No. Somebody is annoyed. We talked about this Stacey. You promised me you wouldn't barge in like this again," Rachel, the poop chair occupant, says.

"No. I promised I wouldn't barge in while you were in session again, and I didn't," I say with a flourish. "That is progress, and you should praise me for it."

So, maybe I had been a heathen in the past, but I was working on it and my attempt at self-improvement should be recognized.

"I will not reward stupidity and stubbornness," Rachel says and throws my-her- half eaten carrot back onto the plate.

"Why so glum, chum?" I ask and earn another scowl. I think Rachel even growls, like actually growls at me.

"Why are you interrupting the one free hour I have during my day?" Rachel asks.

"Hour? Puhlease, you take the longest lunch breaks of any doctor I know."

"Stacey?"

"Okay, okay," I say because it's clear I have hit a nerve with her today. "Is everything alright with Jules? The kids?" I ask, trying to buy me some time before we dive right into things.

"Stop stalling," Rachel deadpans. She knows me too well. She is my oldest friend after all. She had known me before...well, before it all.

5

"I can't just visit my friend on her lunch *hour*?" I joke which only earns me another tight-lipped scowl.

"Be careful, your face might get stuck that way," I chide and abruptly stand from my chair. I wander around the office for like a second before Rachel sighs and demands I answer her previous query.

"I'm having those thoughts again, okay," I finally admit.

To my friend's credit her face softens, and she leans forward in her chair, her attention fully on me, concern in every muscle. She gestures to the chair I had just vacated, and I roll my eyes. She is no longer my friend now but the professional. Still, I sit back down.

"For how long now?" Rachel asks, her hands folded on her desk.

I shrug.

"Stacey," she says sternly.

"A couple of months."

"Have you reacted?"

I laugh because only Rachel would pose the question in that manner. *Had I reacted?*

"Describe reacted?" She doesn't because we both know what she is talking about.

"No. I haven't reacted. That is why I am here, so I don't react."

Rachel nods, unfolds her hands, and then folds them again. She is processing. My friend likes to process things before commenting on them. I should probably be more like her. If I was maybe I wouldn't be seeking her out now.

"I can recommend"-

"No!" I cut her off. I know what she is about to say because this is how it played out the last time I came to her. I had done as she had asked then but I knew now what had worked in the past would no longer work. Things are different now. I am different now.

"Stacey, you can't be a patient of mine. We have a personal relationship and it would breach all forms of ethics protocol in my field. I could lose my license," she states. It's the same argument she

6

gave me last time. Last time I conceded because I too knew the dangers of personal relationships with patients. The last thing I ever wanted to do was put my friend in jeopardy, but things were different this time. I didn't need a therapist; I needed a friend…that had formal training.

"Don't you see, that is why I came during your lunch hour? I'm not a patient. I'm just a friend, visiting another friend that happens to be a psychologist." I smirk at her because it's brilliant. She does not return my feelings to my brilliant solution to our current predicament.

"I can't."

"But you can."

"No, I can't," she says and stands from the poop chair. Rolling my eyes I turn so I can follow her movements. She is walking to the door, opening it so she can dismiss me. I can't allow that to happen.

"I lied!" I blurt out.

"What?" she asks me, her hand stalled on the handle.

"I reacted. But not in the way you think." It works because Rachel abandons the door to return to her poop chair.

God, I hated that chair.

"What did you do?" she asks.

"Brace yourself, friend, because it's a doosey."

"Why don't you just tell me what it is?"

"I can't. Not yet. It requires back story," I say and throw my legs over one arm of the chair I'm sitting in. Rachel squints at me but she does not protest.

"Why do I have a feeling my lunch hours have been overtaken?"

I grin at Rachel because she knows me so well. Still, she isn't kicking me out and I take that as my opening.

"I should probably start at the beginning," I say.

"I wouldn't expect anything less," Rachel comments and she listens as I go back to when it all began. Back to when I started to lose myself.

7

-2-

<u>Drifting Away</u>

I was fifteen when he got sick and I was fifteen when he died. Within a five-month span my father went from a vibrant, active parent to a sunken corpse. Cancer is relentless in its pursuit to produce faster than healthy cells. Eventually the cancer cells become so vast that they corrupt the healthy cells and all that is left is a mutation of what is meant to be. That is how I would describe what happened to my father. He mutated and became so unrecognizable to everyone around him.

I am ashamed to admit that I was afraid of the man he had become. I remembered him as strong and handsome but in the end, he was bedridden, bald and thin beyond belief. He couldn't keep anything down because the chemotherapy was destroying whatever parts of him hadn't been touched by the cancer, and there weren't many. It had been my mother that had wanted him to do the chemo. I remember my father asking what was the point? The doctors had provided his diagnosis – stage four colorectal cancer. My father had roughly a ten percent chance of surviving his cancer. Father had never been a betting man and in the end, he didn't take any chances.

Cancer didn't kill my father.

My father died by his own hands.

I guess he had lived his life the way he wanted, and he made sure he died the same way – on his terms.

Fuck cancer!

Yep, my father gave a big fuck you to cancer and overdosed on his medication instead. He left a note. It was actually a pretty nice note.

He said he loved me and my mother. He said he was sorry that he had to do things this way but he didn't want us to remember him like that. His letter said he wanted us to remember him like he was when he was alive not when he was dying. He was right. I had already started to think about him in terms of pre and post cancer. There was the father I had before and the father I had after he got sick.

Before cancer he would hug me and do things with me. We were always going on some new adventure like skydiving or box car racing. He chased life, the next big thrill, and I was always by his side.

After cancer his biggest thrill was watching the birds outside his window get into a fight. Eventually he even stopped watching the birds and insisted the curtains remain closed. He said the sun hurt his eyes, but I knew better. It was my first experience witnessing defeat.

Witnessing his defeat.

Before cancer he would run daily. He was active, fit and an avid health nut. He ate all the right things and didn't poison his body with things like energy drinks and sugar.

After cancer he rarely ate and allowed poison to be pumped straight into his veins in order to give his wife some semblance of hope. He did it for us because after cancer he hadn't seen the need to hold out false hope.

I wondered if he had made his decision the day he had received his diagnosis or had he decided to end his life later. The first round of chemo didn't work. Mom wanted to try again but Dad didn't. They argued about it and eventually he said he would try again.

He was dead three days later.

Maybe he decided to kill himself after he argued with my mother about trying another foolish last-ditch effort to save his life. To save our family.

Or maybe he had decided to kill himself after I told him things would be better off without the cancer. I hadn't actually meant things would be better off without him. I just meant that cancer was causing his sickness and causing my parents to fight. Our lives had been uprooted by cancer, and I was tired of being strong all the time. So, in a weakened moment, I told my father our lives would be better off if the cancer was gone.

Two days later he was dead.

Then again, it could have also been the news he had gotten from his oncologist. Not only had the chemo not worked but the cancer had spread. My father had been right all along. There really was no point fighting cancer because in the end, it always won.

He was dead the very next day.

As for me, I didn't start to lose myself right away. It wasn't like I had an immediate break from reality and morphed into a completely different person. The changes were far more subtle. So subtle in fact that my own mother never noticed them.

Like my father I stopped chasing the next big adventure. There were no adventures I wanted to discover if I couldn't have him beside me. I pushed away friends that had been in my life since I was little. Friends I once thought I couldn't live without. I stopped talking to my mother about things that really mattered. I still gave just enough to keep her from wondering but I often told half-truths or cleverly worded platitudes. My grades didn't plummet overnight. They just slowly dipped downward, and I was able to disguise it as a simple misunderstanding. So, I had to repeat a grade, big deal.

I'm not sure when the thought came to me, but I do remember thinking that pain is life. My father had rejected the pain and ended his life. He couldn't handle the pain anymore and I felt he was weaker for it. I was determined not to be like him. I would embrace the pain. I would live. So, I picked up the razor that first time and

10

after some initial hesitation I pushed it into my skin. Despite my failing grades I was a clever little self-mutilator. I only did it to my inner thighs because no one ever saw that part of my body. I always made sure I had on clothes that protected that area from prying eyes, and I was able to keep it hidden for two years before I was discovered.

Those two years are a blur of tears, blood, metal, and ecstasy. I found pleasure in the pain and was captivated by the sight of my blood dripping from the cuts. I would often watch the trail of the blood as it ran down my legs. I made sure I only used that razor when things were just too much for me. I wasn't stupid and I knew what I was doing was dangerous. I researched the parts of my body I needed to avoid and just how deep the cuts could go before I sliced into a life-giving artery. My goal had never been to die but to experience life and pain was life.

I learned many things from my father before he killed himself. I knew how to throw a decent curve ball. I knew how to rig a parachute. I knew which carbohydrates were good and which were bad. I knew that sometimes love wasn't enough to make people stay. I also knew that I didn't want to die.

The razor became my lifeline and I brandished it against my skin to prove to myself, to prove to my father, that I wasn't like him.

I wasn't a quitter. I would live through the pain no matter how much blood I spilled.

-3-

Recognition

After retelling the story of my father and the origins of my cutting addiction?therapy?coping?malfunction?disorder? I waited for Rachel to react. Typically, in the past my previous therapists would have one of two responses:

1. They would rest their chin on their folded fingers and purse their lips, pretending to be in thought about what I had just revealed

2. They would immediately show some form of empathy in an attempt to connect with me.

Both reactions became predictable and trite to me. What did they possibly have to think about? It was obvious I had issues since I was seeking them out to begin with. And unless they were closet cutters the empathy was a complete fabrication designed to garner my trust. Both were a manipulation, and I had developed a distaste for such reactions to my past.

Rachel, on the other hand, was not my therapist. A point she kept reminding me of on a regular basis. In fact, some days she would tell me she needed a break from being my friend because I was being too pushy. I never held it against her. My own family told me I had a tendency to *"be too much"*. Whatever that meant.

"Well? Aren't you going to say something?" I finally ask when Rachel continues to remain silent and seated in the chair the color of fecal matter.

12

Rachel groans, throws her head back against the chair and looks up to the ceiling. She raises her arms and holds her hands up, palms skyward. I tilt my head and look up at the ceiling with her. A few of the tiles needed to be replaced. They were looking a little yellow, but this was hardly the time to be contemplating tile repairs.

"What have I done to offend you? Tell me, please, and I will correct it," Rachel calls to the tiles.

I turn back to her and narrow my eyes.

"Who are you talking to?" I ask.

"God. The universe. Whoever is out there listening to my cries for help," she replies and finally looks at me.

Needless to say, I am not amused.

"I am hurting over here Rachel. You are supposed to be my friend and after I tell you about a traumatizing event in my life you ask the heavens why they are punishing you? Listening to me in my time of need is that terrible? Maybe you would prefer it if I just went home and sliced my wrists. That way you won't have to suffer anymore," I say and lean forward in my chair, my gaze penetrating my best friend's wall.

"Stop the bullshit."

Okay, maybe I didn't penetrate her wall at all.

"You forget that I was there for all of that. I witnessed your descent. And suicide isn't a joke so stop talking like that right now. You aren't convincing me to entertain this little drama by poking fun at my profession," Rachel finally gets out of the post flatulence chair to come around the desk. She leans against the edge of the desk and takes my hands in hers.

"I love you. Probably more than I should given what a terrible shit you are, but I can't keep doing this with you. If you want to resume your therapy, then I recommend you go back to Dr. Perkins. You saw him for three years, the longest of anyone, so you obviously liked something about him. Call him."

Rachel is still grasping my hands, and she is looking at me with

13

deep concern. She really is a good friend, and she isn't wrong. I can be pretty shitty. In fact, I'm about to do something really shitty at this moment.

"I slept with him," I say, and she immediately drops my hands. Her body recoils from me and she looks upon me with complete shock. I let that sink in for a minute before I burst out laughing.

"You should see your face right now. You look like I killed your puppy," I laugh.

"Stacey, this isn't funny. Dr. Perkins violated so many protocols by engaging in a sexual relationship with you. If he did this with you who knows how many times he's violated APA's codes," Rachel says. I can tell she has found her next cause, and it is up to me to keep her from going off the rails.

"Oh, relax. I didn't *actually* sleep with him. There's no need to notify the American Psychological Association."

Rachel looks at me out of the corner of her eye, her lips pursed. She knows what is coming because, as she said, she has been there since the beginning. She knows me backwards and forwards.

"I thought about it though. I dreamt about it too and that is why I had to stop seeing him. You know that whole inference thing," I say because I know my 'mistake' will piss her off.

"Transference," she replies tersely. *Right on cue.* She likes to think I make fun of her profession because she isn't a 'real' doctor like me, but she's mistaken. I make fun of her profession because it pisses her off and an angry Rachel makes me laugh.

See – a shitty person.

"Bottom line, you're stuck with me kid so get used to it. I'm on the edge here and if you turn me away now who knows what might happen," I say and swing my legs off the arm of the chair and stand up.

"I can't tell anymore when you are serious or when you are joking," Rachel says from behind me.

"Gotta keep 'em on their toes or they lose interest," I say,

14

snapping my fingers and smirking at her. I'm about to open the office door and make my exit when Rachel gets the last word in.

"The only one that has ever lost interest in you is you."

My 'session' with Rachel leaves a bitter taste in my mouth. I usually made it a point to always get the last word in a conversation because I never wanted to walk away on somebody else's terms. My family treated it like some strange quirk, and they laughed it off; when they weren't frustrated by it. It had never bothered my husband because he was just so laid back. There were times I wondered if anything ever bothered him. But Rachel recognized my desire to always have the last word as just another form of control. In other words, I never felt like I was in control so by walking away from a conversation with the last thought I was ensuring control of the situation. I had promptly told her that her theory was hogwash. She shrugged me off and I oinked at her. Not exactly my most shining moment but at least I got the last 'word'; even if it was a farm animal sound. Control maintained.

Currently, I am struggling to find my balance again because I had been so stunned by Rachel's parting words that I hadn't responded. Instead, I left her office after blinking at her a couple of times. I didn't even give my customary middle finger gesture to Gladys as I left the reception area.

Gladys and I had a great relationship. I annoyed her and she annoyed me, and we both didn't try to hide our dislike for the other. I gave her the middle finger as a token of our affection and in return she would hang up on me whenever I called the office. Her cu de gras was when she 'mistakenly' sent my invitation to Rachel's wedding to South Africa. In my defense I hadn't started the middle finger wave until after that incident. Prior to that I simply called her by the wrong name. She made sure I remembered her name though and I made sure I waved goodbye every time I left the office.

I was reeling from Rachel's words that I hadn't remembered to wave goodbye to Gladys. I imagine I left her stunned and hopefully a bit disappointed that I had forgotten about her. She really was forgettable but that wasn't my fault. She was just so beige. Which is a step up from the poop chair but not by much.

Now I'm back at the hospital, listening to my nurse prattle on about our next patient. Maybe I shouldn't say prattle. That sounds a bit insensitive but after nearly twenty years of the same scene day in and day out the constant drone of my nurse's voices often blended together and became prattle. I picture her head is guillotined off and all I can see is her bottom torso, much like Charlie Brown's teacher.

Waa waa waa.

Oh, crap, she's telling me something important.

"Dr. Levy wanted you to examine his patient because her blood work came back a little concerning and he felt your expertise could shed some further light," Chastity says as she hands me the patient's file.

I glance down at her name tag and shudder. If my parents had given me that name I would not proudly display it upon my breast. What were they thinking? My thoughts drift to poor teenage Chastity making her way through the rough halls of high school.

She was either a complete slut or the consummate virgin. With a name like Chastity there simply was no in between. I'm not judging. Nothing wrong with a healthy sex life, or no sex life, but there is something wrong with setting your child up for failure.

Poor Chastity.

"Dr. Levy wanted to lighten his case load and figured flattery would grease the wheels. This has nothing to do with his respect of my skills and more to do with the golf trip he has planned for next week. Last thing he wants now is a complicated case. Let's see," I say and flip through the chart.

16

I quickly glance over the background information. 66-year-old Caucasian female, no family history of heart disease, cancer or other major events. She is currently taking some medication for high cholesterol, but the dosage is manageable and could even be discontinued through diet changes. I spend more time examining the blood work results that Dr. Levy is so 'concerned' about. Other than a slightly elevated white blood cell count and a marginally low red blood cell count her CBC was unremarkable. Her LFT, or liver function test, had me re-examining the CBC. According to the LFT her ALT and AST levels were elevated. I can see why Dr. Levy had been concerned but when I flip through the chart for the follow-up tests that are typically ordered before a patient is referred to me, I discover that none are present.

Slowly, I lower the chart and glare at my nurse. Chastity is already looking contrite and apologetic. She's worked with me enough to know that I am not going to be pleased with her.

"I know, I know. I tried to call Dr. Levy's head nurse, but they kept telling me both her and Dr. Levy were unreachable. What was I supposed to do? Send the patient away? She was already here," Chastity releases in a mad rush, her cheeks turning red.

Great, I've made the slut/virgin nervous.

"Doctors. That is what is wrong with the medical profession," I mutter.

"Ma'am?" Chastity asks timidly. Like a mouse.

Definitely a virgin.

"Nothing. I'm going to need a second LFT to confirm these results. Coag panel, bilirubin, LDH, the whole she-bang. And get a stool and urine sample. Dr. Levy sent her our way, so let's give her the A-list treatment. Let's do this," I say and enter the room my new patient has been placed in.

"Good afternoon, Ms...," my voice trails off as I once again flip through the chart to find the patient's name, "Farley. My name is Dr. McNill. I'm going to"-

17

"Stacey?" A kind voice says from within the room, and I look up for the first time since entering.

Staring back at me are two people I had known for years. In fact, my brother-in-law considered them family, and they were at every family gathering since my stepsister had married Brad nearly thirteen years ago.

"Reyann? Jeff?" I don't know why I posed it as a question. It was very clearly Reyann and Jeff before me. Reyann was sitting on the exam table, smiling at me. She looked happy to see me but Jeff, on the other hand, was scowling at me something fierce.

"Jeff, it's Stacey. You remember her? Bradley's sister-in-law," Reyann says and slaps Jeff's chest with the back of her hand.

Jeff instinctively moves a hand to the area his mother had just tapped, and I watch as he scratches it like something other than his mother's hand was irritating him. He continues to glare at me as he says, "I remember."

I quickly rack my brain trying to identify the thing I said or did in the past to bring such a look of disgust to his face, but I can't seem to recall anything. My shittyness tended to blend together over the years that I often lost track of how I had offended people. Just as quickly as I try to identify the offense, I brush it aside and get back to the task at hand.

"Hello, Reyann. Jeff," I match his scowl because two can play this game, "I wish I could say it is nice to see you, but it seems you are here due to some test results Dr. Levy was concerned about. I've gone over the results and unfortunately, they don't provide enough details to adequately identify what is ailing you. What originally brought you to see Dr. Levy?" I move towards Reyann and out of the direct line of sight of Jeff, since his death glare is starting to piss me off.

"He did," Reyann says and points at Jeff standing behind her. Finally, his gaze leaves me and goes to his mother. His face softens and I decide that I am not imagining the hostility emanating from

18

him in waves.

"You've been eating less and getting tired more," Jeff states.

"Okay. Both are normal occurrences in woman of advanced age," I say and earn another death glare from Jeff.

"See. I told you there was nothing to worry about. And I will forgive you for that advanced age comment because you are family," Reyann says to me, still smiling.

I'm a bit taken aback by her description of me as family because even though she is always present at family events I never once equated this woman as a family member of mine. She was always Brad's family. Their relationship was actually quite strange to me.

They weren't related in any way and in fact had only met because Brad started working for Reyann when he was sixteen. Over the years they had developed a strong friendship and both Reyann and Jeff had been showing up ever since. I knew Reyann had a second son, but I couldn't recall his name or a face. Jeff was the only one that ever accompanied Reyann. Right now, however, I am wishing the other son had chaperoned his mother today.

"Forgive me, I meant no offense. It is common for a woman's appetite to decrease as they age. As for sleeping, every person needs more sleep as they age. This alone isn't cause for concern," I state, and Reyann looks back at her son triumphantly.

"Well, that's that. Let's go," Reyann says and starts to move off the exam table.

"She passed out yesterday. She was talking to me and then she just collapsed," Jeff blurts and glares down at his mother. His stare causes her to stop her movements.

I look back to Reyann, the actual patient, and resume the exam. "Is this true?"

"Yes, but it was really hot out yesterday and I had been working in the garden all day. It was just heat exhaustion. I needed to drink more water. I was fine later," Reyann says and uses her hand to brush aside the air, effectively dismissing the incident as insignificant.

"Have you ever fainted before?"

"Sure," Reyann says, also dismissively.

"How many times have you fainted in the last six months?" I ask.

This time Reyann hesitates. I notice how her eyes shift slightly towards Jeff, and I recognize the gesture for what it is. She doesn't want to talk about this in front of her son.

"Chastity, why don't you take Mr. Farley,"-

"Collins," Jeff corrects me.

"Mr. Collins," I resume talking as if his interruption didn't faze me, "to the waiting area and discuss the emergency contact forms with him."

All bullshit.

There were emergency contact forms, but the patients filled them out. Over the years I had developed this rouse with my nurses when we had to distance what I called a 'helicopter' from a patient. The helicopter was a person that was too involved in my patient's medical affairs when they had no right to be. Often times my patients were too afraid to ask their family member to leave the room. This fear either stemmed out of a desire not to offend or because the family member held all the control. Either way, my nurses and I were equipped to handle these cases.

"I'm sure you can explain the forms to me later, after this," Jeff says and crosses his arms over his chest. The death glare is back.

"Jeff, do as the doctor says," Reyann tells her son. "I'll be fine." She pats his arm and his rigidness relaxes. He nods his head at his mother and follows the chatty Chastity out of the room.

Chatty Chastity. I liked that.

"How many fainting spells have you had lately?" I repeat once we are alone.

"Probably ten in the last six months," Reyann admits.

"Are you taking any medication that you haven't disclosed?"

20

"No. I told the truth on the forms," Reyann adamantly declares.

"Very well. Jeff said you haven't been eating as much."

"I eat. I just have a hard time keeping it down is all."

Reyann is avoiding my eyes, and I also recognize this behavior. She is ashamed that she has to reveal all this because she hasn't sought treatment before. Many of my patients tended to blame themselves when they sought help late. It wasn't their fault. After all, who goes around thinking that they are sick or that they might die? Human behavior tends to avoid seeking out death and the mind can explain away anything it wishes to suppress.

"Reyann, I'm not judging you. I just want to have all the facts, so I know what to look for. How long has the vomiting been occurring?"

For the next twenty minutes I ask her questions, and she answers them. I make notes, ask follow-up questions and mentally check off boxes as I eliminate possible causes. I conduct a physical exam and notice when she winces at my touch as I palpate her lower abdomen. In the end, I determine that Reyann is going to need more advanced testing than I had originally thought. Perhaps Dr. Levy hadn't been thinking about golf after all when he referred Reyann to me.

As I'm finishing up my notes Reyann speaks softly from the exam table. I had just concluded my physical examination of her and was documenting it when she spoke.

"Please forgive Jeff for his rudeness earlier. He's just worried about me," she says.

I pause my notetaking to give a small sweeping gesture with my hand to let her know it isn't a big deal. Frankly, I could care less about Mr. *Collins* and his bad attitude. It was of no consequence to me.

"His father left us when the boys were still little. We divorced and I went back to my maiden name. Jeff was never exactly thrilled that we had different last names. After all these years it is still a sore spot," Reyann says.

It's nervous chatter and I stop my writing to reassure her wandering thoughts. This too was a common occurrence with my patients.

"We'll know more once we get the tests results. Chastity will take the blood tests, and she'll escort you down to radiology. I'm going to request they conduct the ultrasound today. You might have to wait for a bit until they have an opening but if you decide to wait for a later date, it could be weeks before you get an appointment," I state.

Reyann nods but her gaze is distant. Sighing, I put her chart down and go to her. Standing before her I take one of her hands and her gaze slowly meets mine.

"Whatever it is, we'll face it together," I say.

I don't know why I said it. In fact, I shouldn't have said it. Immediately my thoughts harken back to my 'session' with Rachel and our conversation regarding treating personal attachments. To me, Reyann isn't family and therefore I am not breaching any protocol. However, my statement is very telling. I can't promise her that. I can't promise this woman anything other than that I will do my job to the best of my ability. Still, I don't backtrack.

"Thank you. I trust you," Reyann says and squeezes my hand.

I quickly release her hand and go to the door. This is becoming too heavy for me and I need to end the appointment.

"I'm gonna have Chastity bring your son back in. We are finished here so you can go with Chastity, and she'll explain the rest," I say.

As I'm opening the door a burly figure steps inside and practically pushes me out of the way. I stumble back and am about to say what I think about this aggressive presence when I realize it is Jeff, followed quickly by an apologetic Chastity. I am starting to hate her name as much as Rachel's fecal chair.

"Mom, are you alright," Jeff goes directly to her, all hint of aggression disappearing.

"I'm perfectly fine but you owe the doctor an apology," Reyann scolds her son.

"Reyann, it's fi-,"

"She's not a doctor," Jeff interrupts me.

"Excuse me?" Now, I am most definitely not fine.

"Not a good one anyway. I've already told the nurse I want another doctor for you," Jeff continues to ignore me and speak only to his mother.

I cast an accusatory glance at Chastity. She has the decency to look sheepish. Her cheeks are red again.

Uggh. I need a new nurse.

"Mr. Collins, I assure you my reputation-," once again I am interrupted by the bear known as Jeff Collins.

"I don't give a damn about your reputation! You didn't even know her name when you walked in the door. I won't allow you to treat my mother," Jeff says. He has since turned towards me, hostility and rage directed right at me.

I take a step forward to defend myself because, well, I feel like I need to. He can question my decency as a human being all day long but the moment he questions my ability as a doctor is the moment I take offense. I may be a shitty person, but I was a damn fine doctor. Turns out, I didn't need to defend myself because Reyann speaks out.

"Enough Jeff. She is going to remain my doctor because I want her to, and I can still take you to my knee so stop throwing your weight around trying to intimidate people. It's brutish and I don't like it. Now, I'm going to go with Nurse Chastity," Reyann looks at Chastity with utter sympathy before continuing on, "and you are going to stay here and have whatever this is out with Dr. Stacey. I can't have you two arguing every time I have an appointment. Figure it out children," Reyann says and walks over to Chastity.

Stunned, I watch Reyann leave the room with Chastity trailing behind her. *Children? Did she just call us children?* I'm nearly forty years old and have a 21-year-old son myself. I am hardly a child.

Now, her son, on the other hand, is clearly a man-child. Said man-child is currently staring me down, his arms once again folded across his chest and his face in a pout like I had tattled on him.

"Right. Well, have a nice day," I say and start to turn on my heels to make my own exit.

"You didn't know her name. She was just a chart to you," Jeff says from behind me.

Okay. Guess we are actually doing this. Fine, it is on. Professionalism be damned.

"I see nearly thirty patients a day and consult with many other cases. I don't remember everyone's names right away. Hence the chart," I say and hold it up as if showing it to him will make my point.

"Maybe you shouldn't see so many patients."

Okay, point not received.

"Maybe people should stop getting sick." I know it's ridiculous. That is the point. His statement is just as ridiculous.

"She isn't another name on a chart. She's my mother," he says. I notice the slight tick in his jaw. I notice it because I'd seen it before on other family members. He was afraid for his mother, but he didn't want to admit it. Anger was easier than fear.

Sighing, I release my impatience and call upon all my training. We will never get anywhere if we are both holding on to anger.

"And I will give her all the attention, drive and care that I give all my patients. You may not care about my reputation, but it speaks for itself. Ask any physician here. Hell, ask any physician in this state. They know me by name, Jeff, and that is because I am damn good at my job. You can go to another doctor if that is what you want but they won't be as good as me," I say with all the confidence I have in my bones.

Jeff just continues to glare at me.

I hold his gaze for a short while before I determine its useless.

24

Just as I'm about to turn on my heels and exit the door for a second time I am stopped by the husky voice behind me.

"You better be."

"I am," I state and pause in the doorway to give my best impression of his death stare.

Slowly, but deliberately, Jeff walks over to me. He towers over me, which isn't a hard feat since I'm barely five feet two, and he glares down at me. He is definitely invading my personal space but I recognize this for the power play it is. I am no stranger to the intimidation tactics of men. My profession is laden with such behavior. If he thought I was going to cower than he didn't know me.

"If you're half as good as the way your ass looks in those scrubs then you'll do for now."

He looks at me with an expression of both desire and pure disgust before he turns and leaves me leaning up against the exam room's door. By the time I recuperate, he is long gone and for the second time that day I don't get the last word, and I'm left wondering what the hell just happened.

-4-

Monotony

Arriving home well past the nine o'clock hour I am surprised to see my daughter rush past me as I open the front door. I quickly step aside and shuffle my briefcase and the other items in my arms to keep from dropping them.

"Rebecca Marie McNill slow down," I say to my teenage daughter.

She is gangly, like her father and her arms flail as she turns to acknowledge me since nearly running me down. She's grinning like she has just been given the best news in the world, and I immediately soften. I never could stay mad at my little muffin. She hated her nickname, but I used it every chance I could.

"Hi Mom. I'm sorry, I didn't see you. Bye," she calls to me and skips down the walkway.

"Hold the phone. Where do you think you're going?" I ask her.

"Moooooooom," she says turning my name into quite possibly the longest word ever.

"Beccaaaaa," I imitate her. This earns me an eye roll of the typical American teenager. I grin back at her.

"I'm going out with friends."

"Uh huh. On a school night? I don't think so," I say and look at my watch to emphasize just how much her going out is not going to happen.

26

"Mom, it's summer. And I already graduated," she informs me
with another eye roll.

Crap!

I forgot. Chalk that up to another of my shitty moments. It isn't
like I intentionally forgot about attending my youngest child's high
school graduation. It wasn't my fault the ceremony was a complete
snore fest. Still, I can't lose face, so I engage in the customary
parent-child ritual.

"Who's driving?"

"Me."

"Who is going?"

"Me, Nooni, Emily, Luke and Cameron," my daughter replies,
shuffling her feet in impatience. When she starts tinkling her keys
together I know she is really impatient.

I forgo the customary joke about her friend Nooni's name and
instead keep my parent hat on.

"Okay. Be safe. No drinking and driving. Actually, just no
drinking. And definitely no sex. I mean it. You tell Cameron to keep
his hands to himself," I point my finger at her to let her know how
serious I am.

"Mooom," she elongates the word again and I laugh.

The truth is I had no idea if my daughter was sexually active. I
knew when my son was because I was the one that kept finding the
used condoms in his room when I went in search of dirty laundry. I
finally hit my breaking point after the third condom and barged into
the living room to shove it in his face and told him, in front of his
sister and father, to use the damn trashcan I had put next to his bed
for the stupid condoms. I then promptly told him I was proud of him
for practicing safe sex.

He didn't talk to me for a month.

"Have fun Muffin. Don't do anything I wouldn't do," I call to
her as she skips the rest of the way to her car. She waves back at me
but does not reply. I watch her pull out of the driveway in the car her

27

father and I had gotten her as an early graduation present.

Rebecca was eighteen years old and she would be leaving at the end of the month to go to college in another state. I wasn't exactly thrilled she had chosen University of Nevada of all places, but it was her decision and who was I to stop her, just her mother is all.

My eldest, Cooper, had left for college three years ago and I thought I had taken that goodbye especially hard. He was my first born and had the namesake of my own father, but I don't remember this feeling of panic with his departure as I've had with Rebecca's impending goodbye. I knew what the experts called it – empty nest syndrome.

Hogwash.

The last thing I wanted was another little rascal running around my house and putting their sticky fingers on my medical journals. I didn't want another baby. And in full disclosure I didn't want my children to stay in my home forever. I wanted them to experience their own lives and have their own adventures. It would also be nice to not have my home invaded every other week by rowdy teenagers. The one thing that those rowdy teenagers provided, however, was a distraction from the reality inside my home.

The reality was that aside from my children and their friends that house saw little conversation. When the kids were gone the only sound in the home was the ticking of the clocks and perhaps the occasional flush of a toilet despite there still being two residents within its walls. I am standing in the doorway now, dreading going inside. It is a feeling I have come to know well. I'm not sure when it first appeared or when I first noticed it, but it is within me now and I can't seem to shake it.

Closing the door behind me I go into the kitchen and put my work items down on the table. I have a full night of catching up on reports and immediately go to the coffee maker. I hate coffee. Have always hated it but it has come to serve me well during my late nights. In fact, my husband was the person that introduced me to

28

coffee. Josh was a computer programmer and often worked late into the night on his various projects. He said he liked the quiet of the night and he did his best work then. Unlike me he embraced the silence. As for me, I rebelled against the stillness of the night.

Early in our marriage I used to stay up with him because I believed it was important I be supportive of his work. That habit quickly ended when I realized I was more of a burden than a supportive wife. I just got in his way. He never said that to me, but his body language was enough to convince me that it was best if I just left him alone when he was working. He returned the favor when I began medical school and had to spend many hours poring over reports, books and journals. He would take the children while I locked myself up in our office and spent hours learning about various diseases and treatment methods.

Josh had always been supportive of my goals and would often say 'whatever you need' when I asked for things. In fact, he never told me no. He just continued to acquiesce to my every whim. I used to test his easy-going demeanor every now and then. Once, I told him our house needed some razzle-dazzle and demanded we paint the walls in tie-dye colors. I hated those walls and had them re-painted a week later. Another time I demanded we get this garish fountain for our front yard. At the time we lived in a three bedroom townhouse and shared a front yard with our neighbor. It was absolutely the most hideous fountain but he said okay and had it delivered to the house. The neighbors complained and the fountain was moved to the backyard. It got 'damaged' by the moving crew when we moved out of the townhouse. The last time I tested just how far he would let me go was three years ago.

I came to realize that my husband would allow me anything, forgive me for anything because nothing fazed him. He was Mr. Chill, and I was Ms. Villain. I was the hothead. I was the crazy wife that put way too many demands on her husband. I knew my family felt sorry for Josh because he had to deal with me every day. At least they got a break, but Josh was in the trenches all the time. My mother had even told me how I needed Josh and his patience. You know, because of how hot-headed I was.

There used to be a time I believed my mother and had even been grateful for my patient and easy going husband. I used to think the only person that ever truly understood me was Josh. After all, he had seen my scars. He hadn't shied away from them. He hadn't exactly embraced them either, but he knew about them. He was the only family member of mine that did know about them. For twenty-three years I had hid the scars and destructive behavior from those I loved. Hiding it had become second nature to me and now it seemed pointless to reveal what I had done all those years ago.

I'm running through my past as the coffee brews and assembling my laptop for some serious work when I hear the shuffle of feet coming down the stairs. I don't look over. I don't say anything. I just wait.

"How was your day?" he asks me as I mirror the words in my head. We've been married for twenty years and for twenty years he has been asking me how my day was when I return home. It's like clockwork. *Tick. Tick. Tick.*

"It was fine until the penguins attacked the nursery," I state.

"Huh?" he asks.

"Nothing. It was fine," I say and pour me a cup of coffee. I offer him the pot, and he takes it to pour himself a cup. "Yours?"

"Oh, good. It was good. Finished the Knight project. So, it was good," he says and replaces the coffee pot.

"That's good," I say and take a drink from my mug. He takes a drink from his.

"Yes, it is good."

Around and around we go, repeating the same dance we have done for the last ten years or longer. The days really do just fog together until I can't even tell you when we last had a meaningful conversation. Some would call it familiarity. I call it monotony.

"Well, I'll let you get to work," Josh says and comes over to me. He kisses the side of my forehead, an affectionate gesture he has done the last twenty years. I lean into the kiss as I have done every time. It's the pat on my head that has me holding my breath. I hated that part of this little play of ours. I wasn't his dog, and it irked me, but I never said anything about it because I didn't want to be the hot-headed wife.

Josh leaves the kitchen and returns to his office upstairs. All of his equipment is housed in that room. A room I never went into. It is his domain, and I am content to never touch any of it. I didn't understand computer code anyway. I had tried to learn some of it when we had started dating but I simply wasn't built for that kind of code. Give me blood tests and medical reports any day but not computer programing jargon.

Determined to finish at least two patient's charts tonight before falling asleep I sit at the table, put my disgusting coffee aside and boot up the computer. A picture of my children greets me and I smile at them. It was taken at Cooper's twenty-first birthday, and it was the 'before' picture. I couldn't help myself and I aided my son in getting totally plastered that night. Of course, I didn't force him to take the journey alone. I matched him drink for drink and by the end of the night both of us had to be escorted home. Josh had gone with us, but he refrained from drinking. It didn't matter that Rebecca was our acting designated driver that night. Josh had said something along the lines of "somebody has to keep an eye on you two". He might as well have patted me on the head. I responded by taking a shot of tequila.

I finish up one chart's notes and open up Reyann's patient file. In this day and age of computer hacking the hospital had so many protections for using the laptops away from the hospital. I have to enter various passwords and keep firewalls and other security features up to date. I complained these added features made the network slower, but Josh just reminded me they were necessary. I

31

had to wait for Reyann's file to load so I replenished my coffee. I wince at the first sip like I always do. I really hated coffee. That is why I kept drinking it. The bitter taste kept me awake. I never drank enough of it for the caffeine to impact me, but the taste was enough to jar me awake.

Returning to my computer I look to see if any of Reyann's test results have returned. Some of the blood work I ordered came back and the second LFT confirms the results of the first one. Her bilirubin test is also back, and the results are not what I had hoped for. Based on her LFT and bilirubin her liver has been comprised in some way. I hoped we had caught it in time and that no surgical option was needed to either correct the problem or prevent it from worsening. Jeff really isn't going to like me when I deliver this news.

Not that I am concerned about him liking me. He had been entirely inappropriate today when he had mentioned my ass like he had a right to. I should have punched him and then claimed sexual harassment. At the very least I should have run straight to Reyann and tattled on his ass. I would have loved to have seen her bend him over her knee and give him a good wallop. He deserved it. His smart mouth needed to be taught a lesson.

I spent the rest of the day trying to think of another time I had witnessed him acting the way he had today, but I couldn't recall a single instance. He was always so respectful to my mother and Kelly, my stepsister. In fact, he would apologize to them if he ever swore in front of them. I never apologize for that. He was the consummate good boy in front of my family so why had he acted like a barbarian today?

Shaking my head I clear it of thoughts of him because I do not want him to have that kind of power over me. In fact, I refuse to let him enter my thoughts again.

But he did many times that night.

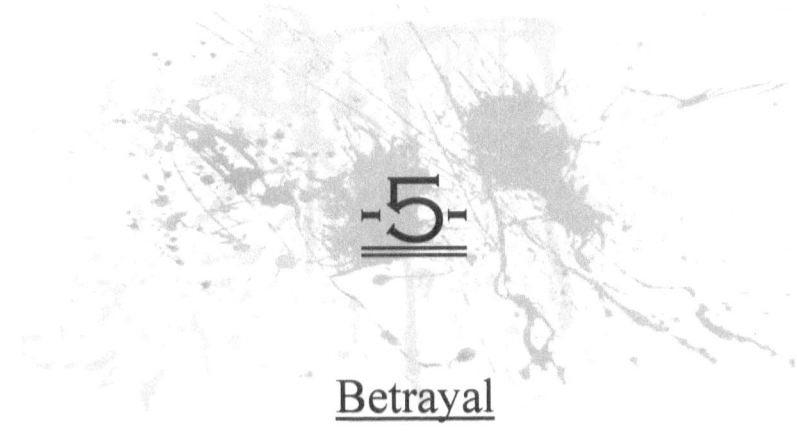

-5-

Betrayal

"No. Not again. Get out," Rachel says to me from her favorite chair in the whole wide world.

"What? I can't visit my friend. I'm just visiting my friend, Gina. There is no need to hover in the doorway. We'll be fine," I say to the sour faced receptionist. Gladys starts to speak, and I promptly slam the door in her face.

"That was unnecessary," Rachel says from behind me.

"She had it coming. You still haven't found the flowers I sent to you on your birthday, have you?" I ask as I plop down in what I have come to associate as my chair. It's purple. I like it much better than Rachel's.

"Are you sure you sent them to my office?" Rachel asks for the umpteenth time.

"Yes, I'm sure. I triple-checked the address. Your receptionist is crap, and you should fire her," I say and use my thumb to gesture to the area said receptionist is no doubt pouting in.

"She's been with me for ten years. I'm not going to fire her. You will just have to do better when it comes to getting along with her," Rachel says and hands me half of her sandwich. I greedily take it and bite into it.

"Why me?" I ask, my mouth full and breadcrumbs flying out

33

onto Rachel's desk. She frowns at me as she swipes the crumbs off her desk.

"Because you started it."

"I did not!" I protest.

"You called her Gloria for months," Rachel points out.

"Because I thought that was her name!"

"When she corrected you, you then proceeded to call her Glinda."

"Glinda, Gladys. They sound alike."

"No, they do not. And that doesn't explain the Gay phase."

"Okay, now hold on just a minute. She is an older lady and in my defense her name is from the same era. Her name might as well be Gay," I explain animatedly as I finish my half of the sandwich. It is tuna salad. I hate tuna salad. A fact Rachel knows, and I suspect is the only reason why she offered me half. She knew I would hate it but that I would eat it anyway. This is her way of getting back at me for interrupting her lunch again.

"You started it. And you just called her Gina," Rachel points out.

"Okay, okay, I started it, but she took it too far. I mean, come on Rachel, South Africa?"

Rachel just chuckles. Accepting that she will never be on my side I move on to the reason I came to her office today. After my last visit on Friday and my encounter with Reyann I knew I needed another session.

"I cheated on Josh," I blurt just as Rachel takes a bit of her sandwich.

She immediately starts choking and I snicker. She glares at me with narrowed eyes as she takes a drink from her eco-friendly water bottle. I wonder if she knew where her tuna came from and if it was environmentally friendly fishing. Doubt it.

"When?" she asks once she has cleared her throat.

"Three years ago." I examine the dirt beneath my nails and set to task to cleaning them.

"Why?"

I shrug.

"Why does anyone cheat?" I ask. Rachel doesn't answer me. She just continues to stare at me. I roll my eyes, stop cleaning the dirt beneath my fingernails and settle deeper into the chair.

Rachel immediately tenses because she knows I'm staying for the long haul now. I've trapped her once again. She wants me to go but she also wants to hear what I have to say.

"I was testing him," I say.

"That can't possibly be your reason," she says in disbelief.

"No, it really is. Remember when I got that hideous fountain to see what he would do?"

"Yeesss," she draws out the word slowly, like she doesn't want to stop saying it because she fears what I might say next.

"Well, this was the same thing."

"It's not the same thing," she immediately states, appalled.

"Yes it is. He never gets upset. Everything is always *'fine'*. Well, I was tired of fine. I wanted to know where the line was, so I crossed one. Only, it turns out I didn't cross anything at all," I explain.

"That doesn't even make any sense. Of course you crossed a line."

"That's just it, I didn't. I confessed. I went to him the next night and confessed my betrayal. I told him it was a mistake. I told him I didn't mean to do it and that it just happened. I told him I was sorry. I cried. I groveled and you know what he said to me?"

Rachel shook her head.

"It's fine."

Silence. Rachel doesn't respond and I take her momentary brain lapse to steal some of her potato chips. They are much tastier than the icky tuna salad sandwich on rye. I'm munching on the chips and reaching for her water when she finally snaps out of it. She moves the water away from me but pushes the plate of chips towards me. I graciously take them.

35

"What else did he say?" she asks.

"Nothing. He said, 'it's fine' and then he got up and left the room," I say in between bites.

"Did you ever try to broach the topic again?"

I can picture the little wheels of my friend's brain spinning and it makes me smile. I loved this woman.

"Of course, many times. He would either repeat 'its fine' or he would change the subject. I'd be like, hey remember that time I cheated on you and he would be like, the lights on the front porch need to be changed. It's like it never happened."

"But it did happen."

"Exactly!" I exclaim, placing the empty plate back on the desk. I use my eyes to plead with Rachel and she gives in, passing me her water. I clap my hands before taking it and gulp down half the contents. Of course, she is glaring at me when I give it back to her, but I just shrug. Potato chips are salty.

"Stacey, why did you cheat on him?"

"I told you. I was testing him," I say.

"Stacey, why did you cheat on him?" she repeats it, and I groan.

I take it back. I didn't love this woman. Right now she is getting on my nerves.

"Because I wanted to see if I could! I wanted to see if I felt bad about it!" I don't know why I'm shouting. It isn't like Rachel doesn't know the kind of person I am. Aside from Josh she is the only other person that truly knows me.

"Did you feel bad?"

"Of course I did," I say and demonstrate just how offended I am by her questions by rolling my eyes at her. She isn't concerned with my offense.

"Do you still feel bad?"

I pause and that is answer enough.

"Do you want to do it again?"

Another pause.

"Did you enjoy it the last time?"

"Oh, sick. Why would you even ask that?" I feign disgust. Rachel gives me her deadpan stare. She is immune to my jokes and deflections.

"I didn't enjoy it like I wanted to. I did it to prove a point, not to enjoy it. But I keep having thoughts about trying it again," I admit.

"What's stopping you?"

"You!"

"No, I'm not. You are stopping you. You feel guilt."

"Of course I feel guilt! What kind of person cheats on their spouse to test them? And what kind of person wants to do it again? I'm scum," I declare.

"Stacey, are you satisfied with Josh?" Rachel asks and this earns one of my deadpan stares because she doesn't need to know about this.

"You want all the dirty details?" I ask.

"Have you told him you are dissatisfied?"

"Yes."

"And?"

"And everything is fine, remember?" But everything wasn't fine, and it hadn't been fine in years. In fact, our troubles began long before my betrayal three years ago. Perhaps it was through youthful ignorance and adulthood denial that our misconnection continued to fester until we just stopped touching one another.

"Are you attracted to him?" Rachel asks. She really won't let this go.

"I used to be."

"What changed?"

"I'm not really sure if anything did. I mean, sure we both put on some weight but we both still basically have the same body type as when we first met. I think...," I trail off because I hadn't admitted this to anyone, not even myself yet.

"Go on," Rachel encourages.

"I think my attraction for him was never really physical. I think what attracted me to him was his affection for me. He has always been attentive and caring. I confused that with passion and love."

"Do you love him?"

"Of course I do."

"Are you in love with him?"

Another pause.

"Are you passionate about him?" She just keeps on asking all the hardball questions today.

"No. I wanted to be. I tried to be, but he doesn't enjoy certain things and he prefers to not engage in that stuff," I say and make air quotes around stuff.

"What stuff?"

"You know, sex stuff."

"You're going to have to be more specific than that if you want me to follow this conversation," Rachel says. She swivels a little in the poop chair and I can't help but think about diarrhea.

"There are exactly two positions he approves of. Him on top or me on top. Even the suggestion of switching it up is taboo. And forget about using toys, blindfolds or other aids of stimulation. He won't even talk about using those things. And on the rare occasion we do have sex it's always in the same place. I can map out in my mind; every move, every sound and how long it will last. I know what he will say when it's over and how quickly it takes for him to fall asleep. I'm just the vessel he uses to empty his seed into. But I can't tell him any of this because then I'm the bad guy who doesn't appreciate what I have in front of me. So, instead, I cheat to jar him into doing something, anything, and all he says is it's 'fine'."

I finish my tirade breathing heavily because I have never shared my feelings with another regarding my marriage and my sex life. It has been a burden I carried alone for so long. After three years of feeling guilty for cheating, for wanting to cheat again and for resenting my husband because he is the barrier to my cheating my

38

thoughts had started to twist and turn until I was once again contemplating returning to cutting. If I couldn't reach ecstasy in a sexual way, then I would do it through scars.

"I'm in a dangerous position here, Stacey," Rachel says.

"What do you mean?" I have no idea what she is talking about.

I'm the one talking about wanting to cheat on my husband, not her. Besides, she was satisfied with her wife, Julie.

"As your friend I want to encourage you to do what makes you happy. But, as a psychologist, I know you are thinking about something that is harmful to you. I'm torn between two roles here and it isn't fair of you to put me in this position," she explains.

She's right, of course. I'm terrible but we both knew that already. No point focusing on the things we already knew.

"Just be my friend then."

"Okay. As your friend I see you are unhappy. If you honestly believe you've done all you've could to save your marriage and if that marriage is causing you to feel like you need to start cutting yourself again, then I say let it go. Do what you need to do to find yourself. But do not start harming yourself again. I don't care how it makes you feel. Slicing up your skin is never the answer, and you must promise me that you will call me the instant you find yourself reaching for the razor," Rachel says sternly.

I can tell now is not the time for my customary jibes so I do as she asks. I promise her I will call her. As for the other parts of her friendly advice I know I won't take it. How could I possibly leave Josh after all he has done for me? I may be a shitty person, but I am not completely cold-hearted.

Family

The results of Reyann's ultrasound have returned, and I wish I could turn back the clock so I could refer her to another doctor. I didn't want to be the one to deliver this news. I'm cursing Dr. Levy again for not following hospital policy and sending Reyann to me directly before completing the usual obligatory tests before a patient is referred to me.

I imagine when Dr. Levy had told Reyann he was recommending she see a specialist she hadn't fathomed he meant an oncologist. But that is exactly what he meant because that is what I do. I'm a cancer doctor. Foolish me thought I could fight cancer, so I spent years studying the various forms and learning how to combat it. My father couldn't beat it but I sure as hell would. While my reputation may have been above reproach, my patient survival rate varied depending upon the cancer they had once they came to see me. The type and stage of advancement factored greatly into what I was able to do for them. After ten years I felt like cancer was still winning.

Based on the images I was looking at before me it seemed Reyann was another patient I would have to deliver bad news to. Dr. Levy's initial suspicions had been correct. Reyann had cancer and it had spread to her liver. Of course, additional testing would be done to confirm what the ultrasound revealed because the images couldn't actually tell us if the tumors were cancerous, but I'd seen enough in my ten years to feel confident I was staring at malignant tumors. Typically, this would be the stage where I would step in with the patient. The patient usually already came to me with the knowledge that they had cancer and not before. I rarely had to be the barer of that initial news. Unfortunately, I didn't have that luxury this time.

Reyann was waiting for me in one of my exam rooms and I knew I needed to get moving but I still took another minute to look at the results again. I was stalling. I knew it. I never had to tell someone I knew personally that they had cancer. My patients started as strangers and while I admit I grew close to some and felt affection for them I knew there would come a day when we would part ways; either through destroying the cancer or through death.

Never before had contact with a patient existed outside the hospital walls. But Reyann was family. I mean, she was family to my family. Our connection would not end in this hospital or stop between us because my family would be invested in her treatment. This was not going to be a routine case at all.

"Dr. McNill, your patient is ready for you," Chastity says timidly from the entryway of my office. The mouse never enters my office. She always just hovers. It was disconcerting and a complete annoyance.

"You can come in Chastity. Stop hovering," I say, perhaps a bit too bitingly.

Much to my surprise Chastity enters my office. Shocking the hell out of me, she actually speaks up when she enters.

"Dr. McNill, I respect you and I think we work well together, but I think it would be best if we both sought a different partnership," she says. Her voice cracks but she still says it.

Her brass pulls me out of my current funk, and I turn to her, grinning like an idiot.

"You do, do you? Well, I don't accept that, Chastity. You're a great nurse and you even out my bullshit. I need you on my staff, so the patients don't see just how much of a bitch I am. What's your middle name?" I ask her. She is clearly stunned by my reaction to her request to be assigned to another doctor, but she recovers.

"Ursala," she says.

"You're kidding me?" I ask. Her parents couldn't possibly be that mean.

"No. My name is Chastity Ursala Morgan." She says it like there is nothing wrong with her name. But there is, there so is.

"Your initials are CUM?" I ask her and she frowns at me.

"Yes, they are. And I've already heard every joke you could possibly say so don't even bother," she sasses me, and I love it.

"Oh, Chastity, you and I are going to be just fine," I say and clamp my hand down on her shoulder. She stares at me in confusion before she notices that I've left her and am walking down the hall-way. I hear her feet shuffling to catch up to me.

"Ms. Farley and her son are in exam room three," she says as she falls in step with me.

"Which son?" I ask.

"Pardon?"

"Which son is with her?"

"The same one that was here last time," Chastity says, once again confused.

"Shit!" This earns me a startled look from Chastity, and I shrug at her. "I'm sure you've heard much worse...CUM."

"Dr. McNill-"

"Call me Stacey."

"Dr. McNill I would appreciate it if you would refrain from referring to me by my initials."

This girl was definitely growing on me.

"Fine. But I can't call you Chastity anymore. And I refuse to call you Ursala. How about a compromise? Morgan?" I ask my best nurse.

"Morgan would be fine," she agrees, and I feel like we are finally in sync with one another as we enter exam room three.

"Dr. Stacey, how are you?" Reyann greets me with a smile, and I cringe inside because I'm about to wipe that smile off of her face.

"I'm fine, thank you for asking Ms. Farley."

"Uh oh. I'm Ms. Farley now. That means you found something," Reyann says.

Of course, she would have picked up on my tone and use of her last name. I was off my game today for sure. Casting my gaze to Jeff, who is standing in the back corner of the room, as far away from me as he can possibly get, I notice how he moves away from the wall at his mother's words.

"Yes. The ultrasounds revealed various growths on the lining of your liver," I begin. I give her the usual prepared speech about further testing and confirmation of the malignancy. I tell her it is too soon to think the worst and that we need to focus only on the next step. I tell her I have the utmost confidence we will have answers for her soon and once we get those answers, we can discuss a proper treatment plan. I tell her she has an excellent support system, and my staff will work with her closely. Basically, I feed her bullshit.

The worst part of the speech is that I know Reyann knows its bullshit, but I can't stop the word vomit from coming out of my mouth. It's what I have always done, and I think Reyann is doing me a courtesy of allowing me to finish. She knows this is more for me than it is for her because when I'm done, she says the kindest thing.

"You're going to be alright," she says to me.

Fuck!

She's the one with cancer but her first thought after hearing the news is to tell me I'm going to be alright. She didn't deserve cancer. She didn't deserve the hell that was bound to follow because despite the bullshit I just fed her I knew her prognosis wasn't good. I just couldn't legally confirm this yet without completing all the steps necessary for a diagnosis.

"What happens if the tumors are malignant?" Jeff finally speaks from his corner. I was a little surprised he hadn't gone to his mother during my speech but it is obvious he had been taking it all in.

"Why don't we just focus on the next round of tests before we jump to conclusions," I say. I've said this before to other family members. I needed them to remain calm because the patient was the one going through the diagnosis and they needed all the support they could get. It worked with the others, not so much with Jeff.

"Damnit! Just tell me!" He starts to move towards me like he is going to wrap his hands around my neck.

"Jeffrey Mitchell Collins!" Reyann scolds him and he immediately stops his advance to return to his corner.

I'm thrown by Jeff's primal response. Even though I had witnessed many family members of past patients react in the same manner it is jarring to see him lunge toward me like he had. For a brief moment, I start to question my involvement with all of this.

"Perhaps we should explore the option of transferring you to another oncologist. Perhaps my presence is only a distraction to your care. I can provide recommendations if you prefer," I direct my comment to Reyann.

Reyann shakes her head adamantly and sends a stern glare over to Jeff before she responds.

"No. I want you to be my doctor. It is my choice, right?"

"Yes. It's entirely your choice," I reply, avoiding the stare of the angry man on the other side of the room.

"Then I choose you."

"Very well. Chastity will get you scheduled for the biopsy. We'll know more then," I say and excuse myself.

I've never before ran from a patient after being the bearer of bad news but I couldn't stay in that room with Jeff another moment. I recognized in him the same anger I had when my father was first diagnosed. I hadn't wanted to accept it either and had lashed out at everyone I could. For ten years I had managed not to identify with my patients in this way but all it took was Jeff and Reyann to make

44

the barriers I had erected come crumbling down.

I return to my office and just pace back and forth because I can feel a panic attack coming. Quickly, I go to my desk and open a drawer to remove my stress ball. If this doesn't work than I will have no choice but to take a pill. I rarely used them, but I still had patients to see, and I couldn't be freaking out will I was talking to them. I'm frantically squeezing the stupid ball when the doorway to my office is filled by the presence of the very man that had initiated the panic attack.

"Go away," I say and continue my pacing.

"No. What are you doing?" he asks.

I stare at him, like really stare at him for the first time. He's tall and wide. His shoulders are massive and everything about him screams 'I work out'. I vaguely recall he does something with rocks. His job requires manual labor, and I imagine he can thank his job for a body like that. His hair is short. Way too short in fact. If he cut it any shorter, he would have a shaved head. I wonder why he just doesn't shave it if he is going to keep it so short. His green eyes are too wide apart as well. It gives him an almost alien looking face. Between that and his hair he just looks absolutely comical.

That is why I am now laughing.

That's what I tell myself anyway. I wasn't laughing because I was on the verge of a breakdown. Nope. I was laughing because there was an alien in my office, and he was asking what I was doing.

"Are you okay?" the alien asks and takes a step towards me.

"Fine. I'm fine. Everything's fine. It's FINE!" I shout.

Jeff glances behind him quickly before shutting my office door and coming over to me. He harshly grasps my arms, trapping them to my sides and gives me a little shake. I drop my stress ball and start to hyperventilate slightly.

"Snap out of it. My mother needs a doctor right now. You told me you were the best, so act like it," he growls at me and shakes me again.

I just start nodding and keep on nodding. I'm staring at his face, but I don't see any of his features because I'm pretty sure I'm about to pass out. Suddenly, a pair of hands grab my ass and squeeze tight. I snap back to reality and quickly push him away before I slap him across the face.

"Keep your hands off of me," I say and take a step away from him.

"Gladly. Are you finished freaking out?" Jeff asks me, rubbing the side of his cheek. He's glaring at me like he was the wronged party. Like he hadn't just groped me in my office.

"I was not freaking out. I was just having a moment," I lie.

"Yeah. A moment where you were freaking the fuck out. I recognize a panic attack when I see one," he says. It takes me a moment before I register what he just said, and he continues when he sees my reaction. "My brother, Tom. He used to get them when he was younger, after our father left us."

"Oh." I'm still stunned by what just occurred between us that it takes me a second to respond in my usually bitchy way. "Did you used to grab his ass too?"

Jeff shocks the hell out of me a second time when he doesn't get upset with my comment. Instead, he laughs.

"No. His cock," he replies.

It's my turn to laugh and before I know it all thoughts of a panic attack are gone. Jeff and I continue to stand on opposite ends of the office but neither of us makes a move. The silence soon becomes awkward.

"I'm sorry for what I said the other day. I was pissed at you, and I wanted to knock you down a peg or two. It was petty and stupid. It won't happen again," Jeff finally says.

At first, I'm not sure what he is talking about then I remember his comment about my ass. The very same ass he had just put his hands on.

"You seemed to like it just fine a few minutes ago," I foolishly say.

Once again Jeff just laughs.

"I didn't say I didn't like it. Just that I shouldn't have said I liked it. As for what I just did here that was done for your benefit, not mine," he says and holds his hands up like he is an innocent man. His cheek is turning red where I slapped him and I delight in knowing that I left a mark on him.

"That may be true but don't do it again," I warn.

"I promise I won't do it again…unless you ask me to," he finishes and turns to let himself out of my office.

"You know I'm married, right?"

"I do."

And just like that he is gone and once again somebody else got the last word in. Twice now he has left me speechless and hanging on to the edge of something I can't identify. I'd been in this man's presence before many times over the years but had never felt the way he has made me feel these last two encounters.

This time when I pick up the stress ball it isn't because I'm experiencing a panic attack. This time it is because I'm frustrated and there is only one way I know of that will release me from this feeling.

Unfortunately, the person I wanted to help me find release had just walked out of my office and he was off limits.

-7-

Rejection

I knew it was a mistake before I did it. Before I made the first move my insides were screaming at me to retreat but I was still buzzing from earlier. I needed a release, and this was the only way I could think of to get what was bubbling up inside me out before I imploded.

Josh seemed willing – at first.

But then I did one of the unapproved acts and followed that up with another unapproved act. This resulted in effectively shutting any further progression of sexual activity down.

First, I bit him on the side. He shied away from me and tried to redirect me, but I dodged him and put my hands on his shoulders and pushed him back on the bed. Then I took his hand and wrapped it around his cock. With my hand over his I guided his movements, so he was pleasuring himself. Then I used my fingers to provide myself some pleasure while I looked on to what he was doing to himself. Or, rather, I looked on while his hand stalled and then he rolled out from under me.

"What are you doing?" I ask him as he sits on the edge of the bed and puts his boxers on.

"You know I don't like that," he says and stands.

"But I do," I say. I'd like to think I didn't whine but I did.

"I'm sorry," he says and goes into the bathroom. He shuts the door, effectively shutting me out too.

Grumbling, I go over to my dresser and pull my vibrator out of its drawer. Then I grab my pillow and the comforter off the bed. He can freeze tonight for all I care. Making my way down the hall I go to the guest bedroom, slam the door behind me and set about finding some sense of release.

I bought my little friend the day after my one-night affair. It was evident that my husband was either incapable or unwilling to pleasure me how I wanted so I invested in plastic and batteries. But the artificial can only carry you so far before you realize you're basically doing it with another robot. It is not an existence I wanted but it was all I had so I gripped Mr. Bullet and let the vibrations do their thing.

Later, I lay in the guest bed and wait. He never comes for me. In fact, I don't see him again until the next morning when I is fixing my bagel for breakfast. He comes into the kitchen looking like he didn't have a care in the world. He pulls out a chair, sits in it and takes a drink of coffee from the mug I had on the table. I want to snatch that mug out of his hands and tell him it is mine, but I don't. I just pour myself another cup and keep on smearing cream cheese on my cinnamon and raisin bagel. There is fruit in it so it will probably be the healthiest thing I eat all day.

"Busy day today?" Josh asks, pulling me out of my bitter silent treatment.

Of course he is perfectly fine. He probably just jerked off after I left the room and fell asleep like nothing was wrong. Because everything is fine and I'm just being too demanding, too unforgiving, too judgmental, too needy. Too. Too. I hated that word.

"Yes. Full case load. Gotta hunt and destroy those cancer cells," I say and wait for his typical twitch when I make jokes. There it is. In the corner of his right eye. Every time.

"That's nice," he says as he turns a page in the paper. He still ordered a traditional daily paper. It was a complete contradiction of his chosen profession, but he said he liked the way the paper felt so he kept ordering them.

"Yes, it is. I just love it when my patients say how nice it was getting to know me right before they die," I bite back. There's that eye twitch again. I'm waiting for him to call me out on my cattiness but he doesn't. He just flips another damn page in that damn paper.

I place my coffee mug a bit roughly on the counter and throw the rest of my bagel away. I'm halfway to the door when he calls out to me.

"Will you be home for dinner tonight?"

"I don't think so," I say, my back still to him. I don't wait for his response. I just gather my things by the door and leave.

When had my marriage started to feel like an obligation and not a choice? When had I started to resent my husband to the point of open hostility? When had I really started acting like the bitch that I was? I don't remember being like this before. So, what had caused this side of me to come out?

This time Gladys didn't even bother to get out of her chair. In fact, she doesn't even acknowledge me. She just keeps her head down and stares at something on her desk.

"Hello, Georgie," I say in an attempt to grab her attention.

Nothing. No reaction.

Hmm. That was strange.

I enter Rachel's office and start talking. I sit in my chair, drape my feet and turn to Rachel. Only, Rachel isn't there. The poop chair is empty. Ahh. So this is why Gladys ignored me. She knew Rachel wasn't here. Touché Gladys.

"Will she be back soon?" I ask Gladys as I return to the reception area.

"Maybe," Gladys shrugs and she licks her finger before flipping a page in the magazine she is reading.

I start to tap my foot on the carpeted floor and look around the reception area. It's boring and grey. It reminds me of the poop chair, and I am not at all comfortable. I debate waiting for Rachel in her office, but I don't like the quiet, so I stay in the reception area with Gladys. Boredom doesn't suit me, and I soon start taping Gladys' desk with my fingers. It isn't until I reach down to grab a pencil off her desk that she acknowledges me.

Gladys grabs a hold of my arm and glares at me.

"Stop that," she says. I nod and she releases my arm.

"I feel like you and I got off on the wrong foot, Gladys," I begin.

"Try wrong everything," she replies. I ignore her.

"But I think we could be friends if we just gave it a shot," I continue.

Gladys just glares at me behind her frog-colored glasses.

"Rachel is important to me, and it is clear you are important to her. We should try harder, don't you think?"

Gladys doesn't have to respond because just then the outer door opens and Rachel walks in followed by her wife Julie. I breathe a sigh of relief and turn back to Gladys.

"Forget everything I just said, Garfunkel," I say to Gladys and walk over to Rachel and Julie.

"Thank god you are here. Gladys accosted me," I greet them.

"I doubt that but if she did you probably deserved it," Julie says to me before she hugs me.

"I'm truly hurt that you think so little of me," I return the embrace and wink at Rachel.

"Don't encourage her," Rachel says to Julie and gets her messages from Gladys. As Gladys is gathering her things so she can go to lunch I stick my tongue out at her. This time Gladys does the finger wave.

Good for you Gladys.

Once Rachel, Julie and I are in her office I plop down on my chair and start kicking my feet out. Julie puts a bag down beside Rachel's desk, kisses her quickly on the lips and steps back.

"I'm going to leave you two to whatever this is. I'll see you at home tonight. Love you," Julie says to Rachel before saying good-bye to me.

Once the door is closed behind her I turn back to Rachel and grin.

"You just had a quickie," I say.

Rachel actually blushes before she turns away from me to go through the items in the bag Julie left behind.

"Don't be embarrassed. There is nothing wrong with grabbing a quick one between patients. Did you have fun?" I ask and Rachel sends evil vibes my way.

"What? You can ask me all sorts of personal questions about my sex life, but I can't ask you one? A bit hypocritical don't you think?"

"Fine. Yes, I had fun. Can we move on to what brought you here today?" Rachel asks and she hands me a plastic container filled with food. I raise my eyebrows at her in question.

"Let's just say I anticipated your arrival," she says and hands me a fork. I take it, open the lid to what has become my lunch and dig in. Lasagna. Yum.

"I think I might have inappropriate intentions towards my patient's son. After I discovered this, I tried to have sex with my husband and he rejected me. Now, all I can think about is boning my patient's son. Like even now, eating this lasagna all I can think about is how delicious he would taste," I say and take a big bite of my lunch.

"Why do you think Josh rejected you? Does he know about your feelings for this other man?" Rachel opens her own lunch. A salad. How boring.

"No. He couldn't possibly. He rejected me because I bit him and wanted him to jerk off in front of me." My friend doesn't even bat an

52

eye at my crudeness. She just munches on her salad.

"He doesn't enjoy doing that?"

"That would be a big fat negative Doc. Like slam on the brakes stoppage. I got off with a vibrator instead and slept in another bedroom. Then he stole my coffee the next morning and acted like everything was '*fine*'," I cringe when I saw the word.

"Did you tell him it wasn't fine?"

"I tried to when he shut down spanky time. But he went into the bathroom and shut the door. I got the message and made myself scarce," I say.

"Stacey, it seems like we keep having the same conversation, but you aren't making any changes. Do you think things will just resolve on their own? Why do you keep coming back to me when you already know what I'm going to say? Why do you stay if you aren't happy?"

Her questions are valid ones, and I have asked myself those same questions many times. Every time I always come back to the same answer. I can't leave him. If I leave him then I truly am the monster I think I am. Because who would leave the man that saved their life?

Savior

The scars kept growing but the hurt never went away. Dad had been dead for nearly three years now and Mom had clearly moved on. She was engaged to Paul now and we lived with him and his daughter, Kelly. He was nice and I liked him well enough. I would never call him Dad but as long as he treated my mother right, I was cool with him.

Kelly was a little younger than me and she was pretty nice too. Sometimes she was almost too nice. She often allowed her friend Jenny to treat her like shit but it wasn't my friendship, so I never said anything. Last thing I wanted was turmoil in our new home. I had enough of an internal struggle going on, so I didn't need an external one as well.

Since we had moved in with Paul and Kelly it meant I was switching schools. I didn't exactly have many friends but the few that I had were now many towns away and I wasn't liking the change. I told Mom I was fine with it, but I really wasn't. My best friend Rachel promised she'd keep in touch with me, but I knew she only said that to make me feel better. I knew it was only a matter of time before she, too, disappeared from my life. It was inevitable. People left all the time. There was nothing I could do about it.

Well, there was *one* thing I could do about it.

The move, missing my friends and feeling like I had no control in anything had me once again putting sharpened metal to my inner thighs. Perhaps it was being in a new home that had me slipping on all my precautions or maybe deep down I really did want to get caught. Either way I left the bathroom door unlocked one afternoon while I was slicing away. I usually waited until everyone was asleep, but the day had been rough, and I couldn't wait. I needed the feeling the razor gave me so as soon as I got home from school I rushed to the bathroom and took out my second-best friend. I had two good lines of blood trailing down my leg when he found me, razor ready for a third cut.

Josh opened the bathroom door and froze. I think he probably thought I was shaving my legs at first because he just kind of smiled at me nervously before looking away quickly. He was there to drop Jenny off. He was her cousin and legal guardian, so he was popping up at our house every now and then. Just my luck, I forgot to lock the door on the one day he had to use the bathroom.

He was about to leave when he suddenly paused and looked back at me. I watched him as he looked at my hand, the razor, my leg, and then the blood dripping onto the floor. I thought he was about to call for my mom but he didn't. In fact, he did the exact opposite. When I heard my mom's voice calling out to see if he found the bathroom he called back to her.

"Yes. I found it, thank you. I'll be back down in a minute," he said and closed the door behind him.

I didn't say anything because I had no idea what he was going to do. It wasn't until he was standing next to me, slowly reaching out for the razor that I reacted. I jerked my hand away from him refusing to give up the razor. Josh took a step back and held up his hands. Then he looked around and picked up a towel resting on the sink.

"We need to stop the bleeding," he said softly and held the towel out to me. I didn't take it. Slowly, he reached forward and placed the towel against my inner thigh, like I was some skittish stray cat that was going to bolt at any sudden movements. I still had my foot on the sink, my leg bent so I could have the best access to my cutting canvas. My work of art was on full display before him.

It was an awkward position to be in, but I didn't move. Josh just stood there, pressing the towel against me to staunch the trickles of blood. Neither of us said anything but I could hear every exhale of our breaths. He was so close to me that I could just turn my head slightly and we'd be kissing. It's an odd thought to have in that moment but with his hand pressed against my thigh I thought about doing it.

"How long have you been doing this for?" he asked. I could see him looking at the many scars that had formed from previous cuts.

When I was sixteen, I had sex with a boy for the first time. He didn't ask about my scars. He just told me I was jacked, and he never spoke to me again. I cut myself after he left. It was slightly unnerving to have a man touching my thigh and asking me about my scars. I was eighteen then but had little experience with the opposite sex. My first time had kind of soured me to pursuing boys. Now a man was showing concern for me; the entire scenario was foreign to me. And, so help me, it was slightly erotic, which only confused me further.

"A while," I finally said.

"Will you stop?" he asked.

I shook my head no.

"Will you stop for today?"

I nodded my head yes.

He held out one hand, palm out, and he waited. Reluctantly, I dropped the razor into his palm, and he deposited it in the sink. He lifted the towel and seemed pleased with what he saw because he dropped that in the sink too. I put my foot back on the floor and watched as Josh started rummaging through the medicine cabinet and drawers until he found what he was looking for.

"Sit," he said and pointed to the toilet. I sat and he started opening bandages. He knelt down, used the opposite side of the towel to clean my cuts and applied the bandages. I found I liked his touch, but I didn't say anything. I just stared at the top of his head as he knelt before me, caring for my wounds. Nobody had ever done this before, and I didn't know what do.

"You shouldn't be hurting yourself," he said once he finished. He picked up the bandage wrappings and stood.

"I need to tell your parents."

A switch had been flipped inside me and I came out of my trance and responded to him verbally.

"Parent," I replied.

"What?"

"Parent. Singular, no s. My Father is dead," I explained.

He looked at me, first with confusion, then with sympathy. "I'm sorry."

"I'll stop. Don't tell my mother. It would only hurt her," I quickly promised.

I could tell he didn't believe me, so I stood up and took the small steps over to him. I grabbed his hands, and I squeezed them as I looked into his eyes, pleading with him.

"I promise, I'll stop," I said. I needed him to believe me. If he believed me than maybe I could believe me too.

"Okay. You'll stop," he replied back, and squeezed my hands reassuringly.

And I did stop. Not right away but Josh kept showing up and asking me how I was doing. I never lied to him. I always told him the truth. If I had cut, I told him. If I hadn't cut, I told him.

Eventually a month went by without me cutting. Then two. Then three. And in the fourth month I finally kissed him. He told me it wasn't right. He told me I was vulnerable, and I wasn't thinking clearly. I told him to shut up and I kissed him again.

Three months after that I was pregnant with his baby. I graduated high school with a giant pregnant belly, but I was never ashamed. I was happy. He had saved me and made me see the beauty in life. We had our son, and we were married a few months after that. Two years later our daughter was born and then I started medical school. The first half of our marriage was good. I hadn't cut myself since I was eighteen but at age thirty, I started thinking about doing it again. Jenny had died and I was reminded of how fleeting life was.

By all accounts I had a great life. I had a loving husband. He loved me so much he had saved me from myself. I had two amazing children. I was at a pinnacle in my career and was making a name for myself in my field. We had just moved into this beautiful home but all I could think about was what if it had been me.

What if I had died instead of Jenny? Would I have died happy?

The answer was unequivocally no. I wasn't happy. I hadn't been happy in years. Instead, I had been pretending. Everything about me was a façade and Josh was the Band-Aid. He had covered my cuts that night and he had been covering them ever since, but a Band-Aid can't stop the bleeding of a gaping wound.

What I used to look back on with a loyal affection now seemed clouded to me. Did he really save me? Or did he just force me to hide who I was? For that matter, who was I? For so long I was Josh's wife, Rebecca and Cooper's mother. Who was Stacey and did I even like her?

None of that mattered though because I owed Josh my life. I couldn't worry about who I was when he had literally saved me from myself. He deserved a wife that was loyal to him and wasn't selfish all the time. What he got instead was a former cutter that cheated on him to test his feelings for her.

I really was the villain in this story. And the villain never deserves a happy ending.

-9-

Empty

I'd told the story of my husband walking in on me cutting myself many times before and always only to my therapists. While I had also told Rachel about it years ago, I had never shared with her, or the others, my true feelings on what had transpired all those years ago. I had never before admitted that in the moment Josh's attention was on stopping the bleeding I was thinking how easy it would be to kiss him. I always felt that if I had admitted that fantasy it would somehow tarnish the magnitude of what he did for me that day. What he continued to do for me.

"You think you're the villain?" Rachel asks me.

She has forgotten about her lunch and all of her attention is on me now. Somewhere between the kissing revelation and my doubts about who I was she had pushed aside her food and leaned forward in her chair.

"Of course I'm the bad guy. In every story there is a hero and a villain. A protagonist and an antagonist. I'm the anti, the other, the dark seed. I mean, I cheated on my husband. I wanted to bash him over the head with my coffee mug this morning. I'm having illicit sexual desires for my patient's son for God's sake. If that doesn't scream bad guy than I don't know what does," I say, finishing off my lasagna. I use my fork to gesture to Rachel's salad. She understands my question without a single word spoken and she hands me the remnants of her lunch.

"Stacey, you aren't the bad guy," she says quietly.

I stuff my mouth full of mixed greens.

"You aren't perfect, and you haven't always made the best decisions, but you are hardly a villain. You are flawed, but so is everybody else. Even Josh is flawed," Rachel says.

I give her my best impression of a '*come on, you can't possibly believe that*' look before going back to the salad. Josh never missed a step. He didn't have thoughts of spousal homicide or cheating. The ugliest thing he had ever done was cut down some rose bushes of our neighbors and he felt so bad about it he replaced the ugly plants.

"He isn't. One of his flaws is that he won't engage with you in meaningful conversation. When you try to broach topics that matter to you, he often shuts down and walks away without allowing you, or himself, an opportunity to fully understand the situation. He allows his discomfort to control his responses to you. You aren't a villain, and neither is he. Both of you are blameless and yet you both must shoulder the burden of what your marriage has become. Not all of this is on you, Stacey," Rachel says.

"If only it were that easy. Sharing the blame would be ideal in this situation but that can't be applied here. I'm not the easiest to get along with, let alone live with. Josh has managed to survive hurricane Stacey for twenty years. My mother always says I'm lucky I found him because I need a patient man. Well, I have him. No matter how much I try to rile him up he won't bite. Mr. Patience," I say and return the now empty food containers to Rachel. She takes them then quickly puts them aside.

"If he were truly patient, he wouldn't have locked himself in the bathroom. He would have discussed what happened last night with you. I fear you've had this image of Josh in your head ever since that day and you've clouded that with the man he really is. You've placed him on this pedestal that is higher than you can reach. So, instead of lowering it, or raising yourself up, you try to tear it down by doing things to convince him you are unworthy of love. You aren't unworthy, though. You do deserve happiness. And you aren't hurricane. Aside from your mother, I've known you the longest. At best, you are a thunderstorm, but hardly a hurricane."

Chuckling at the way she says such a comical thing with a completely straight face, I reply, "You have to say that because you're my best friend. It's BFF code."

She frowns at me.

"Why did you want to kiss him that day in the bathroom?" One track mind, this one.

"Why does that matter?" I ask. She doesn't answer me. She just waits for me to answer her because she knows I will. I was seeking her out for a reason after all.

"Because he was attractive and the first man to not avoid my scars," I explain.

"No. That isn't why. And you can't use that explanation because before Josh you only had one other sexual encounter. Two men do not make a pattern," Rachel says.

"Says who?"

"Says science. Now tell me the real reason?" She easily dismisses my deflection.

I hesitate. I'm not sure if I'm ready to reveal this to her. I'm not sure if I'm ready to reveal this truth to myself. It's a heavy one and I've managed to suppress it for years now. Saying it out loud, sharing it with someone, would make it real and I am terrified of its power.

"I wanted to kiss him because I was already turned on by the cutting and from the blood. I didn't just cut because it gave me control. I cut because it made me feel pleasure. When I would see the blood I would relish it because it was something *I* had made. I was proud of it. When he touched me, I was feeling all that and it felt exhilarating. I wanted more of that feeling," I admit. I can't look her in the eyes.

61

Essentially this confession revealed that my initial feelings towards my husband had nothing to do with him and everything to do with my need to feel pain. The pain brought me pleasure and Josh just happened to be in proximity of those strong feelings one day. Since then, I've been trying to chase that feeling but I hadn't come close. I thought the one-night stand would have provided some semblance of what I remembered but the feeling never came. All that encounter left me with was disgust and guilt.

"Stacey, have you ever considered that, maybe, you never really loved Josh like you thought you did? Maybe what you loved was the thought of sharing the pain and pleasure with another and Josh just happened to be present when you thought this," Rachel gives voice to the very thing I had feared for years.

"I can't think that way. That would mean these last twenty years were a lie. That would mean I lied. I can't accept that."

"Why not?"

"Because then I really would be the villain. It would mean I tricked him into a life that was completely false and only existed because of the one thing he tried so hard to save me from. If that is true than he never really saved me."

I get out of my chair and start to move around her office. Rachel isn't disturbed by my jittery movements. She knows that when I get uncomfortable, I am unable to stand still. So, she simply turns in her chair and follows me with her gaze.

"Would that be so terrible?"

"Yes," I whisper.

"Why?"

I'm fiddling with the books she has on a shelf. I examine two before I respond to her. With my hand still on the last book I turn to her and softly say, "Because it would mean I'm still lost."

Days pass and I do not return to Rachel's. I tell myself it isn't because I'm avoiding her after our last meeting. I'm just busy. To support this, I delve further into my work and put in extra hours at the hospital. If Josh is upset by this, he doesn't share it. He offers to save dinner for me a few nights, but I tell him not to bother. I am used to grabbing quick bites throughout the day and often just go immediately to sleep when I arrive home.

While I fully intended to avoid the silence of home I end up regretting all the hours I spend away because the summer ends and my daughter leaves for college. We went to dinner as a family the night before she left. Our son, Cooper, even came out with us. He drove the three hours from his university to give his younger sister a proper farewell. My parents, Kelly and Brad and their daughter came to bid Rebecca goodbye. It was a nice dinner and afterwards my stepsister and brother-in-law came over to our house for some after dinner conversation.

Brad doesn't drink alcohol due to his past issues with substance abuse, and I think Kelly stopped drinking it too out of solidarity or something. I, on the other hand, had no such obligation and was freely drinking wine in front of Brad. To his credit Brad encourages people to act normally around him and to not make allowances due to his past mistakes. I was glad he wasn't a tool about it, and I silently thanked him as I took another sip of wine.

"I'm so excited for Becca. She's gonna do great at college," Kelly says.

We are all seated in our living room and just catching up on life events. We live fairly close to one another but due to various obligations we typically only see each other on special occasions. I love her like a sister, but we have never really grown close like some sisters I know. We definitely weren't like Julie and her sister, Addy. Now those two were true BFF's.

"Yeah. My baby girl is going to kill it. Hopefully she doesn't get too distracted with the party scene," I say and sit down in the single armchair we have in the room.

Brad and Kelly are seated next to each other on our smaller sofa, and they are holding hands. It's sick-cute how they are still so affectionate with each other after being married for so long. Don't get me wrong. I'm not disgusted by their affection for one another but just once I'd like to see them fight or just disagree. It was like they were one mind in two separate bodies and I wanted to scream at them to loosen up.

"She'll be fine. She's got a good head on her shoulders," the other person that I wished would loosen up says. Josh is sitting on the larger sofa, looking dwarfed by it.

The furniture set was another one of those silly purchases meant to test my husband. The leather couches were just massive, and they swallowed everyone. Sometimes it took me a few attempts to get up because I just sank into them. Josh got around this problem by always sitting on the edge. That, of course, bothered me because he always looked like he was ready to bolt. It seemed he could never relax and was always looking for an avenue of escape.

"I know that. I just meant it is easy to be distracted by that kind of atmosphere," I say defensively. It is Kelly's widened eyes that make me realize I was being harsh. Josh doesn't comment.

"What do you two plan to do now that you will have all this time to yourselves?" Brad asks; the peacemaker of our family. He had been settling disputes between family members for years, from everything to Pictionary battles to silly sibling squabbling between myself, Kelly and our brother, Gregory.

"I'm not sure," Josh responds.

I take a giant gulp from my wine glass, my third, and nearly choke on it. *He's not sure?* We don't have any plans because we can barely be in the same room together. Three sets of eyes are on me and I just shrug.

"Went down the wrong pipe," I say and take another drink.

"Maybe you should slow down," Josh says.

"Maybe you should mind your own business," I say flippantly and finish off the rest of the wine. Josh just stares back at me. I stare right back at him and shake my empty glass.

"Empty. Need a refill. Anybody else want a glass? Kelly? Brad?" I ask, knowing full well they will both decline.

"No, thanks," Brad says.

"Too bad," I say and begin my multiple attempt struggle to get out of the chair. Once I've finally developed enough momentum to propel myself up I sprout out of the chair and go up the three steps to our kitchen area. It isn't until I'm getting the wine out of the wine cooler that I noticed Kelly had come with me.

"Oh. You want a glass?" I ask her, surprised to see her.

"No. And I don't think you should have another either," she states.

"Ughh, not you too. I already have one babysitter. I don't need another one," I say and make sure I pour the wine up as far as it can go in my favorite Santa snowmen stemless wine glass. Everyone else may be grumpy but my snowmen were all smiles. Just to irate Kelly further I carefully lift the overly full glass to my lips and take a noisy sip. She glares at me with narrow eyes.

"Lighten up little sis. This is a night of celebration. My baby girl is going to college," I say and pump a fist into the air. The movement causes the wine to jostle and a little of it spills on Kelly's shoes. She gives me her best look of disappointment, and I give her my best 'oops, sorry but not sorry' look. She isn't amused.

"What is going on with you? You seem extra testy lately," she says.

"Extra. That's a step up from too, right?"

"What?" Kelly asks, confused by my riddle.

65

"Nothing. I'm *fine*. Just wanted a little wine tonight. I had hoped I could enjoy it in a judgment free zone but it would appear that isn't going to happen tonight. Sorry to dip out on all this *fun* but I'm going to retire to my boudoir. You cool cats enjoy yourselves and don't get too wild," I give her a gun salute as a goodbye and walk around her to the stairs.

"Stay golden Brad," I call to my brother-in-law as I walk past the living room stairs.

"Take care, Stacey," Brad calls back.

Ignoring the daggers I know Kelly is staring into my back, I go up the stairs to the bedrooms and forgo the master bedroom. I have been sleeping in the guest bedroom ever since the night of rejection. I've moved quite a few of my belongings in here and survey the clothing I have yet to place in the closet. No time like the present.

After I put the clothes away, I turn in a circle trying to find something else to occupy my time. Unfortunately, nothing springs forth and the only sight I am left with is the open bathroom door. As if in a trance I walk through it, turn on the light, set my wine glass down on the sink and open the medicine cabinet. Sure enough, I find what I'm looking for. I don't know why they would be in the guest bathroom.

Frankly, I'm surprised we have any in the house at all. Josh uses disposable razors. I know why he does that of course. It's the same reason why Kelly doesn't keep alcohol in her house. Why would you want to tempt an addict with the object of their obsession?

Gently, I place my snowmen wine glass on the counter top and take one of the thin metal razors out of the protective sleeve and just turn it in my hands. The bathroom lights catch the smooth surface, and a seductive shine calls out to me. Moving my gaze upward I stare at myself in the mirror holding the blade. I don't know who is staring back at me, but it isn't me. There is only one way I know of to try to get back to a place of recognition.

With this thought in my mind I lift my foot, use the countertop

66

for support and bare my thigh. How convenient I wore a skirt tonight. I push the fabric aside and use my free hand to glide over the scar tissue. I may not recognize my own face but this, I know to my core is all me. Placing the blade against my skin feels so familiar to me and I swear I inhale like a woman does just before she orgasms. I apply some pressure, and the first drop of blood appears. I stop advancing and just take a moment to admire my creation.

Next, I squeeze the area a little to increase the droplets and watch as they drip to the countertop. The design they make is like abstract art, only I can see what they mean, and they are beautiful. I put the blade back and increase the line. Once I'm satisfied with the rest of my masterpiece, I drop the blade onto the stark white counter and just watch the scene before me. At one point I even dip my finger into the red paint and taste it. It tastes like salt and remembrance.

I may not know who Stacey is, but I do know this and just like I did so many times before I wait for the feeling. But I keep waiting because the feeling I had been chasing doesn't come. I even pick the blade back up and make a second cut but aside from the first inhale of breath there is no more spark. Instead, all that occurs is a mess on my bathroom floor and me staring at it like it has betrayed me.

With my foot still propped up, my thigh bared and blood dripping down, I once again look at my reflection. This time I don't even see my own face staring back at me. All I see is a void and all I feel is empty. Now the smiling snowmen just seem to be mocking me with their jovialness. Still, I reach out for the glass and take another sip of wine, swallowing it down just as I have swallowed down the hollowness I've felt my entire adult life.

-10-

Tempting

It's been two months since Reyann walked into my exam room and one month since I confirmed that she has cancer. Initially we discovered the tumors on her liver, and I suspected they were metastases, secondary cancer caused by a primary cancerous site. Further testing revealed that the initial site of cancer was her intestines. Instead of simply battling colorectal cancer she was now in stage four since the cells had spread to her liver, a distant organ, and she had a battle from various locations. A treatment plan was discussed, and she chose which course she wanted to take.

Chemo.

She wanted to see if the tumors would shrink before she underwent any surgical removal option. I wasn't optimistic about the odds, but I kept that to myself. It was still her life, cancer didn't control her, and I would do as she directed because in the end it was Reyann that had to live with her decisions. Or die with them.

I didn't know if she had told Brad or Kelly about her diagnosis and I didn't ask. I also didn't reveal it myself because I believed firmly in patient-doctor confidentiality. And the law believed in it just as firmly as I did. As far as I knew the only people that knew about Reyann's condition was Reyann herself, me, and Jeff. Perhaps her younger son had been told but if he had he hadn't made his presence known. Her hair was thinning by now and I knew it was only a matter of time before she would have to tell others in her life about her diagnosis.

The only person that ever accompanied Reyann on her appointments was Jeff. He came to every one and sat with her while she underwent her Chemotherapy. Today, she was scheduled for another round, and I wanted to check on her status. I wasn't surprised to find Jeff sitting at her side. Reyann was watching the television and Jeff was reading a book. Only Reyann acknowledged my presence as I approached. She muted the television and gave me her customary smile.

"Good morning, Dr. Stacey," she says.

"Good morning, Reyann. How are you this morning?" I ask her with a smile that even I know is more honest than the ones I usually gave to my patients.

"Oh. As well as can be expected. It's nice of you to come check on me," she says. She is hooked up to various machines and has IV lines attached. Patients aren't exactly in the most comfortable position during Chemo, but Reyann doesn't seem to be pulsed by the precarious lines.

"Anything for my favorite patient. How were you feeling after the last session?" I ask her and sit down in the empty chair to her right. She turns her head towards me and I notice the dry lips and slightly sallow appearance in her face that is accompanied with Chemo therapy.

"It was a little rough in the days following but Jeff has been a godsend and saw me through it," she says affectionately about her eldest. Jeff is still reading his book. Either he is oblivious to our conversation, or he just doesn't care.

"I'm glad to hear that. It is always good to have someone with you immediately after treatment. Don't let my presence interrupt your show. What are you watching?" I ask and she laughs slightly.

"The Real Housewives of New Jersey," she admits.

"Oh. I've never seen it. Where are the fake housewives?" I ask. Reyann laughs again.

"You're being cheeky. I know it's mostly a soap opera and even trashy at times but it's my guilty pleasure."

"Well, if you enjoy it, I'm sure I will too. Hit unmute and lets enjoy the trash," I say, earning another laugh.

Reyann turns the volume back on and for the next forty minutes I watch a show that I will never again watch in my life. However, this isn't about me, and I can tell Reyann really enjoys the show. She often provides me back story to explain why the women are arguing or someone is upset. She knows all their names and who is legit and who is just blowing smoke. When the show ends, I ask her what is next, and she shoos me away.

"You don't need to waste your time sitting with me all day. I'm sure you have plenty to do," she says.

"Nonsense. I'm not wasting anything by being here with you. I cleared my schedule so don't you fret. Maybe next show we can watch something with a little more *class*," I suggest, and she laughs at me again.

"Jeff, why don't you take Dr. Stacey to get some lunch? It doesn't seem like we will agree on entertainment and I'm sure you both could use something to eat," Reyann says, her head turned towards her son.

The stone figure in the corner chair finally looks up from his book and he glances at me, looks me up and down, before turning back to his mother.

"She appears to be fully capable of fending for herself," he says.

Jerk. He definitely just implied I am fat.

"Jeffrey Mitchell Collins you get your lazy butt out of that chair and buy the nice doctor some lunch," Reyann orders in the best mother voice I have ever heard.

I'm grinning and doing a terrible job of hiding it because this is a grown ass man getting scolded by his mommy, and I am loving every moment of it.

Jeff doesn't reply. He simply puts his book aside and stands. He starts to walk around the hospital bed and towards the door. He stops at my chair and gestures with his hand.

"Well, aren't you coming?" he says impatiently.

"Oh, you don't have to trouble yourself. I can grab something later," I say with a tight smile. Inside I'm fuming at his fat comment but I wasn't about to lose my cool in front of a patient.

"Nonsense. Go with him. Make sure he eats something healthy and not a burger. He doesn't eat nearly enough vegetables," Reyann tells me.

How could I possibly deny her?

That is how I find myself walking through the hospital cafeteria with Jeff at my side. As Reyann predicted he gets a burger and fries. I choose a piece of cake and chocolate milk. Jeff raises his eyebrows at my choices, and I lower my eyes to his burger. Without a word he adds pickles and lettuce to his burger and then he grabs an apple and hands it to me. Reluctantly, and with an eye roll, I take the apple.

When we get to the cashier, he starts to pay for mine too but I stop him. I tell the cashier I will pay for myself and Jeff shrugs before taking his food choices to a table. After I pay, I'm about to make my exit when he calls to me.

"Doc, sit down," he says and points to the chair across from him.

After a longing gaze at the exit doors, I warily sit down.

He starts to eat his meal, and I just sit there awkwardly. I'd had a carnal dream about this man just the night before and now I was sitting across from him while he stuffed his face. I was not at all comfortable and I blurted the first thing that came to my mind.

"It could be considered a gift if you bought my lunch and that's against hospital policy," I say.

"Okay," he shrugs, dismissively.

"I wasn't trying to be rude. I just didn't want to violate policy," I state.

71

"Okay." He says just as dismissively as the last time and I purse lips at how easily he is unconcerned about what I am saying.

"Not that I would let you buy me lunch anyway because I'm married and that would also be inappropriate."

This time he raises one eyebrow but still he says nothing. His face is cast down and his attention remains on the plate of food before him.

"I don't think my husband would like it very much."

"I got it," he says.

"Okay. I just wanted to make sure you knew why. I didn't want you to think I was being rude. It's just that I'm-," The man has an annoying habit of interrupting me.

"Married. I know. Do I make you nervous Doc?" Jeff asks, his burger all but forgotten.

"What?! No," I say a bit too emphatically.

Jeff grins at me.

"I'm not going to do anything you know?"

"What?" I ask. My eyes are darting everywhere but towards him.

"It's obvious you want me. But you don't have to worry. I don't mess around with married women," Jeff states. This has me snapping back to reality and to myself.

"How magnanimous of you. On behalf of all married *fat* women everywhere thank you so much for that."

Jeff chuckles. Now I am staring right at him, enraged by his careless dismissal of me.

"You're funny. I love a woman with jokes," he states and goes back to his lunch. He keeps his gaze on me though as he eats his fries.

"I'm sure you do. About as much as I love a man with chlamydia."

"See. Hilarious. It's true, though, you know."

"What is true?" I ask feigning interest.

"That you want me. And who called you fat?"

"Excuse me? You did about five minutes ago."

I glare a little harder at him because he is being a dick. He knows it too because his eyes shine with delight at my annoyance with him. He really is nothing but a giant man-child.

"No, I didn't but I can understand why you would get confused. You're distracted by your attraction for me. You can't help yourself. It's purely biological," he explains.

This time I'm the one laughing.

"Right. Because my little brain is incapable of controlling my basic instincts."

"No. I'm sure you're fully capable of controlling your instincts but where is the fun in that? Sometimes you just need to give in and live a little."

I swallow down my instinct to punch him and glare at him.

"But you don't mess around with married women," I repeat his words.

"I know. It's a shame. I'm not sure how we are going to move past this attraction you have but we are just going to have to do it. I know it's going to be hard for you but I'm here for moral support. Anything you need," he says, his eyes twinkling.

He thinks he's got me in a corner, but I'll be damned if I let him have the better of me for a third time. If he thinks he can just say these things and not suffer any consequences than he definitely needs to be taught a lesson.

"Anything I need?"

"Of course. I'm very active in community outreach," Jeff smirks.

"What I need is a good fuck. The kind where we are both spent and sweaty but no matter how many times we cum we keep going back for more. What I need is to feel a hardened cock deep inside me, filling me up. I want hair pulling, biting, marks and pain to the point of ecstasy. I want the both of us to be hurting because it feels so good. That is what I need," I say and stand.

Jeff is staring down at the seat I just vacated, still and silent. I can tell he is processing what I just said and trying to come up with a response. I wait but he doesn't speak. Now I'm smirking and I walk over to his chair. Leaning down I whisper in his ear.

"Don't make promises you can't keep."

His gaze follows me as I stand back upright. With his eyes on me I take a bite out of the apple he handed me and walk away from the table. I'm still smirking when I exit the cafeteria.

The score is now two to one and I'm gaining on him.

-11-

Projection

Despite my own internal reassurances that Reyann is not my father and Jeff does not represent adolescent me I can't help but continue to identify with their situation. After all, Reyann's initial cancer mirrored my father's and with every passing day her prognosis appears to be a reflection of his. Randall Cooper, my father, had initially sought medical care once he realized he was losing weight at an alarming rate. For a man that was extremely health conscious and concerned with his muscle mass a few pounds lost was extremely concerning. He went to the doctor one day and two weeks later he had his diagnosis. Within months he was gone from the world, and I was thrust into life without him.

I know I should have informed Reyann that I couldn't continue as her doctor because of the stirrings of emotions I began to experience early on in her treatment, but something stops me every time. I convince myself that my reaction has nothing to do with my own history but with how invested I am in my patient's outcome. The argument I keep relying on is that I am the best in my field in the local area and it would be harmful to my patient if I step down as her primary physician. My decision to remain her doctor is for her benefit, not for my own.

Lies, of course.

Over the years I have become adept at coating my true motives with altruistic considerations. I wasn't hiding my scars from my family for my own benefit. It was paramount they remain hidden so I did not cause my mother any additional harm. Entering into a relationship with Josh wasn't done to prevent myself from dealing with the pain of losing my father. No, the relationship occurred because I was moving forward by joining my life with a good man who deserved my gratitude. Remaining Reyann's doctor was not so I could have continued access to Jeff, a man that had seeped into my dreams, but was necessary to ensure she received the best care possible.

Every decision I made, every course of action, had a deeper explanation that could overshadow my own selfish desires. I had spent years perfecting my screenplay of justification that I didn't recognize the destruction to my psyche until my habits were all but formed. When, and why, I began to recognize my behavior for what it was I tried to tell myself that this wasn't me. I could change. People change all the time and now that I was able to identify the repeated behavior I could prevent it.

Yet, here I am, making the same mistakes and trying to convince myself that my choices are justified.

Rachel finds me sitting in my usual spot in her office. It has been weeks since I last visited her on her lunch hour. After discussing how my husband had found me in that bathroom all those years ago and how my feelings for him had been influenced by that first encounter, I stayed away. She tried calling me, but I failed to return a single call. Even her wife, Julie, had attempted to reach me but I knew their numbers and hit ignore every time.

Family was supposed to be the people in your life that could look into your soul and recognize your essence. I had kept so many things hidden from my family for so long that I knew what they saw when they looked at me was not the real me. I lived two lives, had two separate existences and I couldn't even recognize which persona was legit. This dichotomy of character is why I had come to Rachel this time. I could have reached out three years ago when I had engaged in an ill-conceived affair, but I had convinced myself that my lapse in judgment had merely been a childish reaction and would not occur again.

Something had changed, however. There was now something growing inside me that kept demanding to be released and I was terrified that the personas I had kept separate for so long would be destroyed and with them my loved ones would suffer the consequences. Despite the hurt I had already brought Josh I did not want to continue bringing him pain. This is why I was back in Rachel's office, fully prepared to grovel.

She pauses in her doorway when she sees me, but she doesn't kick me out. Instead, she sighs, closes the door and walks to her chair. She sits down, puts her purse in her desk drawer and sits back, waiting for me to begin.

"I owe you an apology," I say.

"You do," Rachel agrees. She knows how much I hate saying I am sorry because when one utters these words they are admitting fault and I have problems admitting I am wrong. Usually, I can string together some words that sound like an apology without actually saying it, but I know Rachel will certainly tell me to leave if I continue to bullshit her.

"I shouldn't have ignored your calls. You have been the best friend I could ever ask for and I take advantage of you too much. I know this. I wish I could say I was sorry for that but you and I both know it would be a lie. Honestly, I'm going to take advantage of you as long as you allow me to. I'm grateful for your friendship and you know I'd bury anybody you need me to in order to return the favor. So, I'm not sorry for coming to you."

Rachel nods but does not comment. I continue.

"Remember when you first told me you were gay?"

"I do," she says softly.

We were thirteen and we were at my house for our biweekly

sleep over when she told me. We had just started high school, and I was going on and on about how great the next four years would be. During my nonsensical prattle Rachel had blurted out that she thought she liked girls. I immediately stopped talking and looked at her. I wish I could say I was understanding and supportive, but my first response was anything but.

"But why? Girls are so vapid," I blurted.

Fully expecting Rachel to be upset with me for my foolish comment I was surprised when she hugged me instead. I hugged her back but didn't know why we were hugging. I was pretty sure I had just insulted her.

"I love you," she said to me with her arms wrapped around me.

"Oh, god. Are we, like, gonna kiss now?" I asked her.

She laughed even louder.

"Don't be ridiculous. You're vapid," she replied. She pulled away from me and wiped away the tears that had started to form because she was laughing so hard. She was in a full on laughing fit and I was just utterly confused.

"What's going on? Don't you like me like that?" I asked, hurt that she was laughing at the thought of kissing me.

"Stacey you are hilarious. I tell you I think I'm gay and your first reaction is disgust. Not because you think I'm disgusting but because you think all girls are disgusting. I tell you I love you, but you get upset when I don't want to kiss you. You're the best," she said.

I didn't understand why I was the best. If I was the best, then why didn't she want to date me? She liked girls and I was a girl but she still wasn't interested. What was so wrong with me that she didn't look at me that way?

"But you don't want to date me?"

"Of course not," she said a bit too quickly.

"Why not? Am I not dateable?"

"Of course you are but I don't think of you in that way because you're my friend. Besides, you like boys."

78

"I could like girls," I immediately responded. She narrowed her eyes at me. "I could," I grumbled.

After a few moments of silence, I managed to sulk for an appropriate amount of time before I rebounded.

"Fine. You can like girls, but I must always be the number one girl in your life. I already gave you my heart and I'm not taking it back. Besides, no one will love you like I do," I said.

Rachel smiled at me and once again she hugged me.

"I'll always be there when you need me," she said by my side.

"Good. And I'll always be there for you. Even if you are gay. Wait! Aren't you dating Miles? Is he gay too?"

Calling upon the memory I remember how Rachel had laughed until she peed herself by my final question. Despite her confession to me she kept her secret hidden for nearly ten more years. When she finally confessed to her family, they disowned her and now she lived a life without them. Her wife and children had never met her parents, but I had. I knew how they had doted on their daughter, and it baffled me how they could so easily walk away from someone they claimed to love.

Love was fleeting and often came with strings. Maybe that is why I had told Rachel I had given her my heart because I knew she would protect it. The love we had for each other was string-less and no matter how many times I disappointed her I knew I could always rely on her. She would not abandon me as her parents had done to her.

"No one will love me like you do," I say to Rachel now. She sighs deeply, knowing that this is my apology to her.

"They might if you let them," she says sadly. I hate seeing that sadness in her eyes because it is one step away from pity. I don't want her pity. I don't want anyone's pity.

When I don't respond to her, she sits forward in her chair and leans her arms on the desk. I notice the shift in her demeanor and recognize the psychologist is now in front of me.

"Why did you stay away for so long?"

"I was afraid. And I was ashamed. I've never admitted to anyone before how I felt about my marriage and the connection to my scars. I broke my promise to you," I say after a brief pause.

Rachel's eyes spark with concern quickly before her training kicks in and the concern is replaced with professional stoicism.

"When did you do it?"

I love how she already knows what I'm talking about without actually having to say the words. This woman knew me better than I knew myself. Sometimes her insight scared me but most of the time I was glad that there was someone in my life that saw the real me and didn't turn away from what they saw.

"Three days ago."

"What precipitated it?"

"It was the night we said farewell to Becca. The night before she went to college. Dinner with the family had gone well and everyone was in a festive mood. Even Cooper came down to say goodbye to his baby sister. Frankly it was all pretty typical. A normal family gathering with laughter and jokes. Later, though, Kelly and Brad came back to our place. Things were fine, I guess. I had been drinking some wine and at one point I got annoyed with something Josh said or maybe I was annoyed at how perfectly cute Kelly and Brad were being, but I started coughing after taking a sip. Josh made a comment about me slowing down and that just set me off. I responded with my customary witty remark followed by abhorrent bitchy comments. Kelly told me she was concerned about me, and I spilled wine on her shoes because well, it's what I do.

"Then I left them downstairs while I went to my new bedroom. I'm sleeping in the guest bedroom by the way. After spending about twenty minutes or so trying to distract myself, I eventually ended up in the bathroom to search for my old friend. I found one. I used it," I finish. It is hard for me to admit to weakness. I had cultivated this persona of strength and when the pieces crumble, I find it difficult to

80

get the words out.

"You still think of the blade as your friend? Do you equate other relationships with this sensation of pain?"

I ponder her question before providing my response.

"In that moment I thought of it as a long-lost friend. I wanted it to give me the same feeling I used to get. The same one I felt on the day Josh found me. But this time that mix of pain and ecstasy didn't come. All that happened was that I ended up bleeding on the floor. As for your other question, the answer is yes. I do equate other relationships with pain. Love is pain. Love is betrayal. Love is death," I say.

"But love is also healing and joy. Love is life," Rachel counters.

I smile at her, but it isn't a genuine one. If anything, it is a smile meant to placate a young child. Rachel's description of love is not reality. She above anyone should know this. After how her parents turned away from her, I can't fathom how she can sit here and say this to me with a straight face.

"You know that isn't true," I say.

"But it is true. Love is everything you just described but it is so much more than that. Yes, love hurts. But love is the reason I'm sitting here right now. Love is the reason Kelly was concerned about you. Love is the reason why you continuously describe yourself as the villain because you refuse to place blame on others. It is your way of protecting the ones you love. It's absolutely foolish but that is what love does to us."

"It makes us fools?" I snicker.

"Yes. But it also makes us heroes. Mothers. Friends. *Wives*." She places emphasis on the last word, and I glare at her.

"Are you saying I love Josh? Seems blatantly obvious that I don't, given my recent behavior."

"Yes, that is what I am saying. If you didn't love him, you wouldn't be struggling with yourself right now. You wouldn't be sitting in front of me questioning everything you've done. You love

81

him, Stacey. The problem here isn't the love you have for Josh or the rest of your family. The problem is that somewhere along the way you stopped loving yourself. That is what is blatantly obvious based on your recent behavior."

"So, I'll be cured once I start loving myself again?"

Rachel doesn't take the bait placed by my snide remark.

"Don't turn this into a joke. You aren't a joke. And you aren't the bad guy either. You are human. You made mistakes and you will continue to make them but that doesn't mean you have to hate yourself too. You are a good person, Stacey. And you don't have a disease. You don't need a cure," Rachel says.

"What do I need then?"

"I can't answer that. Only you can." To her credit she genuinely looks hurt that she can't wave a magic wand and fix everything for me.

"What am I paying you for then?"

It's easier to joke than it is to stay in this fog of seriousness. Rachel is smiling now because she knows I've heard her but that I've reached my limit.

"You aren't paying me."

"Well, good."

We are both smiling now. I didn't turn from her when she trusted me with her secret, and she has never once turned from me. Everyone always talks about soul mates in a romantic setting but I had never fully accepted this theory. I don't think soul mates are strictly assigned in romantic relationships. My soul mate didn't even like me in that way. But she did love me, and I loved her.

-12-

Attempt

It's been one month since I returned to Rachel's. I haven't cut myself again, but I also haven't removed the razors from my bathroom. Sometimes I will sit in there and stare at the medicine cabinet that holds the blades. Rachel knows I do this. I told her it is because I want to prove that I don't need them anymore. She told me to get rid of them because I was tempting myself, but I refused. After years of therapy and doing exactly what was suggested I decided that it was time I chose what worked best.

One month and no cuts.

If I could do this than, perhaps, I could do other things too. I got rid of the broken fountain I had once used to test my husband's patience. I posted an add and some other fool paid me money to take it off my hands. The profits were used to replace our hideously large living room furniture. The offending pieces were banished to our basement and much more practical furniture took its place.

I'm not sure what I was expecting from Josh once I made the changes around the house, but I know I hadn't expected what he did.

Nothing.

In fact, he never commented on the changes. Even when I brought up the new furniture, he simply looked at it, nodded and then asked me a question about our son. Maybe I was being petty and childish, but I felt he should have at least commented on how this furniture was better. He could have told me he hated it too and that would have satisfied me. Instead, he barely acknowledged it and I felt we were once again stuck in this awkward place of being married but not really communicating.

Not sure what to do, I simply rely on an old classic and spend an afternoon making him his favorite dinner and figure we can maybe watch one of those sci-fi movies he enjoys. I enjoy the occasional monster movie, but he prefers the ones that rely heavily on technology and a science I just don't understand. This night is supposed to be something nice for him, so I fully intend to suggest we watch one.

The dinner is made, and I am waiting for him to come home from his meeting. Even though he mostly works from home his consultant work often takes him to other locations and I know he had meetings throughout the week. I made the dinner and dressed up in my best cocktail dress. He comes home in a suit, and it is all working out so perfectly. I meet him at the door with a glass of wine and a smile. He is initially surprised and the look on his face has me laughing.

"Here, let me take that," I say and reach out for his briefcase. He releases it without objection. I put it in the hall closet while he just stands by the front door, wine glass in hand, confused.

"I made dinner," I say and gesture towards the kitchen.

"Okay," he replies.

With a chuckle I grab his hand and lead him to the kitchen and his chair. He sits, still looking confused. He doesn't say a word as I place his plate in front of him and take my seat. I have some music playing in the background, candles lit on the table and the lights turned down. I thought it was soothing and displayed the attempt I was trying to make. This was my olive branch. A last-ditch effort at initiating intimacy.

I encourage him to eat when I notice he is just sitting there staring into space. He startles when I touch his hand, and I swallow down the hurt. Rome wasn't built in a day.

"How was the meeting?" I ask. Baby steps.

"Fine. Their software is functioning, but they agreed to upgrade their systems to compete with the markets. It's a good thing they are investing in the new technology because in five years theirs would have been obsolete. In a business that relies heavily on internet traffic and web transfers it is something they need to stay current on," he explains.

I praise him for his latest achievement even though the magnitude is lost on me. Aside from the hospital medical charting software I used I knew nothing about computer programming and business. I wait for him to ask me about my day or to mention the dinner, but he never does. He returns to silence.

In the beginning of our relationship, I did the majority of the talking. I had to pry details out of him and during one of those instances he had revealed how his mother used to make him beef stroganoff every year for his birthday. I made it today even though it isn't his birthday. I wanted him to know that I was trying and preparing his birthday meal seemed like the right thing to do but I notice how he is just moving the meat around on his plate and isn't actually eating it.

"Is something wrong with the food?" I ask.

"Huh? Oh, no. It's fine," he says and puts a noodle in his mouth. He swallows it but it looks forced.

"If something is wrong with it than tell me."

"No. It's fine. It's just...," he trails off and I begin to feel the prickles of annoyance under my skin.

"What?" I ask.

"I don't like beef stroganoff," he says.

I feel my heart slam against my chest, and I'm reminded of those cartoons when the character has fire coming out of their ears because they are mad. While I don't have actual fire coming out of my ears, I can feel them burning.

85

"But it was your birthday meal?" I know he told me this. I remember us discussing it vividly.

"What?"

"When you were younger. Your mother used to make it for your birthday."

"She made it for everyone's birthday. It was my father's favorite, and we ate it on every birthday," he explains.

The only explanation I have for what happens next is sheer frustration. We had been married for almost twenty years and in all those years he had never once told me this. In fact, the few details he had told me about his family and his past had only been revealed after I had asked pointed questions. He never freely divulged information, and I had started to feel like I was bothering him, so I had eventually stopped asking. In that moment I realized that not only did I not know myself, but I didn't know my husband.

I quickly stand up, my chair falling backward as I stand. Josh's gaze quickly turns to the fallen chair and then lands on me. I have my hands flat against the table and I am bent forward a little, but I am staring at the flickering light of the candle.

"Then what the hell is your favorite food?" I ask between clenched teeth.

"I don't have one," he replies and my head snaps to him.

I imagine I look like one of those monsters from the movies I enjoy but he doesn't. Perhaps I was the girl from The Exorcist and my head would spin three hundred and sixty degrees before the night is over.

"Everyone has a favorite food," I say.

"I guess I don't," he shrugs and stands. He picks up his plate and starts to throw the remnants in the trash.

I'm just standing there, watching as he throws away the dinner I had prepared in the hopes of doing something nice for him. The anger continues to grow and before I know it, I'm picking up my plate too. Only, I'm not throwing the food in the trash. I pick up a messy glob in my hand and chuck it at my husband. The sloppy noodles and meat hits him in the side of his face.

Thank you, Dad, for teaching me how to throw.

Josh drops his plate in shock, and it shatters when it hits the floor.

"What the hell, Stace?" he asks as he's wiping the mess off of his face.

"What is your favorite food?" I ask, my voice raised and quite possibly crazed.

Josh looks at me like I've lost my mind. His cheek is dripping from the cream sauce, and I see a flash of anger in his eyes. Instead of shying away from that flash I think to myself, *Finally.* But just as quickly as it appeared the look vanishes, and he walks to the sink and begins to clean the mess off his face.

"What's your favorite food!" I yell.

He ignores me.

I pick up my bread roll and hit him in the back of the head with it.

"Stop throwing your food at me," he says and turns to me.

I'm searching his expression for just a hint of the passion I am feeling in this moment but I'm not finding any.

"Answer my damn question!"

"You're being ridiculous. Stop it," he says and once again turns his back on me.

This time I pick up my plate and chuck it against the wall opposite me. It slams against the wall with a sloppy crash and shatters before the shards fly onto the floor. My dinner is slowly dripping down the wall and my husband is staring at the mess I made like he has just seen an assassination before his very eyes.

Perhaps he did witness an assassination. To him I'm simply having an overreaction to a silly question. To me I am seeing the destruction of my marriage and the life I had spent twenty years believing in. With one simple revelation he has shown me that everything I had built was nothing more than lies.

"Are you crazy?" he asks, turning away from the mess and to me.

"Yes! I've always been crazy. You knew this. You knew this and you married me anyway. But for some reason you kept the fact that you hate beef stroganoff from me for twenty years! Two kids! We have two kids, but you couldn't tell me you hate beef stroganoff!" I'm shouting and my hands are fisted at my sides.

"Stacey, calm down. It's not that big of a deal. We can eat something else," he says. His voice is calm, and his stance is no different than it normally is. I hate how normal he looks right now because nothing about this, about our marriage, is normal.

"You think this is about dinner? I don't give a fuck about dinner. I want to know how the man I've slept next to for twenty years has managed to remain a stranger. How could you build this life with me when you couldn't even tell me that your mother made you a birthday meal you hated?"

I'm baring my heart to him, baring my soul, and his only response is to shrug. He fucking shrugs his shoulders like I'm not falling apart in front of him. I had literally thrown a plate against a wall and his only response is to shrug his damn shoulders!

"Shrug your shoulders one more time!" I hold up one finger and shake my hand. This time he does react.

"I don't tell you a lot of things. That doesn't mean you have to throw food at me. This is stupid. I'm going to bed," he throws the dish towel he had used to clean his face into the sink and starts walking to the stairs.

"Don't you dare walk away from me. We aren't finished," I say and grab a hold of his arm. I pull him back and he sighs.

"I'm not going to fight with you," he says.

"Why not? Fight with me! Yell at me! Do something, anything because I'm drowning here." I'm trying desperately to get him to see how everything is falling apart and that I am on the brink, but my

88

words fall flat.

"You know I don't like fighting. You'll feel better tomorrow after you've had time to calm down." He once again starts to walk to the stairs, and I pull him back for a second time. I know what he means when he says I'll feel better tomorrow because for many years I've allowed the doubts to be pushed back down with the passing of the days. No longer will I allow myself to let the passage of another day silence me.

"No. No more walking away. We have to deal with this. I know you are capable of more than just scowling and walking off. You've told me," I say referencing a time many years ago when he had got into an argument with his cousin and slapped her. He had told me how she had accused him of some terrible things and even though he begged her to stop she kept coming at him. At his wits end he had slapped her. It was not a moment he had been proud of, and it had haunted him ever since. It isn't right for me to bring it up now, but I am tired of him always walking away from me. For my passive, non-confrontational husband bringing up the one moment in his life where he lost control is a low blow, even for me.

"That isn't fair, Stacey. We are done here," he says and tries to walk away for a third time.

"You know why I cheated on you?"

He stops moving.

"Because I could. It was easy. You barely notice me and when I try to talk to you, you dismiss me. You are a robot. You are just like those computers you love so much. You don't even care," I say. I'm crying now but the anger is still very strong inside me.

"You think I don't care?" he asks and turns to face me. He isn't crying but he doesn't look angry either. In fact, his eyes look completely devoid of any emotion. They are cold, hard steel.

"I know you don't."

"All I've ever done is care about you. From the moment I met you, I've done everything I could to keep you safe. I gave you everything you ever asked for and never once did I demand anything in return. If anyone doesn't care, it is you. I've been faithful. You cheated," he says and this time he is the one pointing an accusatory finger. All the time his eyes remain dead.

"I just wanted you to notice me."

"Well, congratulations. I noticed you. God, Stacey, what more do you want from me?"

"I want you to love me!"

Until I say the words I hadn't actually known that was what I had been struggling with. Yes, Josh cared about me, and he had helped me when I needed him but all this time I never actually believed that he loved me because how could he possibly. He didn't even really know me. Every time I tried to show him, he would shut me down or turn away. It seemed even in my marriage there was a dichotomy of character. Josh only saw the wife he believed he had but not the person I truly was.

"I do love you," he says.

"No. You don't. You love the image you've created of me. You love the woman you think you saved. But you didn't save me Josh. I cut myself again last month. I'm just as damaged now as I was then but you refuse to see it because that doesn't fit into your world."

His gaze travels to my thighs when I tell him what I did. He doesn't move towards me though. He just remains standing near the stairs as if distance is the only thing he needs right now, whereas, my body is begging him to come to me.

"Is that why you moved into the other bedroom?"

"No. I moved in there because you keep rejecting me."

"No, I don't."

"Yes, you do. If I do something you don't like you just push me away and shut down. You've done that for years, but I kept telling myself it was my fault. I was the damaged one after all. The desires I had were just wrong because what kind of person enjoys pain. But, Josh, I'm tired of feeling like what I want is wrong. I'm tired of

90

being pushed away." I sniffle and take a step toward him.

When he takes a step back, I know that this isn't going to end well.

"I can't change how I feel. I don't enjoy the same things you do. I can't do them. I won't do them," he says softly.

"I know," I sigh and wipe away the tears before I straighten my back and harden my stance. "But I can't stay in a marriage anymore where I have to hide who I am. I can't do it. I won't do it." I repeat his words back to him.

He lifts his head and instead of dead eyes I see sadness. I want to comfort him, but I know that the time for comfort has passed. Twenty years was far too long to deny the truth.

"What are you saying?" he asks.

"I'm saying I'm leaving. I'm saying this is the end."

With those final words I walk towards the front door, grab my keys and purse from the hooks they are hanging on and walk out of my house. I get into my car, pull out of the garage, and drive away.

Never once do I look back.

-13-

Truth

The first person to call me after I walked out on Josh is our daughter. She discovered my departure after calling the house one day to ask about us sending some of her belongings to her. When Josh had tried to understand what she had been describing she had asked to speak with me and he told her I wasn't there. Becca pressed him for further details, and he revealed that I had left the week before and was staying at a hotel. She immediately called my cell phone.

Trying to explain to my eighteen-year-old daughter why I had to leave without actually divulging the ugly details was difficult. In the end she didn't understand why I had left, and she told me to go back and work things out with her father. I told her there was no fixing this but that we both loved her very much. She told me I was being selfish. I told her she was right but that it still didn't change my mind. She hung up on me.

I didn't blame Becca for her reaction. Josh and I had been very good about keeping our problems secret from our children. Aside from the incident with Brad and Kelly a couple of months ago I had never displayed my resentment and doubted the rest of my family would have suspected me of leaving. Now that Becca knew, however, it was only a matter of time before the rest of my family would discover what I had done. I loved my daughter, but she had a big mouth.

Morgan, formerly known as Chasity, had even inquired about my well-being one day while we were going over records. At the close of each day, we would discuss the day's patients to ensure we hadn't missed anything. While we were discussing our latest patient, she expressed her concerns.

"Are you alright, Dr. McNill?"

"Of course. Did you submit the latest bloodwork for Mr. James?" I ask and open up his file.

"Yes. Are you sure you're alright? You aren't acting like yourself," Morgan says timidly.

I throw Mr. James' file down and give Morgan the best impatient stare I can muster. She sputters a little and this has me smiling a bit. For all her recent bluster she is still the same little mouse.

"What would you like me to say Morgan? Should we have a sleep over and tell all our secrets while we braid each other's hair?"

Morgan is no longer looking at me with concern. Now she is throwing daggers at me with her eyes.

"I don't know why you have to be so nasty. I was only asking because I don't want your personal problems to impact our patients' care," Morgan says and picks up the next file.

With a heavy sigh I do something I have never done with one of my nurses. I admit fault.

"You're right, Morgan. I haven't been myself, but you don't have to worry. This won't affect my performance. And, if for some reason, you think it is I want you to tell me."

Morgan stares at me in disbelief. I had never given one of my nurses permission to chastise me or correct me. In fact, I often responded negatively if they did. I didn't like having my authority questioned.

"I will speak up if our patients' care is jeopardized," Morgan agrees, and we move on with our task.

It takes another three days before my mother calls me. Becca had finally told her that I had left Josh and she wanted to meet me to discuss it. I loved my mother, of course, but we weren't exactly close. In fact, she was closer to Kelly and Brad than we were. You'd think I would have clung to her after my father passed away but for some reason, we never really bonded like I had with my father. She was a fantastic mother and was always trying to get closer to me, but I kept her at arm's length.

I agreed to meet her for lunch. After talking to her I called Rachel to let her know I wouldn't be seeing her that day for lunch and she laughed at me.

"Lunch? You and I both know you don't come for lunch," Rachel says.

"Says who? Jules is a great cook."

"Right. Talk to your mother. Tell her the truth. And don't do what you normally do," Rachel instructs me.

"What do I normally do?"

"Deflect with sarcasm."

"What? I never do that! And I'm hurt that you would suggest I do."

"Don't be a bitch to your mother," Rachel ignores me.

"That is strictly reserved for you my dear."

My mother and I meet at some Italian place near the hospital, and I give Morgan strict instructions to call me the moment one o'clock hits. I decide my mother has me for two hours and not a moment later. This lunch is not going to be a heartfelt mother-daughter intervention. I just want to state the facts and return to my patients. When I arrive my mother, Tasha Johnson, is already seated at a table.

She had married Kelly's father, Paul, when I was seventeen years old and nearly two years after my father had died. I had never held any ill feelings towards Paul for being the new man in my mother's life. I wanted her to be happy and if anyone deserved happiness it was her. In the beginning I hadn't exactly been thrilled she started dating so soon after my father had died but now that I was an adult I understood why she did it. She was lonely and she needed human contact. I was fortunate that the man she chose for her second marriage was Paul Johnson. He was kind and patient. He never once made me feel like he was trying to replace my father, and he opened his home to me willingly. While it had never really felt like home, I still appreciated the effort he made to make me feel welcome. He was good to my mother, and I loved him for that.

"Stacey, over here," my mother calls to me even though I have already spotted her and am walking towards her table.

"I see you," I say and quickly make my way to her so she will stop waving. My mother is very animated. Where my father had been the adventurer my mother is the social butterfly. She would accompany us on our adventures sometimes, but she mostly preferred things like parties and places where she could interact with other people. She thrived on attention. I, on the other hand, preferred anonymity.

"I'm so glad you agreed to meet me. I don't see you nearly enough. The hospital must be keeping you locked away," she says and hugs me when I approach.

I hug her back and we sit. I pick up my menu and start to look through it.

"I have been pretty busy," I say. The truth is I should see my mother more. We live in the same town, and I don't have an excuse for staying away as often as I do. When my kids were younger, I used to see my mother and stepfather regularly but when they grew older, I started to drift away as well. There was no reason for it other than I found it easier.

My daughter is right, I am selfish.

"Well, I'm glad you had time today. How are Becca and Cooper?"

I know she is genuinely asking about her grandchildren, but the question only reminds me of the real reason for this lunch visit, and I decide I might as well just dive right in. No need to postpone the inevitable.

"I left Josh. I'm not going back. The marriage is over and I'm okay with it," I say, folding my menu and placing it back down on the table.

"Oh, well. Um…I guess…," her voice trails off because she is uncomfortable and unsure what she should say.

"I know you know. Becca called you," I decide to give my mother a break from her tap dancing.

"Yes. She did call me. She was worried about you. Is this what you really want?"

Once again, I know she is only doing the motherly thing, but the question upsets me. Am I somehow incapable of knowing what I want? I'm thirty-nine years old and not a child that is confused about what toy to get. I didn't just wake up one morning and say I wanted to walk away from my twenty-year marriage on a whim. Just once I wanted my mother to come out with support for my decisions right from the start, instead of her usual doubt in my life choices disguised as motherly concern.

"Yes, mother, this is what I want."

"What does Josh want?"

And there it is. Her true motives. Josh and my mother had always been close. It wasn't his fault, really. She was also close to Kelly's husband, Brad. My mother had a way of connecting with others and they all loved her. She was super nice so why wouldn't they love her. The nice genes had skipped a generation bypassing me to go straight to my daughter. Ask anyone in my family who the bitch was, and they would all drop my name. Except for my husband. Josh would just change the subject so he wouldn't have to provide an answer.

"I don't know what he wants. The marriage is over. We barely talk to each other and when we do it is usually about bullshit. I'm not happy and neither is he. It's time to recognize the end was here years ago, and cut our losses," I say and wave a waiter over.

"It's only over if you let it be. Marriage shouldn't be so easily discarded," she says just as the waiter appears at our table.

"It's my marriage, Mother, not yours," I say sternly.

The waiter looks from me to my mother before clearing his throat. I imagine he has stumbled on many awkward conversations between people in his profession.

"Would you like to hear the specials?"

"Could you just give us a few more minutes Jeremy?"

Of course my mother would know the waiter's name. He smiles at her before agreeing and disappearing. I just roll my eyes. Even the waiter likes my mother.

"Josh loves you and you have two children together. You should at least give counseling a try," she says and picks up her menu.

I stare at her menu because I can't stare at her now that she has effectively blocked my view. It is reminiscent of how Josh dismisses me when I try to talk to him. I can feel the anger bubbling up inside me. This is not how I wanted this lunch to go at all.

"I have done counseling," I say.

"I meant marriage counseling not individual counseling," she says so calmly and without missing a step that I'm not even sure she said it.

I have never told my family that I had gone to counseling. The only person that knew was Josh and that was because he had asked me to go that first time. It had been after we were married, and Cooper had been born. I was feeling the pressure of being a new mother and trying to keep up with college courses and he was afraid I'd fall into old patterns. He asked me to go see a counselor and I agreed because I loved him and wanted to reassure him that I wouldn't harm myself. I asked him to keep it between us, and he had promised he would.

"He told you?" I'm pretty sure I whisper it because my mother puts her menu down.

"What?" she asks.

I don't whisper it this time.

"He told you. When did he tell you?" I'm glaring at her now. My mother recognizes my anger, and she reaches across the table to place her hand over mine.

"It doesn't matter. He was concerned about you, and he wanted to make sure we knew you were okay. And you were able to stop hurting yourself with the counseling so maybe that will help you again," she says.

She doesn't even know how her words are cutting me right now. Forget about the scars I had placed on my thighs. These wounds hurt me more than anything I had done to myself. The one thing I had believed was true and sacred between me and Josh has just been obliterated. He had never kept my confidence. He had told my mother and others in my family about what he had found me doing in that bathroom. He had been reporting back to them all these years and I never knew about it. Was anything in our marriage true?

"How long has he been spying on me for you?" I ask and slowly move my hand out from my mother's hold. She dismisses my comment with a wave of her hand and a scoff.

"Really, Stacey, there is no need to be so dramatic. He wasn't spying on you. He was just worried about you. I wish you had told me yourself, but you didn't. I was just glad somebody was telling me what was going on with you," she says.

"You're right. It should have been me, but it wasn't. It was him and he promised me he wouldn't tell anyone. I have to go," I say and start to stand.

"What? Why? Because I know the truth?" she asks and stands with me.

98

"No. Because all I can think about when I look at you right now is how everyone has been talking about me behind my back. My husband gave my mother reports on me like I was just some project for him."

"Stacey, you are blowing this all out of proportion. That isn't what happened at all. We just wanted to make sure you were okay. Josh wanted us to know you were getting help. All he did was care for you. We all love you," she says and tries to reach for me.

I step away from her, pulling my hands out of her reach.

"Love is betrayal," I say and ignore the hurt I place in her eyes. I'm hurting and it serves her right that she feels even an ounce of what I am feeling.

I leave my mother in the restaurant and go back to the only place that has given me solace over the years. I bury myself in my work and take comfort in knowing that the battle I fight within the walls of the hospital is meaningful. Here I am not some broken, damaged girl that had been spied on by the man she believed had kept her confidences. Here, I was the strong one.

-14-

<u>Fire</u>

Avoidance is one of the tricks I've kept in my bag the past twenty years and that is exactly what I am doing with my family. I won't answer my mother's calls. I told Paul to stop calling me after he begged me to talk to my mother. I hung up on Kelly when she told me I was acting like a churlish child. Brad, thankfully, hadn't even attempted to reach me. I spoke to my children, but I refused to talk about my marriage to their father and its impending end. Cooper accepted this after the first time I told him some things shouldn't be shared. Becca, on the other hand, refused to accept it and our conversations usually ended with her upset with me.

The days continued to march on, and I had moved out of the hotel and into a rental property. It was considerably smaller than the home Josh and I had shared but it suited me. I even brought the ridiculous furniture set that I had banished to the basement with me. It completely dwarfed my new living room, but it brought me comfort. For the first time I didn't view the furniture as some silly purchase but as a reflection of my true character. I loved ridiculous things. Sure, getting out of the sunken cushions was an ordeal but it was an ordeal I had chosen and sometimes enjoyed. There were times I found myself laughing at my various attempts to get up from the couch. The laughter was welcomed as I had so little to laugh about lately.

I hadn't ever lived on my own and despite my initial misgivings I was finding I enjoyed the solitude and having a space that was completely mine. I hung pictures that had no sense to them but made me smile. I had a poster of a cat that said *hang in there* on my front door so I would see it every time I left. It was immature and I loved it. My apartment was quickly becoming my sanctuary.

Josh and I had only seen each other twice since I had left. The first time was when I picked up the coach and the bedroom set from the guest bedroom. He had just asked how I was doing as the movers worked around us. I told him I was fine. He said good and then we parted. The second time I saw him was when I picked up my mail. I had been driving away from the house while he was driving towards it. He waved at me. I didn't wave back.

I knew it was only a matter of time before my sanctuary was invaded by my family, and I wanted to avoid the intrusion for as long as I could. I hadn't exactly shared my address with them and often told them I was working late, which was true but entirely deliberate on my part.

So, I was in my office late when I got the call. Reyann had been admitted to the hospital. Immediately, I called admitting and got her information. Then I called the doctor that had admitted her to get the history of the incident. Thankfully she had simply been admitted due to some minor complications with her chemo and was expected to be released in the morning. The doctor had just wanted to keep her overnight for assurances.

She was approaching her third month of chemotherapy and had since lost her hair. The rest of her family, including my own, knew of her condition and I wanted to make sure I saw her before any of them showed up and I was forced to interact with them. I went to her room and was pleased to find her sitting up in the bed, flipping through channels. She looked much different from the woman who had initially been sent to me. She was bald and her eyebrows were practically gone. Her eyes were sunken, and she had lost weight. Chemo was not a kind treatment. Despite the differences in her appearance, she still maintained her sunny disposition and she smiles when she sees me.

"I told them not to call you," she says as I approach.

"Nonsense. They know I would have their hides if they didn't. How are you feeling?" I ask and check her vitals on the monitor.

"Tired. I guess I was dehydrated. I wasn't sure what was happening so I came to the ER to be sure," she says and pats the bed next to her. I laugh but do as she is asking and sit beside her.

"I'm glad you did. Dehydration is serious for someone in your condition. Have you been vomiting more?"

"No more than usual. I will just have to increase my fluid intake. That is what the ER doctor told me. He was nice enough, but he doesn't have your bedside manner," Reyann jokes with me. She knows how blunt I can be, and I also know that Dr. Trudy, the ER doctor she saw, is more pleasant than I am.

"Your next treatment is this week," I say. Reyann already knows this. I'm just talking because I'm not really sure what to say to her.

"I'm dying, aren't I," she says, demonstrating her own no-nonsense manner I had come to appreciate from her.

I don't dodge and I don't give her some rehearsed answer that I would normally give. I do give her the same courtesy she once gave to me when I was struggling with her condition.

"You're going to be alright, for now," I say. She smiles at me sadly and takes my hand.

"I've lived a good life. I won't say I'm ready to die because who is ever ready for that, but I can say that I am satisfied with the life I lived." She squeezes my hand and before I can stop myself tears start to fall.

"It isn't right. You don't deserve this," I say.

"Does anyone really *deserve* cancer? I don't think this is about some cosmic retribution. It's like bingo," she says.

102

I look at her questioningly.

"Bingo?"

"Yes. My number was called is all. Instead of a pile of money, I get cancer," she says, and I snort. I quickly cover my mouth with my free hand because who laughs at that.

"It's okay. You can laugh. Sometimes the only thing that can make us feel better through the pain is laughter. I know you did all you could, and I thank you for that. This couldn't have been easy for you."

I roll my eyes at her because once again she is concerned about me when she is the one lying in the hospital bed. This time she laughs.

"Can you promise me something?" she asks.

"I don't know," I respond truthfully.

"Don't stop laughing. Whatever happens with me, with your life, don't stop finding the humor in everything. Laugh as much as you can and love with all your heart, and never apologize for being who you are," she says and brings my hand to her lips. She kisses it and lays her head back down on her pillow.

Before I can respond the room is filled by the presence of her son. Jeff comes barreling in like a bull that has escaped from a rodeo. His eyes are wild, and his movements are jagged. He is clearly worried about his mother.

"What happened?" he asks the both of us. Reyann looks at me and I take her cue.

"She's fine. Just a little dehydration is all. She'll be released in the morning," I say and move away from the bed so Jeff can be by his mother. He takes my place and takes her hand in his.

"You worry too much," Reyann says to him. Her words say one thing, but her eyes say another. She is grateful for her son and for his worry.

"It's what I do," he replies, and Reyann places her head on his shoulder.

"Call me if you need me, Reyann. Goodnight, Jeff," I say and start to exit the room.

"Wait. Can I talk to you?" Jeff calls to me.

Surprised, I simply nod. We had seen one another since the cafeteria incident during Reyann's appointments but neither of us have spoken alone together since then. I am not sure what he could possibly have to say to me but I'm not about to run away. I wait for him in the hallway.

"Thank you for being here," he finally says when he joins me.

"It's fine. I was here when I got the call. She's going to be released in the morning," I repeat.

"Yeah. Look, I'm not blind. I can see what is happening," he says and looks back to his mother sitting in the hospital bed.

"What do you mean?"

"She's sicker than the two of you are letting on. She's doing it because she thinks she's protecting me, but I don't know why you are doing it. Why are you keeping it from me?" he asks, turning back to me.

"Reyann is my patient. I can't discuss her care without her consent," I say. Relying on policy may have been cowardly but I wasn't about to defy Reyann's wishes.

"Fine. Don't tell me. I already know anyway," he says. Jeff rocks a little on his feet before placing his hands in his pockets. While he's doing this awkward movement, I examine him. His hair has grown out and the new length flatters the shape of his face. He no longer looks like an alien and his features have settled. It is actually quite remarkable how a hair style can alter one man's appearance.

He is wearing jeans and a tank top that fit loosely on his body. The muscles on his arms are in clear display since he has virtually no material covering them and when he turns a certain way the shirt moves away from his chest and I can see the muscles beneath the fabric.

He catches me staring.

I look away.

He chuckles.

"See something you like, Doc?"

"Stop it. You should wear appropriate clothing," I say, and he just laughs again.

"I don't usually get any complaints."

"You're impossible," I say and start to walk away from him.

"Hold up," he calls to me.

"What?"

"I just wanted to say I was sorry to hear about your divorce," he remarks and begins to smirk.

I narrow my eyes.

"I'm not divorced," I say.

"Oh. My mistake. Sorry to hear about your marriage, then."

I turn away from him and start walking down the hallway and back to my office. I hear him laughing behind me, but I don't acknowledge him. The last thing I need is to be involved in a scene in the halls of the hospital.

Thirty minutes later, I'm finishing up in my office and decide to call it a night when my doorway is filled by the very same man I left laughing in the hallway. I don't say anything to him when he saunters in and plops down on the sofa I often took naps on during long shifts. Continuing on with my business I let him sit there and look around my office.

"Let's go out," he blurts.

"No," I say quickly and shut down my computer.

"Aww, come on, Doc. I was only teasing you earlier. I think it would do the both of us a world of good if we got some dinner and had a few beers. You know, just two friends sharing a meal," he says.

"Friends?"

"Yeah. Aren't we friends?" he asks innocently.

"No. We aren't friends," I say and stand. I pick up my purse, work bag, and keys. He follows me out of my office, and I lock it behind us.

"Mom thinks we're friends," he says from behind me.

"She's mistaken."

I turn on my heels and walk down the hall to the elevator. Truth be told I am not sure how Jeff continuously manages to get to my office. The offices are kept separate from patient areas and the only way to access them is with keyless entry from a hospital badge. I am contemplating this when I se Jeff wave and wink at one of the nurses we pass.

Ahhh.

He was apparently becoming friendly with the nursing staff.

"You're disgusting," I say.

"Why? Because I appreciate a good-looking woman?"

"Because you think you are some sort of prize."

"Hey, I am a prize. I own my own business and have my own house," he replies, pretending offense.

"Both of which belong to your mother," I reply.

"Details," he waves me away.

Until his mother had gotten sick Jeff had lived in an apartment, but he moved in with his mother to help care for her. As for the business he owned, it was originally his mother's. Brad had informed me that Jeff managed the landscaping business his mother had inherited from her father. I imagined it would one day be in his name. I had skillfully managed to gather more information on him after Reyann had told Brad about her condition and I was finally able to come clean about being her doctor. I wasn't interested in him specifically. As Reyann's doctor it was important I familiarize myself with her support system. At least, that is what I tell myself.

As we approach the elevator Jeff moves in closer to me and I take a step to the side. Pushing the button to go down to the staff parking garage I glare at him. He chuckles and leans against the wall. His stupid shirt moves loosely to the side and one of his nipples

106

is visible. Once again, he catches me staring.

"Just come out with me," he says.

"No."

The elevator doors open and I step inside. I hit the button I need and just as the doors are about to close Jeff stops them with his hand.

"My mother is dying," he says.

I stare back at him and breathe in sharply.

"I know she's dying. I need a friend that also knows this. Just be my friend tonight," he says. All presence of the flirt that had just been before me has vanished. The man before me now is displaying his vulnerability and I don't have the heart to turn him away again.

I nod in agreement.

Jeff steps on to the elevator and we ride it down in silence. Neither of us says anything until we are both seated in my car. Not sure where to go I turn to him.

"Where are we going?"

"Ever been to Tuckets?" he asks.

"Tuck-its? Is it a strip club?" I ask, horrified.

"No. But I'm up for one if you want to go," he says with a smirk.

I shake my head, and he laughs at me.

"Tuckets is a small neighborhood joint. Nothing fancy but it has good food and the people are tolerable. I'll tell you how to get there," he says and for the next fifteen minutes I follow his instructions until I pull into a tiny rock paved parking lot.

The building is hidden partly behind some trees and the only indication it is a bar is the small neon sign that says open. Frankly, the place could be straight out of a horror movie. There is no lighting in the parking lot and it seems deserted despite the various cars around us.

Jeff notices my hesitation and he laughs at me. I really am getting tired of him constantly laughing at me.

"It isn't as scary as it looks. Come on," he says and grabs my hand. He pulls me forward and I stumble on the gravel. He catches

107

me and puts me upright. I'm cursing my heeled shoes and business casual skirt. I was not dressed to walk across gravel.

"I can walk on my own," I say and pull my hand from his grasp. He just shakes his head and continues to walk towards the building. Despite my misgivings, I follow him.

As soon as he opens the door music drifts out, and I hear voices. The place is dimly lit but it seems inviting. Much to my chagrin voices call out to Jeff when he enters. He returns the greetings and goes straight to the bar. The bartender offers his hand, and Jeff grasps it firmly in greeting.

"Haven't seen you in a while," the bearded bartender says to Jeff. He is just as physically imposing as Jeff is. In fact, his arms appear to have a larger muscle quantity than Jeff's and I imagine the two of them will break some fingers as they shake hands.

"Yeah. Been taking care of Reyann," he responds. I've never heard Jeff refer to his mother by her first name before and I find it odd.

"How is the old wench?" the bartender asks, and I look to Jeff, expecting him to respond angrily. He doesn't.

"Same ole ball buster just with cancer," he returns.

As he is talking to the bartender Jeff pulls out a stool and gestures for me to sit. It is something someone with manners would do and completely contradictory for a man that stood by and let another man call his mother a wench. The whole scene is jarring to me.

"You alright?" Jeff asks from his own bar stool.

"Yes," I say and quickly take my seat.

"Stacey this is Yoder. We went to school together," Jeff introduces me and I offer Yoder my hand. He takes it and gives me a friendly shake leaving all of the bones in my hand firmly intact.

"You've been friends since high school?" I ask.

"High school? Nah. I didn't know this jack ass then. We met in business classes," Yoder replies. He turns and pulls a bottle of beer

108

out of a cooler, opens it and puts it before Jeff. Jeff accepts the beer and takes a swig, all while looking at me.

"Business class?" I ask.

"The illustrious doctor here thought my education ended with the twelve grade," Jeff jokes with his friend. They both enjoy a laugh at my expense.

"That isn't true. I just don't know that much about you," I admit.

"Can I get you a drink?" Yoder asks me.

"Do you have any wine?" I ask.

"I do. Nothing fancy though. What kind would you like?"

"Merlot would be fine," I say.

"That's the red one, right?" Yoder asks. He bursts out laughing when I stare at him in disbelief. "Kidding. One glass coming right up."

"You look uncomfortable," Jeff says once his friend has gone to retrieve my drink.

"I am. Everyone here knows you," I say and glance around. It is an eclectic crowd of young and old. There is a group in the corner playing pool. A few of the booths are occupied and a couple is dancing on the floor that seems to have been cleared by pushing tables together.

"So? You would be more comfortable if they didn't know me?"

"I just feel like you took me into your cave or something."

Jeff bursts out laughing and Yoder decides to reappear at this moment.

"She telling jokes?" Yoder asks.

"She thinks your place is a cave," Jeff responds.

"No. That isn't what I said at all. Your place is lovely," I say to Yoder.

"Now I know you are lying. It's a hole!" Yoder says and puts a wine glass down before me.

"No. It is…charming," I say, and this earns me grins from both Jeff and Yoder.

109

"Thanks. It's no empire but I like it," Yoder says as he looks over to Jeff. I see the exchange between them and know there is something more going on here.

"What? What does that mean?" I ask Jeff. He shrugs. Yoder is the one to answer me.

"Jeff expanded Farley and Sons from a simple family run business to three locations. He is the primary landscaping company that all the construction guys use, and he even has contracts out of state. Last I heard you were looking into further expansion. That true?" Yoder turns back to Jeff.

"Maybe. Maybe not. Mom is more important," he says, and Yoder gives him a sympathetic nod.

"Yeah, she is. Let me know if you two need anything," Yoder says, knocks his knuckles against the wooden bar and ventures away to help the other patrons.

"He seems nice," I say in an attempt to breach the silence that has developed.

"He's a giant ass hat, but he's good people. Why did you become a doctor?" Jeff shifts the conversation.

"You aren't interested in that," I say and take a sip of my wine.

Jeff turns to me, beer bottle in hand, and drapes his free arm along the back of his stool.

"I wouldn't have asked you about it if I wasn't interested."

"Alright. I wanted to fight cancer. No, that isn't entirely accurate. I wanted to fight cancer and *win*," I correct.

"And?"

"And what?"

"Did you win?" he asks, still staring pointedly at me.

I avert my gaze and look down at my wine glass.

"You know I didn't," I say, referring to his mother.

"Winning isn't everything," he says, and I turn back to him, startled.

"What does that mean?"

110

"I mean sometimes it's more about the journey than it is about the end result. You may not always win but that doesn't change the good you've done. Mom adores you," he says and takes another swig of his beer.

"She's amazing," I say, and he smiles.

"Yeah, she is."

"Where is your other brother?" I had wanted to ask Reyann this many times, but I didn't want to pry. Being here, sharing a drink, I find it much easier to broach the topic with Jeff.

"Tom is...Tom. He doesn't do well with the heavy stuff. He's visited her twice but after the last time I could tell he was having a hard time seeing her like this. He calls her often and she talks to his kids all the time. He lives in Milwaukee," Jeff says and turns in his seat to face forward again. I can tell he has mixed feelings about the way his brother is handling their mother's condition.

"Siblings are hard. Except for Gregory. I swear he came out of the womb perfect. Kelly, however, is my stepsister and there are times I just need a break from her," I say. While many years separated me and my younger brother he held a special place in my heart. After all, he grew up with my own son and they are the best of friends. While I had always been close to Gregory, Kelly and him struggled initially to find a connection. They are closer now that they have both matured.

"Yeah? I never understand why it took Brad so long to go after her. He wasted many years," Jeff says, and I am taken back to all the years Brad had pinned after Kelly but never told her how he felt.

"Fear keeps people from taking what they want."

"Yeah. What do you want?" Jeff asks and turns his head slightly so he's looking right at me.

It seems the flirt is back because his stare is boring into me and I adjust in my seat because my body is definitely reacting to the hard stare. He knows what he is doing too because he smirks at me. It's the smirk that has my ears heating up.

"You weren't shy about telling me what you wanted before."

He is talking about what I had said to him in the hospital cafeteria about needing a good fuck. I had said it because we had been engaged in a game of skill and deflection. But I was tired of playing games. After all that had transpired in my life recently, I didn't want to keep pretending my life wasn't changing drastically.

"I was only trying to get you back for all the times you had stumped me. It's true I am attracted to you but I'm not completely moronic. I know nothing good would come out of me pursuing you," I say and finish my wine.

"I can think of a few good things," Jeff says and waves for Yoder. I wait while Yoder replenishes our drinks and leaves before responding.

"We are too connected by family. Nothing good could possibly come from whatever this is," I say and gesture between us.

"You are making things more complicated than it has to be. We are attracted to each other, and it is clear we both could use a little distraction. You're divorced and I'm not married. There is no complication," he states.

"I'm not divorced yet."

"Details," he says, and I snort. He grins at me beneath his beer bottle as he takes a drink.

"Did you always want to take over the family business?" I shift the topic because I need a distraction from my distraction. He really is a charming man.

"Yes. I knew when I was a kid that I wanted to work in the dirt. After good ole Dad high tailed it out of town I started to help Gramps and Mom as much as they would allow. Gramps died when I was fifteen and Mom took over permanently. I was pretty much full-time staff by then. I'd go to school and rush over to help her as soon as I got out. I wasn't the greatest student, but I graduated," he admits with another of his famous grins.

"It's good that she has you," I say.

112

"What about you? Did you always want to be a doctor?"

"Actually, no. I wanted to be an Olympian."

"Really? What sport?"

"Kayaking."

"No kidding. Why kayaking?" Jeff asks, turning his entire body so he is fully facing me now.

"My dad and I used to do it all the time. I was pretty good at it, and I loved the water," I smile at the memories.

"So why did you shift gears?"

"My dad got sick. Cancer," I say softly.

"Ahh. Life punched you in the face," Jeff says, and his statement pulls me from my sadness.

I laugh. "Yeah, you could say that."

"Well, I'm not glad your father got sick, but I am glad you got punched in the face because my mother needs you," Jeff says and tips his beer bottle towards me in a gesture of thanks.

"He killed himself," I blurt.

"Who did?" Jeff asks.

"My father. He would have died anyway. The cancer was making sure of that but before it could he killed himself," I explain.

Jeff sits beside me, his chest rising with every breath. I can tell he isn't sure what to say after I drop this bombshell on him. Honestly, I figured he would have known since he was so close to Brad and Brad was close to my mother. Apparently, unlike my husband, Brad was capable of keeping things to himself.

"I'm sure he had his reasons," Jeff finally says.

"What?" I ask, my voice rising. What a terrible thing to say to me.

"It isn't easy to be the one looking into the eyes of the ones you love as you fade away. It can break even the strongest person."

"It hasn't broken your mother," I say quietly.

"Well, Reyann isn't like most people. She's been through a hell of a lot, and she has her faith. I don't think she would be able to carry on without it," Jeff states.

"And you? What about your faith?"

"Me? The only faith I've ever had is in the woman that raised me. You want to know how your father could give in so easily? Ask me again after my mother dies," Jeff says. He is still turned towards me and is looking into my eyes as if he is looking into my soul. It's the heaviest stare I've ever experienced with another person, and it frightens me.

Quickly, I stand from my stool and stretch.

"You said they had good food here?" I ask.

"Yeah. Let me get Yoder," he says and stands as well. He doesn't acknowledge my quick shift in demeanor, and I am grateful for that. I have no doubt he recognized my behavior for what it is; a reaction to being uncomfortable with sharing personal details about my life.

I watch as he walks to the other end of the bar and engages in some conversation with other patrons along the way. He must know that I need a break because he takes his time returning to me. When he gets back, he is carrying two new drinks for us. I thank him and he sits back down.

When he had been gone my thoughts had drifted back to the days following my father's death. I had never considered how my mother had been feeling in those days. I was young and completely focused on the war raging within me. Now, however, I am left wondering how she was able to move past it all to find the life she now had. She is happy, I know this, but I don't know how she was able to reconcile her past with her present. I imagine a large part of it had to do with her marriage to my stepfather, Paul, and the child she had with him, my brother Gregory.

Those are the thoughts running through my head when Jeff rejoins me and maybe it is his easy confession of vulnerability regarding his mother's impending death that has me revealing another secret of mine or maybe it is the wine. Either way I speak

114

without a second thought.

"I used to cut myself after my father died. I didn't know why I had started doing it. I just knew how it made me feel when I did it. Everything was out of control but that was something I had absolute control over. I have scars," I say and my hand brushes against the fabric of my skirt as I speak of what is hidden beneath. Jeff's gaze follows the movement of my hand.

"Many think scars are ugly. Josh wouldn't touch them or even talk about them. But I don't think they are ugly and when I look at them I'm not ashamed I put them there. There are times I even think they are beautiful," I confess.

I wait for the moment when Jeff tells me I'm crazy or damaged or some other form of abnormal. They were words I had heard before. Words my own husband had said to me at one time or another. I wait for the concern, for the sympathy, for the disgust, but it never comes.

"They make you think of your father, don't they?"

My head swiftly moves up and I see Jeff is looking at me and not away like I had expected. I nod my head to let him know that my scars are a reminder of the father I had loved and lost, as well as a visual representation of how dangerous love can be.

"He probably wouldn't like you hurting yourself. There are other ways to honor his memory," Jeff says, and he reaches a hand out. He takes the hand I still have resting on my thigh, and he locks his fingers with mine. I keep my gaze on our locked hands as he places them on his leg.

"I don't know how," I say in response to his comment.

"Kayaking," he replies.

Once again, my head lifts and I find myself staring into Jeff's eyes.

"You haven't done it since he died have you?"

"No. I haven't done a lot of things since he died," I admit.

"Would you like to?" he asks.

115

Slowly, I smile and say, "Yes. I would."

"And so, you shall. But first, we eat."

Suddenly, Jeff releases my hand, and Yoder sets two plates down in front of us. I am staring at a plate of steak, fries and corn fritters. Not a single vegetable in sight. I turn to Jeff, and he grins.

"Dig in. It's good for you," he says and places a bite of steak in his mouth.

Just as I'm about to cut my own steak, another plate is put before me and I'm staring at a single slice of chocolate cake with an apple slice on it. Turning back to Jeff I smile brightly and he reaches out with his fork to take a piece of the cake. He holds his fork out before me, and I don't even hesitate to take the bite of cake in my mouth. I'm laughing as I chew when Jeff uses his thumb to swipe away some chocolate on my lip. I watch as he brings his thumb to his mouth, and he sucks the chocolate off.

Damn, this man is good.

-15-

Dancing

"Tuna," I say from my bar stool.

"Tuna? Why? There are so many worse foods," Jeff says from his stool.

I look at the various bottles before us and giggle a little. At some point I had switched from wine to the beer Jeff had been drinking. It had been disgusting at first but after my first beer I was forgetting how I didn't really care for beer. Or maybe it was the shot we had shared. It didn't matter. I was having a good time.

"It's my choice and my choice is tuna," I say.

"It's a bad choice," Jeff says.

"Well, what would be yours?"

"What food makes me gag?"

I nod. We have been asking each other random questions for the last hour or so. It is entertaining and I had learned quite a bit about this peculiar man. He hated wearing sleeves and owned only a couple of shirts with long sleeves. He preferred listening to women singers because he liked their range. The only books he ever read were about business or landscaping. He couldn't stand politics and rarely voted. He had never been married but was engaged once. She had broken it off after she had cheated on him. His favorite food was deep dish pizza, and I was about to find out his least favorite.

"Penis," he says, and I snort.

"No, it isn't." I playfully slap him on the shoulder. Sure, I was drunk but so the hell what. I was freaking thirty-nine and an adult. I could get drunk if I wanted to.

"Right. That's you," he says and smirks at me. I slap his shoulder again.

"Be serious," I say.

"Okay. Seriously I can't stand pickles," he says.

"But I saw you put them on your burger at the hospital."

"Yeah, and I hated every moment of it. As soon you walked away from the table, I took them off," he says.

"You're an odd duck, Mr. Collins." I laugh and it turns into a hiccup. I cover my mouth with the back of my hand, just in case the laugh turned hiccup turns into something else.

"Better an odd duck than a limp dick, Mrs. McNill."

I cringe at the use of my last name and Jeff notices.

"Sorry," he says.

"I'm gonna go back to my maiden name."

"What is it?"

"Cooper. Like my son. I named him after my father," I explain.

"Okay, Ms. Cooper. What is the one thing you have always wanted to do but never have?" This man is so adept at keeping my mind off of things I would sooner not think about.

"Just one? There are so many," I say.

"Okay. Tell me them all," Jeff says and leans back in his stool.

"I've never been to Italy. I've been to Africa though, so I guess that doesn't really count. Okay, I've never…," I can't seem to think of a single thing. I start glancing around the bar for something to trigger a response and Jeff starts laughing at my obvious panic.

"Don't strain yourself," he says.

"I'm not. I'm just thinking."

"You're thinking so hard you have smoke coming out of your ears," he jokes and lightly flicks one of my ears. I swat away his hand and then an idea comes to me.

118

"I've never made out in a bar," I say.

This sobers him up and he narrows his eyes at me in disbelief.

"I don't believe it. If you wanted to make out all you had to do was say so. You don't have to make things up," he says and takes a drink from his beer bottle.

"I'm not making it up. I had a baby at nineteen and was married before I was twenty. I never actually went to a bar with Josh before. He doesn't like scenes like this. I've never had an opportunity to make out at a bar before," I explain.

Jeff stares at me blankly for so long that I start to regret ever admitting just how little experience I actually have. I grew up to fast and yet there is so much I have never done that others my age have done. I may not have been innocent, but I certainly wasn't experienced. I'm about to change the subject when Jeff stands and grabs a hold of my hand.

He steers me towards the juke box, and I watch as he deposits some money and chooses a song. Then he takes a hold of my hand again and pulls me to the makeshift dance area. It has now been left empty as the few remaining patrons are all seated at the bar. The song Jeff picked starts and he pulls me against him, one hand still locked with mine and the other around my waist. I settle my head against his chest and together we sway with the music. It's not exactly a love song but the words the woman sings describes our night perfectly.

As we move together, I close my eyes and take in his scent. He is wearing a thin tank top, and I can feel his skin against me. It is hot, musky and all man. Even though he isn't at work he still carries the scent of pine with him, and it reminds me of Christmas, my favorite holiday.

"Stacey," he says my name and it pulls me out of my trance, and I open my eyes. I pull away and look up at him.

He doesn't say anything more. He just moves his head down to mine and joins our lips. We are no longer swaying to the music, but our lips begin a dance of their own. Jeff is the fourth man I've kissed in my life. The first was during a time when I thought giving myself to someone else would heal me. That boy rejected me. The second man had been Josh, who was still my husband. The third man had been a stranger I had never intended to see again. All of them were significant in their own way but none of them had ever made me feel the way this man was making me feel in this moment.

I feel like there is no one else in the room. Everything and everyone else disappear. We are all that remain and we are engaged in a seductive dance that I have never before been a part of. His presence makes me brave, and I tentatively bite his lip. He doesn't pull away from me or try to shift my focus. He moans into my mouth and then he bites me back. I am so stunned by his reaction that I break free from the kiss and look down at his chest while I try to catch my breath.

"I'm sorry. Did I hurt you?" Jeff asks, his hot breath landing on my face.

"No. It's just that no one's ever let me do that before," I explain.

"You can do whatever you'd like. This is about you," he says.

I look up at him and I smile. He smiles down at me, and I use one hand to caress my way up his chest until my hand is around the back of his neck. I push against his neck, and he grins when our lips once again touch. This time I deepen the kiss and remove my hand still clutched in his so I can grab a hold of his side and pull his body closer to mine. I feel his erection against me, and it empowers me to keep going.

I move my hand underneath his shirt and feel his hot skin as I continue to lick, bite and taste his lips. His hands are now clutching my sides, steadying us both. It isn't until the hand I have beneath his shirt starts to travel down that he pulls away from me.

"I'm sorry," he says again.

I chuckle because for someone that has a difficult time uttering those words it is strange to see how free he is with them; especially since he has nothing to apologize for. He was only giving me what I wanted and then I had to take it too far.

"What for?" I ask.

"For stopping. I really want to keep going but you've had a lot to drink, and we have an audience here," he says and turns his head towards the bar.

I follow his gaze and see Yoder and the three remaining patrons all staring at us. They are grinning and laughing.

"Don't let us stop you. We were enjoying the show," Yoder says and the other patrons howl with laughter.

"That's the downfall to making out in a bar. There are always onlookers with nothing better to do than gawk," Jeff says loudly.

"Hey, no one forced you two to swap spit," Yoder calls back.

I start giggling because, well, I have had a decent amount of alcohol and also because this is so perfect. I had made out in a bar and was a part of friendly banter. Other than with Rachel I never really got to do this. Josh preferred to stay at home, which didn't really lead to many social encounters. Aside from my colleagues and family I didn't really have much interaction with others. I am enjoying this.

"Maybe we should go back to the bar?" I say and Jeff groans.

"I don't think I should move right now," he says and his eyes dart down towards the front of his pants. He is still clearly aroused.

"Just walk behind me," I say and take his hand.

We walk back to our stools with Jeff behind me the entire time. Yoder laughs at him as we make our way back to the bar. He knows what Jeff is hiding but he doesn't share his thoughts with the others.

"Two waters Yoder," I say when we are both seated.

"Water?" Jeff turns to me.

"Yes. I need you sober."

"Me? I'm fine. You're the light weight," he says, clearly offended.

"Hey, I don't know what effects alcohol may have on your

121

stamina," I say and glance down at the seat of his pants.

Yoder chuckles as he sets the waters down before us.

"I like this one," he says to Jeff. Jeff glares at him.

"My stamina will be just fine," he says. He still drinks the water though.

We stay for another hour and drink coffee with our water. Jeff pays the bill, says goodbye to his friends and I hug Yoder goodbye before we leave. Despite my initial misgivings I had come to enjoy the small, tucked away bar and the people in it.

"Give me your keys," he says holding out his hand.

"No way," I say and pull my hand back.

"You had more than me in there."

"No, I didn't. You had more than me," I say.

"Stacey, give me the keys. I've been drinking non-alcoholic beer all night," he says.

I stare back at him, a little hurt that he had been sober this whole time. If he had been drinking non-alcoholic beer than the only alcohol he consumed had been the one shot we did hours ago. That also means that only one of us had been buzzed during our make out session while the other had been completely sober. Which meant he did it because he wanted to and not because he was influenced by beer.

I give him my keys.

"Where are we going?" I ask.

"I could take us to my place," he says.

I shake my head no. I couldn't possibly do what I had planned in Reyann's house. It seemed disrespectful to her.

"Your place?" he asks.

I shake my head no again because even though I was now in an apartment I didn't want my sanctuary to be invaded. I wanted to keep it to myself for just a little bit longer.

"Hotel?" Jeff says.

I agree and he drives a couple blocks until we spot one. Neither of us says anything on the drive, or when we walk in and Jeff secures us a room. Not a word is spoken as we walk to the room. Jeff holds the door open for me, and I walk through the threshold and into the dark room. Jeff turns on the lights and looks around the room. It is a typical hotel room which is good because if I had been surrounded by familiar things I probably would have changed my mind.

"You don't have to do this," Jeff says as he comes up behind me. I feel his chest against my back, and I lean against him. His hands go to my sides and I feel his fingers tighten against me. I lay my head back, my neck exposed. Jeff leans down and kisses my neck gently before he nibbles on it.

"I want to do this," I say.

With those words any hint of the man concerned about my misgivings is gone. Jeff turns me so I'm facing him and he crushes his mouth against mine. He moves his fingers, and they grab a hold of my shirt. In one quick motion he has it over my head and off my body. The shirt flies across the room and he bends his head so he can continue his trail of kisses down my neck, to my shoulder, to the tops of my exposed breasts. I'm breathing heavily from the anticipation and when he takes a nip at the top of my left breast my breath catches in my throat.

In response Jeff reaches down with his hands and takes hold of my ass. He grips it and lifts me off the ground. I wrap my legs around him and he walks to the nearest wall. With my back pressed up against the hotel wall he continues his onslaught. My legs and arms are wrapped around him, holding on. I can't reach him with my own lips, so I just rest my head against the wall and enjoy the sensation of what he is doing to me. Once he has his full, he uses one hand to pull the cups of my bra down, exposing the rest of me to the cool air. He doesn't even hesitate. He takes my nipple into his mouth and he sucks. It's painfully exhilarating, and I savor every moment of it.

When he bites my breast, I cry out.

"You like that?" he says against my skin. His hot breath mingles with the trail his lips have made, and the air makes my skin buzz.

"Yes," I whisper out breathily.

"What else would you like me to do?" He kisses the side of my neck, and it takes me a moment to recover.

"Will you put your fingers inside me? Right here?" I ask and show him where I want him to touch me.

I'd never before made requests during sex. I had never felt I could, but Jeff made everything feel normal. I wasn't afraid of rejection with him. I didn't fear his reaction to my desires.

"Like this?" he asks as he reaches one hand down. He pushes my skirt up until it is bunched around my waist and I feel his fingers searching beneath the material of my undergarments that remain between us. His fingers graze me, and I nod.

"You have to say it. It doesn't count unless you say it," Jeff says.

"Yes. Like that," I say breathlessly when his fingers push inside me.

"Open your eyes, Stacey. I want you to see how this turns me on," he commands.

My eyes snap open and I am met with his steely grey stare. The entire time his fingers move inside me we maintain eye contact. When my breathing starts to increase because it feels so good he keeps his gaze locked on mine. And when I finally cry out because his fingers worked their magic he demands I keep my eyes open through it all.

"You're beautiful when you cum," he says, his lips pressed against mine. I press my lips against his and hungrily suck on them.

"You feel amazing," I return the compliment.

"Baby, you haven't even begun to feel me," he says and lifts me away from the wall. He takes me to the hotel bed and essentially throws me down on it. It's not gentle at all and I laugh because it's everything I want.

Jeff reaches out and unzips my skirt before pulling it down the length of my legs. He starts to lean over me, but I shake my head no and prop myself up on my elbows.

"Not until you take those off," I say and point at his pants.

"You're killing me," he groans and tries to reach for me.

"Nuh, uh. Lose the pants." I'm giving the commands now.

"You drive a hard bargain," he says but does exactly as I want. He takes off his jeans and I'm shocked to find he isn't wearing anything underneath.

His erection springs forth and I'm just staring at him in shock.

"You can touch it if you'd like," he says it with a laugh, but he has no idea how much I want to touch him. I move to the edge of the bed, my gaze still firmly on what he has presented to me. I reach out slowly and take him in my hand. He groans and moves closer to the bed.

He is a beautiful man. He is all hard lines, muscles and perfection. His entire body has been carefully maintained and is now before me, my own private playground. I move my hand along his length and examine every inch of him. He is truly fascinating.

"If you keep looking at me like that than this is going to end much sooner than either of us wants," Jeff says. I turn my head up towards him.

"You're beautiful," I say in awe of him. He smiles and his hand reaches out to caress my cheek.

"No one's ever called me beautiful before," he says.

"Why not? You're magnificent."

"Magnificent, huh? I could get used to that."

My hand moves up and then down his length and this time his eyes close. I'm excited by what I'm able to do to him and I repeat the movement. Then, on instinct, I lean forward and take him into my mouth.

"Oh, God, Stacey. You really are trying to kill me," he says.

I continue my exploration. I taste what I want, touch what I want and revel in the sounds I bring out of him. Just when I think I'm about to give him the ending he had given me earlier he gently pulls away and carefully lifts my face so I'm staring up at him.

"I love what you are doing to me but that isn't how I want tonight to end," he says.

"Okay," I reply.

"Move back," he says, and I scoot further back on the bed.

He kneels down on the bed before me and reaches out. It is then I realize that my bra is still awkwardly on my body. He releases the clasp, and it falls away. He then uses his hands to feel every inch of me. The movements of his hands also act as an instructional guide, and I move my body to complement his movements. Eventually I am lying down on the bed as he removes my underwear. He is now kneeling between my legs and his hands are making the journey back up my leg and into the area where my scars are. I tense and try to pull my legs up, but his grasp closes on my knees.

"Don't do that. Don't pull away from me," he says, and his eyes hold my own gaze. I don't respond to him with words. Instead, I relax my body and sink back down into the pillows.

Jeff continues his movements, and his fingers move over my scars. He touches every single one and when he leans forward and starts to kiss every one of them, I can't help my reaction. I start to cry.

"You're beautiful. Every inch of you," he says against the patchwork on my thigh. With every gentle kiss another tear falls. Once he has placed a kiss on every one of my scars, he moves up the rest of my body and places a kiss on my lips.

"Please don't cry. I can't stand to see you cry," he says and wipes away the tears with his thumb.

"I'm sorry," I whisper.

"What for?" he asks and smiles at me.

"For waiting so damn long," I utter, and he chuckles.

"No more waiting," he replies and starts to reach for his pants

126

and his wallet.

"No!" I grab his arm and stop him. He looks back at me in his halted stance.

"I want to feel you. I need to feel you. I've been tested. I'm on birth control," I continue to blurt things out. I'm nervous. I fully expect him to reject this latest request, but he doesn't.

Jeff just nods and comes back to me. He settles against me and uses his knee to move my leg so he can get into a better position.

"You're sure?" he asks.

"Yes. Please," I say and before the last syllable leaves my lips he thrusts into me.

It isn't a gentle entrance, and I bite my bottom lip when it happens. Jeff doesn't apologize and I'm glad he doesn't. This is exactly what I want, complete release. He doesn't say anything. Instead, he covers my lips with his and he bites my bottom lip for me. He moves inside me, and I adjust my legs so I can take him in deeper. His lips move away from mine to my shoulder. He kisses my shoulder twice and continues to thrust inside me. I can feel every retreat and advance in the depths of my core. My entire body is on fire, and he is the flame feeding the blaze. I can tell he is waiting for me before he allows himself to find his release. His movements have become more deliberate and when I suck in a breath at the moment my center is reached, he increases his speed.

"Oh, God. Yes!" I scream and Jeff bites down on my shoulder.

Once. Twice. Three times he retreats and advances. With a cry he pulls out of me and empties himself on my stomach. Another first for me. Once he has finished milking himself, he falls onto the other side of the bed and throws his arm over his eyes.

I lay there for a minute just glowing from the sensations I had just experienced. Slowly, however, doubt starts to creep in, and I go to move off of the bed. A hand reaches out and grabs a hold of my arm.

"I thought I told you not to pull away from me," he says.

"I was just-"

"Running. You were running. Don't," he says and releases my arm so he can drape his behind me. He wraps his arm around my shoulders and pulls me into his side.

He kisses the top of my head, and I just lay against him. Rigid. This is new to me. I hadn't cuddled against a man for years. I wasn't sure how long I was supposed to do it for. With Josh it had always been brief. He usually excused himself to clean up so quickly after we were intimate.

"Do I make you nervous, Doc?" Jeff had asked me this question once before and I had told him no.

"Yes," I say this time because I really was finished playing games.

"You don't have to be nervous around me. What are you thinking?"

"That I don't know how to do this."

"Don't know how to do what?"

"This. Cuddling," I say.

Jeff chuckles and kisses my head again.

"You're doing it just fine. But if this makes you uncomfortable don't worry. We won't be doing this for much longer. I just need a few more moments, we'll get you cleaned up and then on to round two," he says.

I lift my head from his chest and stare into his eyes.

"Round two? Already?" I ask, surprised.

Jeff grins at me.

"I told you my stamina was just fine," he says and rolls on top of me. "Now, what is something you have always wanted to do in a bed but haven't ever done?"

This time I'm the one grinning.

-16-

Repercussions

It isn't until the next morning when I wake up naked in a hotel bed next to a man that isn't my husband that I realize I was wearing my wedding ring the entire time. When I see the golden circle catch the light of the rising sun I sit up in the bed, look frantically at the softly snoring form next to me and rip the ring off of my finger. I'm looking around the room for a place to put it when I feel Jeff beginning to stir next to me. In a panic I quickly throw the covers off of me, pick up my stray clothing items on my way to the bathroom and lock myself inside.

I throw the bundle I collected into the bathroom sink and start to sift through it. I throw my bra and other clothing items behind me; including Jeff's silly tank. I find my skirt and search for some sort of pocket but there isn't one. I drop the skirt into the sink, clutch the ring in my fisted hand and back into the tub. My gaze continues to move around the bathroom in frenetic movements because I'm not sure what to do.

Sure, I had cheated on my husband before but that had been done for a specific purpose, and I hadn't actually enjoyed it. In fact, I made sure I hadn't enjoyed it. I chose the man I was least attracted to and barely participated in the events that had transpired in that hotel room. For the life of me I couldn't even call forth the man's face from memory. It seemed I had blocked it as soon as the encounter had ended. My sole purpose for completing that act hadn't been for pleasure. It had been to get a reaction out of my husband and to prove that some form of passion still existed between us.

But this night, this man was already seeping beneath my skin, and I knew I didn't want it to end. This couldn't be the first and last touch between us. I was already craving him, and I had just left his side. This was a feeling I was not used to and the familiar out of control haze I knew in my teen years was overpowering me and I was desperately seeking an escape.

"Stacey," Jeff calls to me as he softly knocks against the bathroom door. I jump from the sound of his knuckles against the wood.

"Yes," my voice cracks out in response.

"Open the door Stacey," Jeff says softly. It isn't a command. In fact it sounds more like a plea and that is why I reach out and unlock the door.

Jeff twists the knob and steps inside. Surprisingly, he closes the door behind him. He is wearing his pants, and he carries a sheet from the bed in his hand. It isn't until he wraps me in the sheet that I remember I am still naked.

I twist my hands in the sheets and thank him. He rubs his hands on my shoulders, warming my chilled body. When I relax, he turns me towards the toilet, puts the lid down and gently guides me to sit on it. Then he crouches before me, puts his hands on my knees and looks up at me from a position that can't be comfortable for him.

"Talk to me," he says.

I sigh, look at him and my shoulders sag as if I'm accepting a form of defeat. My escape into the bathroom was so I didn't have to have this very conversation, but he sought me out. At first, I debate deflecting but I dismiss that option when I hear Rachel's voice in my head telling me not to be a bitch.

"It just all became too real. I needed a moment," I reveal.

"I know. Last night wasn't just sex for me. I hope you know

130

that," Jeff says as he shifts his weight. He's trying to maintain eye contact with me, but I can tell he is starting to feel the effects of his awkward position.

"I don't have any expectations. I'm hardly in a position to have any," I respond.

"Okay. Well, I think I do have expectations," he says and reaches up to my fisted hand. He gently takes my hand and pulls my fingers apart to reveal my gold wedding band sitting on my palm. He takes the ring and holds it out in front of us.

I stare at the ring, not sure what he wants me to do.

"Is your marriage really over?" he asks, turning the ring in his hand.

I nod.

"It doesn't count unless you say it," he repeats the same words from the night before that had turned me on. In the harsh light of day those same words make me wince.

"Yes. It's really over."

"Twenty years is a long time. A lifetime for some. I don't expect this to be easy and I'm a patient man, Stacey. But I don't want to waste our time if you can't be in this with me. Say the word and I'll walk out of this room and your life, no questions asked. If, by any chance, last night means as much to you as it does to me than I'll stand by you. I'll give you whatever you need, be whatever you need. All you have to do is decide," Jeff says, takes my hand to turn it palm up and places my wedding band back in it. He closes my fingers around the ring, encapsulating it in my fisted hand.

"My marriage is over," I repeat but I avert my gaze from Jeff's.
"But?" he asks.
"But I'm not ready for what you are offering."
"What are you ready for?"

I pause because I am not entirely sure how to answer him. My marriage is over and I have no intention of returning to Josh and the life I had walked away from. But I also know I am not sure what kind of life I really want. Does this new life include space for another person? I haven't even gotten used to the idea of having space for myself, let alone another person.

"I think I just want to do more of what we did last night. I want to experience things I've never done before. I want to go kayaking and hiking and go to a sporting event and cheer for opposing teams just because I can. I want to have fun. I want to get to know *me* again. But I also don't want to say goodbye to you. I just don't think I can offer you any more than that," I say. I wait for him to get up and walk out. Who would possibly stick around after being told they would be nothing more than a distraction.

"Whatever you need. What do you want to do right now?"

"I should probably-"

"No," he interrupts me, "don't think about what you should do. Tell me what you *want* to do." His fingers clench a little tighter around my knees, drawing my attention back to him.

"I'm hungry," I say. He blinks at me. I doubt he expected the answer I gave.

"Okay. Let's get some breakfast," he says once he has recovered and stands. He holds out his hand to me and I look at it before looking at the closed bathroom door.

With a grin, I stand and plunge my fingers under the seams of his pants. I use the material of his jeans to pull him up against me as I kiss him deeply. He doesn't even skip a beat, and his arms wrap around me as he kisses me back.

My hands are now on the zipper of his jeans. He hadn't even bothered to button them, and they easily slide off his body. I shrug out of the sheet still draped around me and now that my arms are free I push against his chest until he is backed up against the bath-room wall.

"Breakfast can wait. I'm starving," I say against his lips.

Jeff chuckles and grabs my ass, pulling me towards him.

Sex in the bathroom. Another first for me and it is glorious.

It isn't until later, when we are cleaning up, that I realize I had dropped my wedding ring onto the bathroom floor.

Eventually we get breakfast. Normally when I share a meal with another person I sit across from them, but I decided to try something new and sat beside Jeff in the booth. I definitely discovered the benefits of sitting next to a man during a meal when Jeff's hand moved between my legs and fed another part of me. My own hand had started to push his away initially but after the shock wore off I realized that this was something else I had never done before. Public displays of affection, especially this sexual, had never been something I was able to engage in during my marriage. Instead of pushing Jeff's hand away I embrace the experience, and it is by far the best breakfast I have ever had.

After, I took him back to the hospital. Reyann is being released, and he is going to take her home. I decide I will collect some work since I was going to be at the hospital, and I park in my assigned spot when we arrive. When I start to get out of the car Jeff grabs my hand and pulls me back in. I am smiling when he leans forward and gives me an affectionate kiss on my lips before kissing my cheek. His hand finds its way into my hair and he is moving his fingers through it, softly caressing my scalp when he speaks.

"Thank you for being my friend last night," he says.

I laugh. Of all the things I thought he was going to say that was not at all expected.

"I'm sure the sexy time was the highlight," I joke.

"Well, I didn't hate it. You do know that wasn't my intention when I asked you to go out with me?" His eyes are pleading with me to believe him. It is obvious it is important to him that I believe this and despite my inner demons I actually do believe what he says.

"I know. I'm glad I was able to be there. And I didn't hate the sexy time either," I smile and give him a quick peck on the lips.

Jeff laughs and pulls away from me to lean back in his seat.

"Will you go to a baseball game with me on Thursday?"

I'm about to turn down his invitation when I once again hear Rachel's voice in my head. *Tell the truth.*

"Yes. I'll go with you," I say.

"Good. It's a date," he says with a grin and gets out of my car. I'm stumbling to get out after him and forget I still have my belt on. It catches and digs into my chest before I release it.

"It's not a date," I call to him once I have freed myself and am able to get out of the car. He is already walking to the elevators, and he just gives me a slight wave as he keeps on walking. "It's not a date!"

When he gets to the elevators he pushes the button, turns to face me and says, "Don't fight this. You know you want me."

"No, I don't."

"You want me so hard you were begging for it last night," he calls to me as the elevator doors open behind him. He gets in and right before the doors close, I flip him the bird. I can hear his laughter as the doors close.

Shaking my head I reach into my back seat and pull out my purse. As I'm locking my car, I see a movement to my left and I turn to see my daughter standing there. She is staring at me and the look on her face displays hurt, shock, anger, and finally pure rage.

"Becca," I say. I'm starting to move towards her when she shouts at me.

"You cheated on dad again!" She turns on her heels and practically stomps towards the vehicle Josh and I had gotten her for her graduation.

"Becca! Hold on," I rush to her and cut off her path. She tries to

134

walk around me, but I match her steps and keep her trapped between cars.

"Move!" she shouts at me.

"No. Not until we talk about what you think you saw," I say.

"What I *think* I saw? I saw you kissing another man in your car in the parking garage of your work while you are still married to my father. I saw you cheating on Daddy, again. That is what I SAW!" Her hands are fisted at her sides and with every shout they shake. It takes me a minute to realize that she is revealing just how much she knows.

"Again?"

"Yes, Mother, again. I know about the first time. I heard you two talking. He forgave you and this is how you repay him? Is this why you left? So you could be free to have your man on the side?"

"Becca, you don't know what you are talking about. There are things, private things, that have happened between your father and me. Jeff-"

"Jeff! Oh my God, you are sleeping with Uncle Jeff?" Becca interrupts me.

"He isn't your uncle," I lamely say as if this particular fact will somehow redeem me for my actions.

Becca just rolls her eyes at me and lets out a cry of frustration. She once again tries to move around me.

"Why were you here Rebecca?"

"Does it matter? I wanted to talk to you about this stupid divorce but clearly nothing anyone else wants matters to you. How do you think Dad is going to feel when he finds out you have been sleeping with Uncle Jeff this whole time?"

"Whole time? Rebecca Marie McNill, you have no idea what you are talking about," I say sternly.

"Using my full name isn't going to silence me Mother. I'm not the one in trouble here," my teenage daughter chastises me.

"I'm not in trouble either. I'm a grown woman and what I do

with my time is not your concern and it isn't your father's concern anymore. I'm sorry this is hard for you Becca, but your father and I are separated. There will be no reconciliation, and you are just going to have to accept that." I use my best serious-mother voice I can muster to let my daughter know just how serious I am. My daughter isn't fazed at all.

"As long as you are happy nothing else matters, right, Mother?" she crosses her arms over her chest and stares at me in judgment.

"That is cruel, Becca. If you aren't capable of talking about this rationally than there is no point in continuing this conversation," I say.

"Go to hell Mother," my daughter says and in my shocked state she pivots and goes to her car.

I'm staring at her departing form and wondering how, just moments earlier, I could be so happy and now all I want to do is erase the last twenty-four hours so I can never have to see the look I just saw on my daughter's face.

Love is pain.

Love is betrayal and it is clear my daughter believes I have betrayed her father and our family.

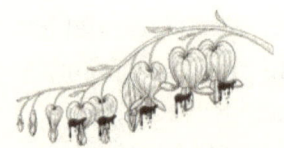

Knocking on the door I go through a series of emotions and almost convince myself to turn around when the door suddenly opens. Jules is staring back at me, and she quickly pulls me inside when she sees my frantic appearance. She doesn't even speak as I follow her through her house and into the kitchen.

Rachel and another young woman are sitting at the kitchen table with cards in their hands and drinks at their sides. There is a cheese plate in the center of the table and as soon as I sit down, I grab a slice of some white cheese. It's gross but I eat it anyway. Jules places a glass of wine down next to me and I manage a quick thank you with my cheese stuffed mouth before I pick it up and down half its contents.

They are all staring at me now, waiting for me to speak but I stuff two more pieces of cheese down my throat and finish my glass of wine before I say anything. Jules refills my glass when I push it towards her, and I take another sip before I swallow the cheese and look at the faces staring back at me.

"What are we playing?" I ask. No one answers me.

"Hey, Molly. I haven't seen you in a while. How have you been?" I ask Jules' and Rachel's niece.

"I'm fine. I seem to be doing better than you are at the moment," the teenaged girl says to me, her brows dropping in concern.

"Oh, I'm fine. I'm getting divorced, sleeping with a man my children consider an uncle, and my daughter just told me to go to hell. See, right as rain. I never understood that phrase. Right as rain. Rain makes you wet and ruins outdoor parties. Why is rain right?" I'm rambling but it brings me comfort.

"I think it has something to do with farming," Molly says, and I snort out a laugh.

"That would make sense. What about when pigs fly? Who even thought of that?"

"Stacey? Why don't we go into the living room?" Rachel says from her chair. She is already putting her cards down and standing up.

"Oh. I didn't mean to interrupt. Finish the game," I say and pick up my wine glass.

"You can bring the wine with you," Rachel says.

"Alrighty," I say and stand to follow her.

Jules and Molly remain in the kitchen while Rachel escorts me to their living room. White couches. I hold my wine glass a little firmer as I sit down.

"So, I take it you had an eventful day," Rachel says from her cushion.

"You could say that. I slept with Jeff last night. You remember him? My patient's son?" I begin.

"And?"

"And it was flipping fantastic! He lived up to every fantasy I had about him," I say and drink some more wine.

"But?"

There was that insight of hers again. She always knew when there was a "but".

"But I think he wants more than I can give him."

"He has feelings for you," Rachel states.

"Doubtful. I'm sure he's just experiencing afterglow or something." I dismiss her statement because Jeff suddenly developing feelings for me after one night together is ridiculous. Sure, I had felt some pretty strong feelings after our night together, but I wasn't about to go confess love or anything like that.

"Stacey, how much do you really know about this man?"

"What do you mean? I've known him for over ten years. He's a good friend of Brad's. They think of themselves as brothers. He's at every family event," I say.

"But how many times have you actually had a meaningful conversation with him?"

I think about that for a little bit. The past ten years replay in my head, and I look back on all the birthdays, holidays and gatherings my family has had. I can't seem to recall a single time I ever had a private conversation with Jeff. When we spoke, it was always with others around and only in a peripheral way. The only meaningful conversation I'd ever had with him occurred last night.

"Once. Last night," I admit.

"It's possible this man has had feelings for you and you've just never known about them."

138

My eyes narrow at Rachel's warning and my shoulders go back defensively.

"What are you saying?"

"I'm saying be careful. You are making a lot of changes in your life right now and it would be wise to make sure you like the changes. I've never met Jeff so I'm not going to pretend I know his character. He may not have some ulterior motives other than wanting to spend time with you but be careful. As for Becca, she'll come around. She's just hurting because of the divorce. Give her time," Rachel says.

Her warnings are being given out of love and concern for me, but I feel wretched after hearing them. Not because she may be right but because I desperately want her to be wrong. Jeff couldn't possibly have harbored secret feelings for me all these years and then acted upon them in my moment of weakness. He couldn't possibly be that conniving. And yet…how much did I really know about him? Is it possible that I was only seeing what I wanted to see? Was I once again shaping the reality I wanted and ignoring the signs before me? Would I ever learn?

"You are supposed say atta girl and give me high five for having amazing sex," I remind her of her responsibility as my best friend.

"Atta girl," she says and lazily lifts her hand for me to slap. I do. "Feel better?" she asks.

I glare at her, then take a careful sip of wine, protecting the obnoxiously white couch.

-17-

Games

Thursday arrived without a word from my daughter. I tried to call her, but she wouldn't answer. I called my son, and he told me Becca had spoken to him and that she was still upset. I asked Cooper to tell Becca I wanted to talk to her. He promised he would. He didn't ask me any questions about Jeff, and I didn't supply any information. I did speak briefly to my mother because she had left me a message regarding Becca being upset. I spoke to my mother about the altercation Becca and I had and she listened. She didn't lecture me on my choices or suggest I go back to my husband. She only asked if I was sure about what I was doing. Maybe I would have preferred it if she had lectured me. I told her no one is ever really sure, but I was going to do it anyway. She didn't reply.

Kelly also called me to give me an ear full. Surprisingly, or perhaps not so surprisingly, my family heard about my… relationship? Fling? Affair?... with Jeff from Becca. Kelly revealed that Brad had been stunned to hear about it too. This told me that Jeff hadn't revealed our night together to any of our mutual connections. I wasn't sure if he chose not to reveal it out of respect for me or because he was ashamed. In the end I decided his motives were irrelevant.

He had called and asked to pick me up at my apartment for our non-date but I told him I would meet him at the hospital and we could leave from there. I said I needed to work late, and he accepted that. Truthfully, I just didn't want to invite him into my apartment. It was still my untouched sanctuary.

I met him in the parking garage and the first five minutes of the ride were done in silence. He kept glancing at me, but I kept looking out the window. I refused to be the one to break the tension.

"Everyone imploded," he suddenly states and once again he manages to shock me. He continues to say the last thing I ever expect him to say.

"Pardon?"

"Your family. Brad called me. He wanted to warn me, I guess. I'm enemy number one it seems," Jeff says and glances at me.

Finally, I look at him. Releasing all tension, I turn in my seat and give him my full attention.

"Number two. The top spot is reserved for me," I say, and Jeff laughs slightly.

"Now I don't feel so bad," he jokes and we both smile.

"I don't know why they all feel like they have any right to be so judgy. We are both grown adults. Becca will get over this," I say.

"She called me," he reveals.

"What?!" I'm utterly stunned my daughter would do that. "What did you say?"

"Well, she yelled at me for about twenty minutes about ruining your marriage and betraying her father's trust."

"Oh, Becca."

"Once she calmed down, I assured her that until you and Josh separated there had never been even a hint of us getting together. And then I told her I'd be willing to talk to her about it more but that I thought she needed to talk to you first," Jeff explains.

"Oh. She won't answer my calls," I say. My daughter is more like me than she realizes. Avoidance is one of my plays and she is perfecting it.

"I meant what I said to you, Stacey. Whatever you need, all you have to do is say it," Jeff reassures me.

My conversation with Rachel is playing in my head and doubts start to surface. Is he playing a game with me? What exactly is his end game? Questions are running through my head when we finally arrive at our destination. I look around and see we are at a local park that has many baseball fields on it.

"What are we doing?" I ask.

"We're going to watch some All-American baseball. Little league style," he says.

"What?" I glance quickly back at him, and he laughs at my horrified expression.

"Come on," he says and gets out of his truck.

Hesitantly I follow him to the back, and he hands me two lawn chairs. He takes a cooler out of the truck bed and instructs me to follow him. I do but I'm already planning my escape. This is just nuts.

"Okay. We have the Red Sox playing the Tigers on field three. Yankees are playing the Mets on field two. And on field one we have the Dodgers against the Giants. Choose your team," Jeff says as we stand in the area that leads to all three fields.

I'm absolutely baffled by his choice of entertainment. When he invited me to watch a baseball game with him, I hadn't expected he'd take me to a little league game. Only parents were supposed to watch these. Neither of us had a child that was playing here today, and I could only imagine what the parents would think of two adult wierdos watching their children play ball.

"We could always just find some central spot and watch all three games but that would make cheering for opposite teams difficult," Jeff says, waiting for me to make a decision.

His comment brings me back to my bathroom confession and how I had told him I wanted to go to a sporting event and cheer for opposing teams. This whole set up was his way of fulfilling one of the items on my wish list. I stop thinking about all the ways this could be considered inappropriate and make my decision.

"Dodgers and Giants," I say.

"Fair choice. I would have gone with the Red Sox and Tigers, personally. I'm just glad you didn't go with the Yankees. This way," he says and gestures to what could only be field one.

I follow him and we pick a prime location along the third base line. Jeff helps me set up the folding lawn chairs and I'm tickled to see they have cup holders. Once we are settled in our seats Jeff reaches down into the cooler between us.

"Your peanuts. A ballpark must snack," he says and gives me an individual size bag. I take it, smiling the entire time.

"You have your choice of lemonade, pop, or beer," Jeff tells me. He waits for me to give my answer.

"Beer. It's a baseball game," I say.

"Another good choice. Now, this is a little league field, and alcohol is technically not allowed so I have cleverly disguised the beer in non-objectionable root beer bottles. Don't tell anyone," Jeff says and hands me one of the makeshift bottles.

"You are absolutely crazy," I laugh as I take the bottle. It is still chilled from being in the cooler and it pairs well with the peanuts.

"Crazy like Einstein," he says and opens his own bottle.

The players take the field, and more fans settle in next to us to watch the game. The sun is shining, the people around us are in good spirits and I can't help but smile.

"Which team are you claiming?" Jeff asks me.

"Dodgers."

"Alright. Come on Giants!" Jeff calls out.

"Your team is going down," I gleefully say.

"Oh, no. I was watching them warm up and I clearly have the stronger team."

"Wanna bet?" I tease.

"What are the stakes?" Jeff asks, intrigued.

"My team wins you have to spend an evening at Tuckets wearing

143

a tu-tu and tights." I don't expect him to accept the wager because that place is clearly his domain, but he surprises me once again.

"Deal. But if my team wins you have to get 'Jeff is best' tattooed on your ass," he counters.

"What? No!"

"Ha, okay, okay. No tattoo. But you will have to say, 'Jeff is the best sex I've ever had' to every person I tell you to for a period of…five hours."

"That's all? Piece of cake. Deal," I say, and we shake on it to make it official.

Five innings later and the score is Giants - three, Dodgers – two. I'm on my feet yelling for my player to run faster. He gets thrown out at second and the inning is over. I plop back down in my seat in frustration and Jeff laughs.

"Looks like you'll be singing my praises sooner than you thought," Jeff mocks.

"It isn't over yet. We still have four more innings," I caution him.

"It's never too early to accept defeat."

"Never!" I cry out.

"I haven't seen you two here before. Which one is yours?" the woman sitting next to Jeff suddenly asks us. I'd seen her eyeing him the entire game, but I kept my opinion to myself. It seems she has other ideas, however,

"That one," Jeff and I both say in unison but point at different children on opposite teams.

"Oh," the woman says, clearing confused. "That's David, Shannon and Bruce's son," the woman says about the kid I had pointed at.

"Don't pay any attention to her. She's nearly legally blind but she wants to be supportive, so she comes out. Our boy understands that Mommy really isn't routing for the opposite team. She just can't see who is out there," Jeff says, his voice dripping with sympathy for

144

my imaginary plight.

"Oh. How terrible," the woman says, feigning concern for me. She gives me a look that says, "poor you", but then she quickly turns back to Jeff.

"It's so refreshing to see a father coming to these things. So few come these days," she says.

"Really? That's terrible. I always make time for my boy," Jeff says.

I make a gagging noise, and the woman looks at me quickly.

"Is she alright?"

"She's fine. Allergies," Jeff says and starts slapping me on the back like this will somehow cure me of my allergies.

"That's terrible," the woman replies because apparently that is all she knows how to say.

"Which one is yours?" Jeff asks her.

"The pitcher," she says brightly and points at the kid on the mound. Crap! Her kid is on my team and he's doing a shit job. Just as I finish the thought the batter smacks a pitch out into the outfield and he makes it to third base before my team can get it back in.

I groan and Jeff smirks at me.

"He's talented," Jeff says to the woman. She beams at him.

"Yes, he is."

Ugg, gag.

"Aww, come on!" I shout as the next hitter is walked to first base.

The woman turns to me, and Jeff pats me on my hand.

"Sweetheart, that's the wrong team again," he says affectionately.

"Bugger off," I say and push his hand away.

The woman looks to Jeff, and he just shrugs. She lets him know how sympathetic she is by batting her eyelashes at him. If she kept that up there would be a scuffle on the sidelines.

"Finally!" I shout when the coach takes the pitcher out and

145

replaces him. This earns me an evil stare from my biggest fan sitting next to Jeff.

Once the pitching change is made my team is able to tie the game back up and we make it to the final inning. My team is last to bat and I'm literally on the edge of my seat, bag of peanuts open and I'm nervously munching on them as my final batter steps up to the plate.

"This is it, the moment of truth," Jeff whispers in my ear.

"Hush," I say and wave him off.

He chuckles, sits back and winks at the woman sitting on his other side. I stomp on his foot and he just laughs. During this exchange my batter receives two strikes on him. When the pitcher releases the next pitch, I cover my eyes because I just don't want to see it. Suddenly I'm surrounded by cheers, and I look through my fingers to see my hitter running furiously around the bases. I jump up, spilling the rest of my peanuts on the ground and cheer.

My player makes it to third base and the next hitter steps up to the plate. I remain standing, clasp my hands together and place them over my lips. Jeff is still sitting but I'm not watching him. My eyes are fixed on the field. First pitch is a strike. *Damn.* Second flies wide and is called a ball. Then the third pitch is released, and the batter hits it. It is a ground ball, and it goes between the first and second baseman. I'm jumping up and down and cheering my heart out as the runner from third makes it easily over home plate.

Final score: Giants – three, Dodgers – four. My team won!

"My team won!" I declare and turn to Jeff.

"It seems they did," Jeff says as he stands.

"You lost," I say and do a little shimmy in place.

"Your wife is one strange lady," the woman next him says as she is gathering her things.

It's the word wife that has me glancing down at my left hand. My wedding band is back in its place. I notice Jeff glance down at my hand briefly before turning back to the woman, a fake smile plastered on his face.

"That's why I married her," he says.

We gather the rest of our things in silence, and I don't say anything until we are back by his truck. After we have put everything in the bed and he closes the hatch, I break the tension.

"Thank you. This was everything I never expected," I say.

Jeff smiles at me but he doesn't say anything. He goes to the driver's side and gets in. Sighing, I get into the passenger seat, and he starts the engine.

"It's not that easy," I blurt.

Jeff has his hand on the gear shift, and he puts it back in park before turning to me.

"I know," he says.

"I've tried to keep it off but something about that finger being bare after this long seems odd to me. I want to remove it," I continue.

"Okay."

"I'm not trying to hurt you."

"I know."

"Say something else," I request because his easy understanding of my neurosis is starting to grate at me.

"What do you want me to say?"

"Not that. Tell me what you are thinking."

"Okay. I'm thinking it really sucks that you keep wearing his ring. I'm also thinking that I've never been married, and I don't know what you are going through. I'm thinking this would be easier if I had met you first," he says.

I stare back at him for a good minute before I respond.

"That's a lot of thinking," I finally say.

"It is. Do you think you'll ever take it off?"

Using my thumb, I twirl the ring on my finger and look at it before I answer him.

"Yes."

"Alright," he turns and puts the gear in reverse. As we are pulling out of the parking spot the woman who sat next to him waves to him frantically. She is walking over, and Jeff rolls the window down.

"Aren't you forgetting something?" she asks and points behind her at the kid Jeff had identified as ours.

"Um, nope. Turns out the kid isn't mine after all," Jeff says. He rolls his window up and leaves the bewildered woman staring at his departing truck.

"You could always circle back and run her over," I say.

"Is that a hint of jealousy I detect in your voice," Jeff teases.

"No. I just found her insufferable. She was so obvious it was embarrassing," I explain.

"Uh, huh, sure."

"Hey, we have some shopping to do," I declare.

"What?"

"You need a nice pink tutu and tights for our next visit to Tuckets," I say.

"Our visit, huh?"

"Oh yeah. There is no way I am going to miss that."

"Alright. This Saturday?" Jeff asks me with a smile on his face.

And that is how I think I started dating Jeffrey Collins without even realizing it.

-18-

Intervention

Three weeks have passed since my daughter revealed my relationship with Jeff to our family. Three weeks of dodging questions, phone calls, inquiries, and demands for answers from various busy bodies. Three weeks of allowing myself to escape into a different world with Jeff through non-dates and wild nightly sessions between the sheets.

It has also been three weeks since my daughter spoke to me last. Today, however, she is no longer able to avoid me. We had a pre-scheduled family event to attend, and I knew my daughter wouldn't miss it. It was her cousin's birthday, and she adored her younger cousin and had been looking forward to this birthday. The entire family was set to gather at Kelly and Brad's house for a celebration fit for a princess.

I had briefly entertained the thought of skipping the event but a particularly aggressive phone call from Kelly put a stop to such thoughts.

"I know what you are thinking and I'm telling you to forget it. You have to come to the party. Jenny Lynn is expecting you," Kelly had said to me.

"Kelly, you know how our family is. This is supposed to be Jenny Lynn's day, but it will turn into a babble fest about me and Josh. I don't want to do that to Jenny Lynn," I said.

"That is complete B.S. You just want to avoid the family. Well, forget it. You are coming and that is final," Kelly declared, and the conversation was effectively over.

So, I found myself standing outside my sister's door, gift in hand, and dread in my knock. I intentionally arrived early because I didn't want to give the rest of the family an opportunity to gossip about me and then ambush me. I knock on that door a good hour before the party is supposed to begin.

Brad answers the door, his aging pooch at his heels. They had gotten the dog before Jenny Lynn had been born, and I knew that when the time came to say goodbye to what had essentially been their first "child" together, Brad would be hit the hardest. I quickly kneel down and scratch the mutt behind the ears.

"Who else is here?" I ask Brad as he steps aside to let me in.

"Your mother and Paul," Brad replies.

"Crap! How long have they been talking about me?" I ask.

Brad shrugs and I follow him through the hallway. He always was a man of few words. Perhaps that is why it took him and Kelly so long to finally admit they had feelings for one another. Our family has never been really great at communication. The strong and silent type is more our repertoire. Until, of course, the flood waters crash through the dam and all hell breaks loose.

"Maybe an hour or so," he says, and I immediately stop in my tracks. He stops with me and just waits. Brad is used to my little peculiarities.

"Hostility level?" I ask.

"No more than usual," he replies.

"Judgement factor?"

"Off the charts," he says, and I suck in a breath.

"Richter scale?"

Over the years Brad and I had developed a system for gauging the tension level over family drama. There were three criteria of concern: how angry everyone appeared (hostility level), who was to

150

blame (judgement factor) and finally how severe the situation seemed to be (Richter Scale). We used the earthquake measurement tool because our family so often treated things like a natural disaster where the literal earth was falling away beneath our feet. A rating of one meant no lasting damage and few discussions would be had regarding the matter. A rating of nine meant complete catastrophic damage to all relationships and that no recovery was evident in the near future.

"Nearing a seven with possible growth," Brad reveals.

"Shit. Damage control?"

"Unavoidable at this point."

"Any chance I can count on your support?" I ask him. He lowers his eyes at me but says nothing. "Right. Kelly's on their side so you must remain Switzerland. Always the peacemaker. Don't you ever just want to pick a side?"

"I have chosen a side. The side that stays out of it." Brad says and continues walking through the house and into the kitchen. I envied him the luxury of remaining on the sidelines. It was a luxury I had yet to experience.

I can hear my family's voices from the kitchen, and I take one last longing look at the front door before I square my shoulders and walk into the lion's den. I'm greeted by the sallow expressions on my mother's and sister's faces. At least Paul smiles at me and stands to give me a hug.

"Thanks, Paul, for the hug. It's nice to have one family member still think I'm worthy of affection." Immediately, I wish I could take my words back. I had intended on coming today and keeping my mouth shut but in typical Me fashion I had laid down the first punch. Of course, my mother isn't about to let this just slide.

"Stacey, nobody here thinks you are unworthy of our love. We are just concerned about your choices. You do have a tendency to react impulsively and not focus on the bigger picture," my mother says from her seat. She is skillfully putting together what looks like party streamers.

"And it starts," I say as I put my niece's gift on the table.

"What is that supposed to mean?" my mother asks defensively.

"It means I'm barely in the door and the intervention has already started."

"Intervention?"

"Yes Mother. The one you, Kelly, and Becca have no doubt been planning these last couple of weeks. Let me be very clear – I am *not* getting back together with Josh. I am getting a divorce. And yes, it is true that I have begun to seek out the company of other men. I am allowed to do this and would appreciate it if all the mechanizations of how to get me and Josh back together would cease. For once can this family just enjoy a nice family event without it turning into some crisis that needs to be managed? Please keep this day about Jenny Lynn and refrain from mentioning my current relationship status."

Both my mother and Kelly exchange looks with one another before returning their gazes back to me. They are silent but their eyes betray them. It is clearly obvious that they had every intention of discussing the very things with me that I didn't want to talk about.

"I think that sounds reasonable, Stacey," Paul says to me. "Tasha?"

My mother looks over at her husband and groans.

"Fine. But only for today. We will need to talk about this at some point. And don't think I've forgotten all about how you refuse to let me see your apartment. Honestly, Stacey, your behavior lately is childish." She is about to continue when Paul clears his throat, cutting her off. My mother sighs and falls silent. It is the only acknowledgement of her agreeing to drop the matter that I will get.

Unfortunately, Kelly makes no such assurance, and she finds me over an hour later. Jenny Lynn's friends have arrived, and other acquaintances of Kelly and Brad's have overtaken the house. My children have yet to arrive, and I am shamelessly gulping down copious amounts of wine in an attempt to ready myself for their accusing gazes. Kelly finds me hiding in the backyard. The weather is starting to turn, and the other guests have decided to remain in doors. I am huddled in a jacket, lounging on a chaise when Kelly joins me.

"Mom is only saying those things because she loves you," she begins.

I snort at her.

"Sometimes her *love* is suffocating," I say.

"She isn't trying to be suffocating," Kelly says as she sits down in the chaise next to mine.

"She is so talented that she doesn't even have to try, she just succeeds," I reply and offer Kelly my wineglass. She shakes her head, and I squint my eyes at her.

"I've always wanted to know. Did you stop drinking because of Brad?"

Kelly doesn't respond right away. Her gaze lingers into the distance before she answers.

"Maybe at first. But I never really was much of an avid consumer anyway so it was easy to just cut it out entirely," she says.

"But it wasn't something you did for you. You initially did it for him," I persist.

"I suppose. You say that like there is something wrong with that." She looks at me, her lips already pursed in preparation for what she thinks I am judging her on.

I shrug my shoulder and take another drink from my dwindling wine glass.

"Don't do that. If you are going to say something halfway then you might as well just say the rest of it," Kelly says.

"Alright. I just don't understand it. You, not drinking isn't keeping him sober. Only he can keep himself sober so why did you alter your behavior?"

"Because I love him," she says so quickly that I actually laugh at her.

"Ooookaaaay," I elongate the word to show just how little I think of her answer.

"You really can be a bitch." The venom dripping from her words is easily detected.

Slowly, I turn to Kelly and blink back at her. She has never once called me a bitch before. Not even when I told her she sounded like a moose when she was giving birth. Not my finest hour, but she was bellowing.

"You think everyone else is judging you but really, Stacey, you are the worst of us all. Even when we were kids you would walk around like the rest of us were just completely ridiculous and you were the only one with any sense. Just because you don't understand something doesn't mean it's wrong or something to be laughed at."

It all comes out of her in a rush and it occurs to me that I never really knew what Kelly had thought of me all these years. Maybe I just never wanted to know because I already had a pretty good idea where her opinions lay.

"I'm not laughing at you," I reply, looking at her so she knows I am being serious.

"Yes, you are. You laugh at all of us. We used to tease you about your habit of blurting things without thinking because it used to be harmless. But it hasn't been harmless in years, Stacey. Words hurt. Your words hurt your family and I'm not going to pretend that they don't anymore."

"What have I said that hurt you?" Other than the moose comment I couldn't think of anything I had said that was hurtful.

"You told me that naming my child after a deceased person would cause irrevocable harm to the psyche of my daughter," Kelly says.

"No, that isn't what I said. I said that there have been reports that people with the same namesake as a deceased relative have felt added pressure to mirror the deceased person's personality and that has caused irrevocable harm."

"You named your son after your dead father!" Kelly responds, irritation dripping with every word.

"I didn't give him the same first name," I say and am rewarded with a punch on my arm. "Ow," I say and rub the spot Kelly punches.

"You don't even see how the things you say hurts others."

"That isn't true. I just don't understand why others feel hurt by them. I don't say them in an attempt to hurt people. I say them because they are important," I defend myself.

"Brad doesn't need to be reminded about the relapse rate of drug addicts," Kelly narrows her eyes at me and crosses her arms over her chest.

"Yes, he does. He needs to know how important his continued sobriety is. He's doing a kick ass job and should be reminded of that," I once again defend my actions.

"That isn't why you do it."

Exhausted, and nearing my last nerve, I say, "Why don't you tell me what you are really saying, Kelly?"

"Fine. You like to remind the rest of us how much better you are at everything than we are. You throw your success in our face and bring up our failures to keep us down and yourself elevated."

"What? Are you kidding me right now? I got pregnant in high school for fucks sake!" I say and stand up from my lounge chair. She is painting an ugly picture of me, and I had no idea that my family actually believed these things about me.

"You think you are the only one that is allowed to have important things going on. You monopolize everyone's time and relish in disaster," Kelly continues as she stands, squaring off with me.

We are facing each other in a tense noontime showdown that is bound to end with a fatal shot. Despite the warning signs, I can't seem to stop myself and I keep firing back at her. One of us will be drawing blood, and I'm determined it won't be my blood that spills on the patio concrete that is in desperate need of a power wash.

"You're one to talk. Your entire adolescence was all about drama between you and Brad. Will they? Won't they? Tap, tap, tap until neither of you could remember the steps anymore. You lived in denial and spent years avoiding the truth. And then you marry him and expect the rest of us to just change our behavior because he has a problem with staying sober? If anyone relishes a disaster, it is you," I say and give her a little shove on her shoulder.

Kelly stumbles back a bit but she quickly recovers.

"You are so completely warped that you pursued Josh even though you knew it would devastate Jenny. You practically threw yourself at him and then got pregnant because God forbid anybody else be the center of attention for once," Kelly fires back.

"Excuse me? You think I got pregnant on purpose? You think I wanted to be knocked up at nineteen and finish school with a walrus belly? You're delusional. I even moved out of the house so you could have your space because I didn't want to be the center of attention."

"Right. You moved out for my benefit. You did that because you knew it would send Mom and Dad into a tailspin, and you wanted one more thing to lord over them. Your Mommy issues are legendary."

"My mommy issues? If anyone here has mother issues, it is you. You always make such a big production when you call Tasha Mom like it's some big achievement for you. Like you have another option or something. Newsflash, Kelly, you don't! Your mother walked out on you! We are all you've got!"

"Ahem, girls."

"What?!" Kelly and I shout at the same time and turn to see Paul and various other party guests gathering around the patio door to watch our family display of sibling warfare.

"Maybe now isn't the time for this," Paul says to us. Of course,

Kelly falls in line, and she quickly paints a smile on her face as she walks back into the house. Always the perfect, obedient daughter.

I'm about to turn my back on the party goers when I spot my daughter and soon to be ex-husband among them. Becca is glaring at me with daggers and Josh is looking at me with concern. Instead of reaching out to them I do quite possibly the worst thing and stick my tongue out at them. Becca shakes her head and then turns on her heels. She walks away and soon others begin to follow her. Josh, however, ventures out onto the patio with me.

"If this is another intervention please stop before you begin. I've had enough family involvement to last quite a while," I say and hold my hand up to him.

"Not an intervention. Just an observation," Josh says and adjusts his gold rimmed glasses, so they sit further back on his nose. That singular habit of his used to make me smile because when I was younger all of his idiosyncrasies were endearing to me but today that same habit makes me sneer.

I shake my head slightly and he recognizes the gesture as an act of permission.

"You're angry," he says, and I chuckle snidely.

"Really? The fight wasn't hint enough?" He is smarter than this and I find his comment quite comical.

"I don't mean with Kelly and your family. You're angry with me. You're angry with yourself."

"What? No, I'm not," I say but my words have lost some of their bite.

"I was angry with you too. I thought all of this was your doing. I thought our marriage had ended because of the choices you made." He pauses and I take that moment to step away from him. Just one more person in my life reminding me of my mistakes.

"But I was wrong, Stacey. You had been telling me for years you weren't happy. I just wasn't listening. I know that now. You're angry with me for letting it get this far. But you're angry with

157

yourself for staying as long as you did. I don't know about you but I'm tired of being angry. It doesn't suit me," he says.

"Of course it doesn't. Because that would require emotion and that just isn't something you do," I snap back.

Josh doesn't respond with his own biting remark. He just nods his head silently.

"You like to think I don't feel things Stacey, but I do. I just don't express my feelings in the same way you do. I don't like full displays of rage and hurt because I don't believe it benefits anyone. You and I have two different approaches to problem solving."

I interrupt him because I can't stand to listen to his prattle any longer.

"God! Why can't you just talk like normal people? Even now you are so formal. It drives me insane!" I throw my hand up before me in frustration.

"Exactly. And your need to inject passion into every conversation exhausts me. I love you Stacey, but I think you are right. We are not suited to be married to one another."

At first his admission brings me a sense of peace but as the words sink in the anger I know so well continues to boil to the surface. These were things I had been saying for years but now, because he said them, they were suddenly true? The nerve of this man.

"I get it. You need to be the one that is right, is that what this is? You come out here and pretend you are on my side when in reality you just want to be the one to end things? Well, tough shit, buckaroo, because I already dumped you," I say and poke him in the chest.

"That's not what I'm doing, Stacey."

"Well, then, pray tell, what are you doing out here Josh?"

"I'm telling you I won't fight you on the divorce. It will be amicable," he says.

I should be calming down. He's giving me exactly what I want

158

but instead of finding comfort the more he talks the more I become enraged. Giving me what I want? Like I wanted my marriage to end in failure with my family barely talking to me? None of this was what I had wanted at all.

"You are the dumbest genius I have ever met," I say and turn to walk away from him.

"Stacey? I'm just trying to keep things civil," Josh says, and I twirl back around, wine spilling on the concrete patio. Oh yes, I manage to hold on to my wine glass.

"Of course you are, Josh, because that's what you do. Mr. Civility. Can't have you painted as the bad guy because that just wouldn't fit with the narrative you've created all these years. Mr. Hero. You tried to save Jenny. You tried to save me. You save every member of this family from time to time because that is what you do. You save people and you are never the bad guy. Nope. That role is reserved for me. I tricked you after all and got pregnant. I cheated on you and forced the end of the marriage. It had nothing to do with how you pull away from my touch or ignore my scars. It has nothing to do with how I have to practically beg you to talk to me. It has nothing to do with how you always change the subject and ignore the things I say because you are just trying to keep the peace. Don't fight for me, Josh. I wouldn't want you to break character and give everyone a heart attack," I say and stomp away from him.

"Stacey?" he says again but this time I speak before he continues.

"I'll have my lawyer send you the papers by the end of next week."

I leave Josh on that dirty patio and walk through the house and out the front door without another word to anyone. As far as interventions go, I would say my family bungled this one.

-19-

Escape

I'm still fuming from the altercations with Kelly and Josh that I don't notice Jeff until I practically ram into him. I quickly close the door behind me and step off the front entrance at the same time, so I end up walking straight into Jeff.

"Whoa there. Where's the fire?" he asks as he steadies me.

My mind is racing, and my heart is bounding from the verbal sparring that upon hearing Jeff's voice I immediately recoil. All my instincts are shouting at me to lash out. His presence is the embodiment of how my life has gone to shit and he didn't deserve to go unscathed.

"Perfect, this is just perfect. As if I didn't get enough from Larry and Moe in there. Now I have to deal with Curly too," I say and step away from him. It is then I realize I am still holding onto the wine glass I forgot to leave in the kitchen. Perfect. Just perfect. I am not going back in there.

He is carrying a silver bag with pink sparkles, and it is a complete contrast to the man that holds it. Jeff is all brawn in a pair of jeans and a t-shirt that, in my opinion, is a size too small. I'm sneering at how it accentuates every muscle in his arms because it seems like something a tool bag at the gym would wear just to make others aware of how much hotter he is than all the others trying to lose those last five pounds of holiday weight. He is the reason why

160

people give up on their New Year's resolutions. How could they possibly compete with him?

"It seems I've stumbled into something here. What happened?" he asks, cool as ever, like nothing in the world could possibly bother him.

"It's a family matter. You aren't family," I spit out.

Jeff blinks at me, purses his lips, but doesn't lash back. He stands there, holding that ridiculous gift bag, staring at me with his stupid grey eyes. The same eyes that he demanded I stare back into when he had me pressed against the hotel wall. I'd seen those eyes staring back at me in various positions of love-making the past month and it is those eyes that has me snapping out of my anger.

"That was cruel," I say regretfully.

"Yes, it was. Do you feel better now?"

"No." I shake my head and hold up the stupid wine glass, releasing a sigh at how silly I must look.

Jeff shifts his gaze so he is staring over my head and at Kelly's front door. He moves the gift bag to his other hand before taking a step towards me. Before I realize what he is doing he is before me, leaning down so his forehead is against mine. I can feel his breath on my face, and I close my eyes. We stand with our foreheads pressed together, breathing softly for a few minutes. I shut out the world and just focus on his breath hitting my face.

"I'm going to go inside and see Jenny Lynn. I imagine Becca and Josh are in there too. They might stop me before I can get back here but I don't want you to leave. Stay. Wait for me and then the two of us can get the hell out of here," Jeff says.

"I don't think that is a good idea. If I had known you were coming today, I would have stayed away. The last thing I need right now is more fuel added to the fire," I reply and step away from our linked bodies.

Jeff remains in his spot, but he is now staring at me with his brooding eyes. I never have to guess what he is thinking because his eyes tell me everything I need to know. He doesn't like what I said, and he wants to argue with me but his quick glances back to Kelly's house tell me he won't make a scene here.

"Don't leave Stacey. I'll only come after you if you do," he finally says before he snatches the wine glass from my hand and steps around me to enter the house. He doesn't wait for my reply, and I don't follow him into the house.

I start to walk towards my car to leave, ignoring his request, when I'm suddenly struck by what he said. He would come after me, but my own husband let me walk out of that house without even considering coming after me. I had told my family that there was nothing that would convince me to remain in my marriage but that hadn't been entirely true. When Josh had revealed he wouldn't contest the divorce I should have been satisfied but instead I reacted angrily. Now I knew why. Somewhere, in the deepest part of me, I wanted him to fight to keep me. I wanted him to run after me and beg me to stay. I wanted someone to fight for me and if Josh had done so I would have remained in my marriage.

Once again, my thumb twirls the ring on my finger as my thoughts wander to my failed marriage. Josh was right. I did want fire and brimstone, but I didn't want to be the one delivering it. I wanted him to spring forth from a vicious flame of desire. I wanted him to want me like I needed to be wanted. I wanted passion and desperation and absolute crazy devotion. He was walking away far too easily and his turned back was a reminder of how the past twenty years of my life had been built on a fantasy I had conjured in my head. He said he loved me, but I wasn't so sure he truly had. Maybe, neither of us had really ever loved the other. Maybe what we had was a sick, twisted kind of need, but that wasn't love.

"Mom?"

Shaking out of my dreary thoughts I turn to see my son Cooper walking up the driveway. I immediately smile and open my arms for the hug. He walks to me and folds his arms around me. I cling to my

162

first born like he is my lifeline to a time that is slowly crumbling.

"Did Becca say something?" Cooper asks me and I laugh at his question.

"Surprisingly, no. Don't you worry about this. I want to hear about you. How's school? Is Gregory with you?" I inquire about my much younger brother who was only a few years older than my own son as I pull out of the embrace.

"School's fine. Greg stayed behind at school because he has some video interview with a company in London. Stop stalling, tell me what happened?"

Both my children resembled their father very much in appearance. They had the same bone structure and there were times I felt Cooper could very much be Josh's clone. Their personalities, however, were not similar at all. Where Josh was stoic and solid, Cooper was worrisome and sensitive. Becca was the brick wall that refused to budge but Cooper was the ocean. He ebbed and flowed according to the tides.

"Just an argument between siblings. You remember those don't you?" I smirk at my joke. When he and Becca were younger, they were constantly getting into silly sibling squabbles. Mostly they were initiated by Becca.

"You and Aunt Kelly had a fight? Was it about Dad?"

"Cooper, please don't worry about it. Go inside. Say hello to everyone and enjoy the party."

"Mom, I'm not ten anymore. I know you and Uncle Jeff are involved and I know the family isn't exactly thrilled about it. Becca lets us know how upset she is about it any chance she gets. You don't have to hide things from me," my son says and my heart breaks just a little.

"I'm not hiding anything. I just don't want you to feel like you are being placed in the middle. Your Father is inside. I'm sure he'd love to see you," I say and pat his shoulder.

"Okay, don't tell me what happened. I'll just ask Becca," he says so flippantly that it causes me to chuckle. He grins at me, satisfied he got me to laugh.

"For what it's worth I get why you and Dad are getting a divorce." His comment effectively knocks the air out of my chest. Stumbling for a response I stutter a bit. My son just laughs at my fumbling before explaining.

"You two think we don't notice things, but we do. You barely talk to each other, and you haven't spent more than ten minutes in a room together in years. I can't say I'm thrilled about things, but I understand it. You both should do what makes you happy. We'll be fine," he assures me.

"Where did my little boy go and who is this man?" I ask my son as I bring my hand to his cheek. Cooper blushes and turns his head to the side.

"Come on, Mom. I'm twenty-one years old. I haven't been a kid in a long time," he says.

"Oh, I know. I found the condoms to prove it."

"Mom!"

"Okay, okay. You know I love you, kiddo?"

"Yeah. I know."

The door to Kelly's house opens and Jeff comes walking out. He sees Cooper, smiles and walks right up to my son to offer his hand. Cooper eagerly takes the hand, and they engage in some strange male fist bump/hand shake thing.

"Hey, Cooper. How's college life treating you?" Jeff asks.

"Can't complain," my son replies.

"And your girl? She still your girl?" Jeff asks.

"Yeah."

"What is that, two-three years now?"

"Yeah. About that. I'm gonna head inside and say hi to the rest of the family. Check ya later," Cooper says to Jeff. "Bye Mom. Love you," Cooper says to me as he gives me a brief hug.

"Love you too," I say and watch as my son enters the house.

"He's a good kid," Jeff says at my side.

"Yeah. You know about his girlfriend?" I ask, turning to Jeff.

"Yep. This may surprise you, but your family used to talk to me. You ready to go?"

"I know they used to talk to you. I just didn't know you knew about those things," I say and start walking to my car. Jeff falls in step beside me. "Did Becca corner you?"

"Nah. They stayed clear. I just said hey to Brad and Kelly and gave Jenny Lynn her gift. I can't believe she is nine already. It was just yesterday she was a little baby."

"Yeah, time sure does seem to be speeding up. Look, Jeff, I'm going to head home," I say when we get to my car.

"I'll follow you," Jeff says and takes his keys out of his pocket.

"No. I meant by myself."

"I know what you meant but I'm still going to follow you. I'm worried about you, and it seems there are some things we need to discuss."

"I don't want to talk. I just want to be alone," I insist.

"Well, tough. Because I don't want to be alone right now and I have some questions. You think you are in this alone, Stacey, but you aren't. I'm right here, every step of the way. Stop trying to push me away and just let me be there for you."

"But why? Why are you putting up with all of this? You've been on the periphery for years and now I'm just supposed to believe that you have feelings for me all of a sudden? Nothing you are doing makes any sense. I've tried to keep this just about fun, but you keep insisting on getting involved. I don't understand your motives and I'm not so sure I can trust you," I reveal all the doubts plaguing my mind.

"That's fair. But you are assuming that I didn't already care for you. I've known you for years. I've always cared about you, Stacey. I care about Becca and Cooper too. Hell, I even care about Josh. You think I wanted to be the guy that tore you two apart?"

"You didn't tear us apart," I say, rolling my eyes at his ego.

"I know that, you know that, and even Josh knows that, but the rest of your family doesn't know that. To them I'm the great usurper and that's fine. If they need me to be the bad guy, I can do that, but I won't let you use their feelings as an excuse to pull away from me. I don't know what this is between us, but I do know I like it. I don't want it to end. I think we could be good together. So, I'm going to get in my truck and I am going to follow you back to your place. We are going to go inside, and you are going to let me be there for you because that's what people do for those they care about." Once again Jeff steps closer to me and places his forehead against mine. He wraps his fingers around my arm and begins to slowly caress it.

"I don't like being told what to do," I reply.

Jeff laughs, his hot breath landing on my face.

"Yeah, you do. But you give just as much as you take," he says as his hand on my arm drifts to my side. He grips my shirt and moves it up, so my skin is exposed. He presses further into me, and my back meets the cold steel of my car door.

Jeff's hand travels under my shirt and up until he has a firm hold of my breast. He flexes his fingers as his head dips and his lips meet mine. His lips crush against me in the same manner that his body is pressing into mine. Without hesitation I eagerly return the kiss and become breathless. When we break apart, we are both panting and I know he is just as turned on as I am.

"There is a reason there is so much heat between us. This can't be just fun. It feels too good," Jeff says against my cheek.

"It's pheromones," I say.

"No, Stacey, it's more than that. Take me to your place and I'll prove it to you." Jeff's hand travels down my stomach to the line of my skirt top. His fingers dip inside, and he teases me with a foreshadow of what's to come. I lay my head against his shoulder and breathe in deeply. We both know he doesn't have to convince me further. I'm going to let him inside.

166

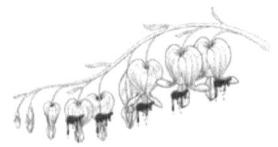

It's been a long time since I could honestly say I was nervous about letting a man enter my personal space. My mother was right at the party. I was deliberately keeping people away from my apartment. At first it had been unintentional but as time drifted on it seemed to be an act of desperation on my part. As long as I could keep those I cared about away from this new place of mine, I could keep the reality of my divorce at bay. As long as I was the only one living in this world than my old life could remain intact.

Having Jeff standing in my two-bedroom apartment was quickly destroying all the safeguards I had erected around my little haven. I remained by the entrance while he wandered the living room. It wasn't a small space but to me, standing in the background, watching this invader explore my sanctuary was painful.

"You look uncomfortable," Jeff remarks.

"I am," I admit openly.

"I promise not to break anything," Jeff chuckles and takes a step towards me. He notices my instinctive reaction to retreat and he stops advancing. I'm pressed against the door with nowhere to go, like a caged animal. I can only imagine the look in my eyes.

"Stacey, this is nothing more than two people who enjoy one another's company spending some time together."

"I know that," I snap. I am met with Jeff's quintessential smirk that clearly states, '*you're so cute when you protest but you are also full of shit*'.

"This has nothing to do with you. I'm just still upset about the fight I had with Kelly," I recover and walk away from the entrance to go into my kitchen. It's larger than the living room and it gives me a few moments to collect myself. I take out a bottle of water from the fridge and gulp down some contents.

Jeff takes a seat on my oversized sofa and to my surprise it doesn't completely swallow him whole like it does everyone else. In fact, he actually looks quite comfortable sitting on the leather sofa. He drapes an arm over the back and turns his head to me. I tip the bottle of water towards him, offering him one and he shakes his head slightly declining.

"Tell me what happened."

"You don't need to hear the ugly details. It was just a silly sibling argument. Nothing worth repeating," I dismiss him.

Jeff sighs heavily. "Tell me what happened, Stacey."

I look over at him and I notice how his usually relaxed stance is now tense. His furrowed brows let me know that he is upset with my dismissal of his request and his clenched jaw tells me he won't give up.

"Fine, but it really was nothing," I say and come out of the kitchen. I sit on one of the breakfast bar stools so I can maintain some distance from him. My living room and kitchen are separated by a long counter that holds four stools.

"The gist of the argument was Kelly basically saying I am a hurtful bitch that spews out horrible things for the sole purpose of hurting my family. I'm selfish, cruel and an attention whore. End of story."

Jeff narrows his eyes at me. "You're holding back," he says.

"Uggh, fine. I may have alluded that she has severe mother issues because her own mother abandoned her and that she is jealous of me." I struggled to get the last bit out. In the heat of the argument I completely believed I was in the right but now, with the ability to calmly examine the events, I realize I was completely out of control.

"Ugghh," I say again, throw my head back briefly before bringing it forward to rest in my hands. I'm ashamed of my behavior.

168

"I didn't know Kelly back then and Brad never really liked to talk about personal things. But he has shared some things with me over the years. Kelly's mother wasn't exactly fully functional in the reasoning department. She had high expectations for Kelly and would withhold affection until Kelly met those standards. From what Brad told me she was never able to meet those standards. And then, one day, her mother just disappeared. I don't know what that would feel like. Never being good enough and then never even being given the chance to at least try," Jeff says all of this while I'm still hiding my face in my hands.

"Oh, crap," I mutter into my hands.

"What's wrong?" Jeff asks.

I lift my head and stare into those penetrating eyes.

"You know more about my sister than I do. We lived together for years, share parents, call each other sisters in all capacity of the word and with the exception of blood we are sisters. But I don't really know her. Sure, we would talk when we were teenagers and she was the first person I told when I found out I was pregnant with Cooper but we were never really close. In fact, I don't know what possessed me to tell her first other than she was the closest in proximity besides my parents the night I found out. I used to believe I went to her first because I trusted her or something but honestly, I think it was just because I needed to tell someone, and she was just there. I'm a shit person," I say and place my head back in my hands.

I'm answered with Jeff's rumbling chuckle and I peak a look at him through my fingers. He is really laughing this up. I'm glad he finds my misery so amusing.

"You aren't a shit person. Did Kelly ever ask you about the things you were going through?"

"Well, no," I say slowly.

"Exactly. The facts are you were two kids thrown together because your parents decided to only have sex with each other for the rest of their lives. You were never best friends. The two of you were just surviving the life handed to you. Could you have opened up more? Sure, but neither of you did. If you are a shit person than so is Kelly, and I know Kelly. She is a great person. I'm also getting to know you and from what I can see you are pretty spectacular too. Plus, you have a great ass," Jeff throws in.

I snort and sit back in my chair as much as I can. My hands are now in my lap, rubbing my legs. Glancing at my surroundings I suddenly realize I am no longer panicking about having Jeff in my apartment. In fact, I'm finding I rather like his presence.

"So, what do you think of my new digs?" I ask him.

He lifts his gaze and examines the two rooms he can see.

"I think I might need your decorator's phone number," he jokes.

"I like her style too."

"Hmm. I especially love the motivational poster and the Rockin' Jesus painting," he says titling his chin to my latest addition to the chaos that is my design style.

"Thanks. Found that gem at a yard sale last week. I think the guitar really makes the scripture pop," I reply and earn a grin from Jeff.

"Give Kelly some time. She'll come around," Jeff says.

"I will."

"Now, why don't you show me the rest of this place? I hear they started including bedrooms in these units now," Jeff says as he stands.

Chuckling, I stand too.

"You would be correct. We even have indoor plumbing now. It is quite the rage."

"Yeah? Maybe you can show me your plumbing after the bedroom," Jeff says, wiggling his eyebrows suggestively.

I take his hand, and he falls in step behind me as I guide him towards my bedroom.

"I think arrangements can be made."

All requests are complied with, and Jeff ends up staying through the night. When I wake there is a note on my nightstand from him that reads:

Thanks for letting me in.

P.s. I took a hostage. You'll get him back once you pay the ransom.

Jeff

Throwing my covers off of me I run into the living room and find that Rockin' Jesus has been removed from my wall. In its place is another note. This one reads:

In retaliation for the humiliation I suffered at Tuckets while wearing the most uncomfortable pink tutu I have ever worn in my life you must complete the following tasks.

Treat your nurse to lunch and apologize to her for making fun of her name. She didn't choose it. It isn't her fault her parents didn't have forethought.

Compliment a random stranger. A real compliment, not those half platitudes you use.

Pay someone's bill.

Talk to Kelly (and be nice)

If you complete these tasks then I will return your beloved Rockin' Jesus to you, unharmed. Fail to complete these tasks and he will forever be enshrined next to my bed for eternity. Imagine the horrors he will see. Don't let him suffer. Save the man!

Signed...the super-hot kidnapper.

-20-

Introspection

Standing in line at the local coffee shop that isn't some franchised, multi-million-dollar company whose employees think "conscious uncoupling" is a real thing, I go over the ransom note Jeff left me. While I slept peacefully in the afterglow of our nighttime activity he had stolen away into the night with my prized painting. He really is the worst kind of heathen to have ever existed. Who steals a rocking Jesus?

Jeff thinks he is being so clever with his little list of demands. Taking my painting as collateral to ensure I pay up is absolutely unnecessary because I have no intention of following through with his demands. He can keep the painting. I am sure I can find another equally fascinating depiction of our lord and savior. I refuse to become a pawn in Jeff's immature game of revenge.

"How may I help you? Sir?"

I'm pulled out of my thoughts by the voice of the teenage barista trying to get the attention of the elderly gentleman at the front of the line. He is squinting at the menu and appears to be confused. The young girl keeps trying to get him to respond but he just keeps scanning the menu, ignoring her requests. The couple behind the elderly gentleman starts to become impatient and I can hear them muttering some choice words under their breath.

I observe the scene, but it isn't until I see the woman try to push around the elderly man to get to the counter that I intervene. I step out of the line and walk right up to the older man. I take hold of his elbow and give the impatient woman my best hateful glare. She glares right back, and her puckered lips make her look like a constipated sea creature.

"Sorry it took me so long, Dad," I say, and the elderly man turns his head slightly to me, still confused. He doesn't pull away from me, but his eyes are pleading. Now that I am closer to him, I am able to see the hearing aid in his left ear. Taking a chance, I start to move my fingers and hands and begin speaking in sign language to him. I learned how to speak it many years ago when I had a patient that was deaf. Cancer is hard enough and I didn't want my patient to have to rely on a translator in order to find out she only had four months left to live.

I am delighted when the older man starts to sign back to me. It seems he forgot his glasses at home, and he is unable to see the menu. In his haste he also forgot to bring his notepad. He is on his way to the doctor to get a replacement hearing aid because his current one has malfunctioned. His hands tell me all this in rapid motion. After he explains the situation, I ask him if he would like me to order for him. After a brief discussion on what he is looking for I turn to the teenage barista and give her the man's order. She looks at me with relief and rings up the man's order.

It isn't until the man starts to pull out his wallet that Jeff's list pops back into my head. Before I know what I'm doing I'm pulling out my own credit card.

"I'll get this one Dad," I turn to the barista and hand her my card. "I'll take a large, iced coffee with two pumps of caramel. And I'd like to pay for their order as well," I say and gesture to the impatient couple behind me. "For being so patient with my Father," I say and smile tightly at the pucker fish lipped woman behind me. She immediately starts to sputter like she is going to argue with me, but her companion places a hand on her arm, and she quiets down.

"Thank you," the companion says.

Jeff may have put that little item on the list in an attempt to get me to do something nice for a stranger but in my own fashion I used this opportunity to stick it to a complete bitch. The list never dictated how I had to go about completing it. If thirty dollars allows me the opportunity to let this woman know just how much of an ass she is than it is a trade I gladly make.

The barista collects everyone's orders, charges my card and brings us our completed drinks. As she's handing me mine, she brightly smiles and gives me a small to go bag.

"Oh, this isn't mine," I say and try to give the bag back to her.

"It's a complimentary scone. I wanted to thank you for coming to help. That lady was getting really mad, and I wasn't sure how to handle the situation. You saved me," the girl says and passes the bag back to me.

I'm literally stunned. I've never been given a complimentary anything for doing something nice before. Sure, I've been thanked for saving someone's life on numerous occasions but that was part of the job. This, however, is not something I expected and I am not sure how to handle it. Then, Jeff's list once again pops into my head.

"You seemed to be handling it just fine. You're really good at your job and with people. Thank you," I look at her name tag, "Danny for always giving me my coffee with a smile."

I take my items, drop a twenty in the tip jar and say goodbye to the young barista. She stares after me, mouth agape after seeing the tip I left. On my way to the door, I see the older gentleman sitting at a table and start to wave to him. He gestures for me to join him and for the first time in a long time I don't give a second thought to how I have a million things to do. Instead, I walk to the table, sit and have one of the greatest conversations with a stranger I have ever had.

Talking to this man, thinking about the young barista and replaying Jeff's list in my mind I can't help but realize how so much of my life had been trying to chase after things I thought were important. It is true that I have always been driven to achieve more, reach the next obstacle and conquer it. Ever since I could remember I'd been running a hundred miles an hour and never slowed to take a moment and just breathe. I had Cooper and started college soon after. Then I became pregnant with Rebecca and still kept up the same pace. I was newly married, had two young children and blazed my way through medical school. Failure had never been an option and through sheer will and determination I accomplished every goal I ever set.

But I had never just sat down with someone and talked to them because I could. I only did things that had a purpose and talking to a complete stranger like we were old friends never had a purpose. Paying for another person's items because it was a kind gesture didn't help me reach my goals. Praising a customer service attendant wasn't productive to my ambitions and it was their job to do those things, so I never before thought about going out of my way to thank them.

Jeff may not think I'm a shit person, but I certainly hadn't been a good one all these years. Success didn't always equate to serenity. I was confident in my professional life and had complete faith in my abilities. My personal life, however, was full of doubt. There had been contention between my mother and me for years. I usually remained on the outskirts of family events and rarely participated in deep conversations. I actively avoided getting to know Kelly and I even did something similar with my marriage to Josh. I believed his lack of openness caused me to stop asking him things about himself but that was really just an excuse. I could have pushed more but it was easier to just give up.

Rockin' Jesus would be returning to me. Jeff's silly list is now something I have to complete but not only because I want my painting back. No. I need to complete it because I need to find me again. I have held on to the resentment I'd been feeling for far too long. It is time I walk through this life with a different purpose – this time I won't push away the doubt. I will embrace it, own it, and identify where it is coming from. Then, I will destroy it and come out a better person.

I will be me again.

-21-

Devastation

Cursing Jeff and my stupid epiphany for the hundredth time I smile tightly at Chastity (my nurse formerly known as CUM, or Morgan) as she regales me with another story about growing up in rural South Dakota. If I have to hear another "aww shucks, isn't my family silly" story I just might vomit. Taking her to lunch was on the list, apologizing to her was on the list, but repeating this torturous event is not on the list and I have already decided Chastity and I will never share another lunch.

"Cousin Stan hasn't been the same since that day," Chastity says between laughter. She is enjoying her free meal and the retelling of family antics.

I, however, keep glancing at my watch and the door of the restaurant in desperation. How I wish I was with a patient, anywhere but here right now. This whole journey only began a few hours ago and already I wish I could make a retraction.

"Dr. McNill," Chastity says. Her tone is no longer jovial, and I tear my gaze away from the door and to her.

"Yes, Chastity," I say before taking a bite of my chicken pot pie. Sometimes the body just needed a nice comforting meal, and this baked goodness fit the bill.

"We got the results back on the tests you ordered for Ms. Farley," Chastity begins. She is still looking at me but now her eyes are sympathetic. I know this look. It is the look she uses on patients that are about to receive a bad diagnosis.

"Why are you just now telling me?" I demand. If she knew this before we went to lunch, why didn't she tell me? I'm nearly ready to explode at her when she suddenly starts to cry. *What just happened? I haven't even yelled at her yet.*

"I know you care for Ms. Farley and her son. I know how personally invested you are in her case. I wasn't sure how to tell you, and I wanted to tell you away from the hospital in case you needed to be alone." Chastity averts her eyes to hide her discomfort. Her body language, however, screams volumes.

"I'm personally involved in all my cases," I state and earn a narrowed look from Chastity in return. Guess she knows about me and Jeff. "Okay. Tell me what they reveal."

"The chemo was unsuccessful. The cells have grown, and they are now present in the lymph nodes and other distant organs. It has spread."

Chastity whispers the last part like the world will fall apart if she says it loudly. I suppose that is an accurate assessment because internally I feel like my world is about to crumble. How am I going to tell Reyann this? And Jeff? How am I supposed to tell my family that someone we all love is going to die?

Why couldn't the list have helped me with this?

And why is Chastity acting all emotional in a crowded restaurant when she doesn't even know Reyann, or Jeff for that matter? This is most definitely a single lunch excursion.

You would think the first person I would have called after hearing about Reyann's test results would have been Reyann herself or even Jeff. But I didn't call either one of them. In fact, I didn't call anyone. I had Chastity call Reyann to set up an appointment. We were simply following the same procedures we had followed for years with my other patients. I didn't call the patients to schedule their appointments; my nurses did that. This was not an unusual practice and I doubted Reyann would take offense to it but that didn't stop me from having a moment of self-loathing for being such a coward.

The next morning, I sat outside Rachel's office waiting for Gladys to appear and unlock the waiting room door. I knew I was going against the non-agreement I had made with Rachel. I was showing up during her clinical hours as if I was just another patient waiting for her scheduled appointment. It was wrong but I also knew my friend wouldn't turn me away.

Sitting in that hallway, I was bombarded with visions from my past and speculating about the upcoming appointment with Reyann. I had no doubt that Jeff would accompany her just as he had done with every other appointment. How could I possibly tell Reyann that based on my calculations she had less than two months left to live with Jeff in the room too? This exact outcome was what Rachel had warned me about. She had told me getting personally involved would only bring complications but I had ignored her warnings because I knew better. After all, I was the *real* doctor.

"Stacey?" Rachel calls to me softly.

Lifting my head from my raised knees I look up at Rachel and Gladys, tears streaming down my face. Rachel's shoulders slump and she turns to Gladys.

"Can you call my first two clients and reschedule them for a later time today?" Rachel asks Gladys.

Surprisingly Gladys doesn't object. She doesn't even sneer at me. Instead, the receptionist nods sympathetically and casts a caring glance down at me as she steps forward to unlock the door.

"Thank you, Gerdie," I say, but my heart isn't it and it comes out

179

weak.

"You're welcome, Nimwit," Gladys says and we both exchange a small smile with each other. This truce may end up being short lived, but I appreciated the distance Gladys quickly gave us, as well as that tiny bit of normalcy when she insulted me.

"Come on, let's go inside," Rachel says and extends her hand to me.

I look at the hand she offers and to my surprise I start sobbing uncontrollably. Rachel immediately drops her bag and settles down next to me on the floor. She pulls me into her side and embraces me. I cling to her as the sobs continue to shake my body.

"Let it all out," she says as she strokes my hair.

For the next five minutes I do exactly as Rachel says and let all the emotions come flooding out of me. My marriage is over, my daughter refuses to talk to me, my sister practically hates me, my mother has no faith in my life decisions, and I am going to have to crush the one person that has been in my corner during all of this. But none of that is the worst part. The worst part is that even though I know Jeff will be devastated and Reyann is going to die, the only thing I can think about is how this is bringing up all the things I had repressed when my father had died. All I keep focusing on is the fifteen year old girl I had been and how I couldn't watch another person I cared about be destroyed by cancer.

"I'm sorry," I sob into Rachel's shoulder.

"You don't have to be sorry. You know I'll always be there for you," she says and squeezes my hand.

"I should have been there for you when your parents kicked you out. I should have been a better friend. Instead, I just stayed away because I was selfish and too scared to be the friend you needed. I'm so sorry I let you down."

"Hey, stop that," Rachel says and turns me so we are facing each other. "You were going through your own shit that was far worse than my own stupid family drama. There has never been a moment

180

where I felt you were a terrible friend. You have been the best friend I could ever ask for and don't you ever apologize to me for that again."

"Okay," I sob and use the sleeve of my shirt to wipe away some snot.

"Now, get up off this floor. It hasn't been cleaned in ages," Rachel says and once again offers me her hand. This time I take it and she pulls me to my feet.

"Hold my calls," Rachel says to Gladys as we pass her.

Inside Rachel's office we find two hot steaming cups of coffee and I quickly claim one for myself. *Maybe Gladys isn't half bad after all.* Taking the mug with me, I sit in my usual purple chair and Rachel surprises me by sitting in the chair next to mine instead of the poop chair. She waits for me to get settled and sips on her own coffee. I am grateful she allows me these moments to compose myself.

"Reyann is going to die," I state once I feel I'm collected enough to speak.

"Yes. You told me about her diagnosis," Rachel says.

"No, you don't understand. The chemo didn't work. The cancer spread and it spread more quickly than we anticipated. I think it has always been worse than I thought. I must have missed it somehow. There isn't anything else I can do. Surgical excision is no longer a viable option. Based on my calculations she won't survive past the next two months. I failed again," I say and cast my glance down to the floor.

"Stacey, you didn't fail. You know perfectly well that this was always a possible outcome. If this was any other patient, would you have been sitting out in that hallway waiting for me today?"

"No," I say ashamed.

"The reaction you are having isn't about Reyann. Tell me what this is really about." Rachel reaches out and lays a hand over mine.

"I told my father our lives would be better off without him. I

181

killed him," I sob and the tears cascade down my face.

"No, Stacey, you didn't do that. You've told me what you said, and his decision had nothing to do with you. He was sick and he was scared. You didn't force his hand."

"I lied to you." Whispered words of truth. Words I have never before uttered aloud out of shame and remorse.

Jumping up from my chair I put my coffee mug down on her desk and begin to pace the office. I rub my arms frantically trying to keep me rooted to this place and out of the raging memories.

"What did you lie about?" Rachel asks. She is now standing too but she remains by the chairs, so she doesn't spook me I assume.

"I told you I said I wished the cancer was gone but that isn't what I said. He had asked my mother to leave the room, and he was talking to me like he was saying goodbye. He was saying things like how proud he was of me and how he was sorry he couldn't be there to see me graduate school, get married and live out my dreams. He took my hand," I lift the hand he had taken hold of and stare at it through the tears in my eyes.

"He tried to squeeze it, but he was so weak that he couldn't even do that. He said he loved me and then he asked me to be there for my mother. He asked me to not let his death keep me from finding happiness. I tore my hand away from him and told him to stop talking. I told him he needed to fight. I told him to fight for us. He said he was tired and that he didn't have any more fight left in him. I told him I hated him. I told him he was a coward and that if he died, I'd never forgive him for leaving me. I told him if he was going to just give up then he should just do it because our lives would be better off without a coward in our family."

Somehow, I had dropped to my knees during my confession and Rachel had come to me. We were both on the floor again. I was rocking back and forth while I continued to stare at the hand I had refused to let my father hold as he told me he loved me and said his final goodbye.

"He called to me as I ran from the room, but I just kept running. I refused to visit him again and then he killed himself. He died believing I hated him. I told him to do it!"

"No, Stacey, no," Rachel reaches out and takes hold of my shoulders. She gives me a little shake. "Your father knew you loved him. He knew you didn't mean those things. And he loved you too, very much. His death was not your fault. Listen to me, Stacey. You were both hurting and you both did what you needed to do to cope with it at the time. It was ugly and unfair, but it was nobody's fault. You didn't cause any of that to happen," Rachel says, and she wraps her arms around me.

My arms fall to my sides, and I allow her to hold me, but I do not return the embrace. I let the tears fall until I run out. The shakes eventually slow and then stop. When I have control once again, I move out of Rachel's embrace and stand. She watches me as I walk back to the purple chair, sit down and pick up the coffee mug.

"Stacey?" she asks with confusion. She is still kneeling on the floor, staring at me like she doesn't recognize me.

"I guess mental instability runs in my family, huh? Dear old Dad at least had the cojones to finish the deed. I just play pretend with a blade. I accused him of being a coward but really, it's been me all this time running from things. I told myself I cut to remind myself I was alive but that was just another lie. I didn't do it to feel alive. I did it because I was already dead and nothing I did to my body mattered. I did it to remind myself that I had died when he died." I say it all into the coffee swirling in the mug I hold.

Rachel lifts herself up from the floor and she slowly walks over to me. Carefully, she takes the mug from my hands and sets it down on the desk. She keeps my hands clasped in hers as she kneels down so she can look in my eyes.

"Call Dr. Perkins. Resume your therapy. I'm begging you, Stacey. Don't fall further into yourself. Get help."

My friend is virtually on her knees, begging me to take the steps necessary to keep from harming myself. She is supporting me and loving me through all this mess and all she wants is for me to be honest with her. A part of me wants to do what she is asking because her love means everything to me. But another part, a stronger part, rebels against that love and everything it has meant to me over the years.

"I will."

I lie.

That's the thing with lies. Once you start telling them you start to believe them and you can't stop telling them. Sometimes I think it is easier to lie to the ones I love because they so desperately want to believe me.

Love is pain.

Love is devastation.

Love is betrayal.

-22-

Children

Two days later Chastity and I are preparing for our appointment with Reyann. My mouse of a nurse had even volunteered to be the one to be the bearer of the news, but I had dismissed her offer. I was the doctor, and it should be me; needed to be me.

"Dr. McNill, are you ready?" Chastity asks from the doorway of my office.

I'm standing in the center, staring out the giant window into the distance. My view wasn't particularly spectacular since half of it was obscured by a parking structure, but I was able to see just enough of the spattering of trees that the changing leaves were visible. The seasons had changed and soon the first snowfall would be upon us. The holidays were right around the corner and this was one corner Reyann would not turn.

"Dr. McNill?"

"Yes. I'm ready. Let's do this," I say and immediately shift into my doctor mode.

Reminiscent of our first appointment nearly five months ago, Chastity shuffles her feet to catch up to me and she hands me the patient's chart. Even though I already know what I will find I open the chart, a formality based on habit and not necessity and I quickly scan through the information. I hand the chart back to Chastity as we come to the room: exam room three. How fitting.

Before I open the door, I take a deep breath and square my shoulders. What I am greeted with is not at all what I had been expecting. The room is full of people. Reyann is sitting in a wheelchair with a small child on her lap and another one standing next to her. Jeff is talking to another man in the furthest corner and a woman is standing nearby watching the children talking to Reyann. Even more shocking is that Brad is also in the room. He is sitting in a chair next to the woman I have never seen before. It is actually Brad who notices my presence first. He nudges the woman standing beside him with his elbow and she startles slightly. Brad points at me and she quickly turns to Jeff and the other man.

"Tom," the woman says, and I watch as Jeff and the other man turn towards me.

Tom. So, this is Jeff's younger brother. I quickly scan the room one more time and put the pieces together. Tom, his wife and their two children have come for a visit.

"Everyone this is Dr. Stacey," Reyann says as she hugs her youngest grandchild to her.

I can see how weak her embrace is, and I force the memories of my father's weakness out of my mind. Today isn't about me and my own demons. Today, I am not Stacey, my father's daughter. Today, I am Dr. McNill, and these people are strangers to me.

"Hello," I say. Chastity must have noticed my discomfort because she steps forward and goes to Reyann.

"I'm Nurse Chastity. What is your name?" she asks the child in Reyann's lap. The child shyly leans into Reyann and does not answer.

"That's Gracie. She's three. And I'm Robyn. I'm five," the other child, also a girl, states proudly as she holds up her hand, displaying all five of her fingers.

"Wow. You are so tall for only being five. Do you think your parents would mind if I took you two to get some yummy treats?"

Chastity asks the girl, but she looks over to the woman standing next to Brad.

"Really? Can we Mom? Dad?" young Robyn asks her parents.

"I don't know. Tom?" the children's mother turns to her husband.

This is my first time ever seeing Tom, Reyann's younger son. He is not as tall or burly as Jeff. In fact, if I didn't know they were brothers I never would have assumed they were related. While I study the contrasts between the brothers, Tom steps to his wife, takes her hand and continues to observe me as well. I recognize the moment he understands what is about to happen. Too many times I have witnessed this realization from a family member.

"I think that sounds like a good idea. Make sure you hold your sister's hand and be good for the nurse," Tom says to his daughter.

"Hooray! Do you want me to bring you a snack, Grandma Rey?" Robyn says to Reyann.

"Oh yes. Bring me your favorite," Reyann says and smiles widely.

"I will. Come on Gracie," Robyn says and holds her hand out for her younger sister.

Chastity takes hold of Robyn's other hand, and we exchange a brief look as she passes me. She is offering me her support, but no amount of silent looks can possibly prepare me for what I have to do next. I wait until the children are out of the room and the door is closed before I speak again.

"How are you feeling today, Reyann?" Like a coward I open up her chart and look inside instead of looking at her.

"Better. I can even walk short distances. I've been keeping my food down too. Haven't I Jeff?"

At the sound of his name I look up from the chart and our eyes find one another. He has come out of the corner to stand beside his brother and sister-in-law. He is glaring at me with hooded eyes that I interpret as accusatory. Once again, I avert my gaze and return to the chart before me.

"Yes, Mom. You've been doing better," Jeff confirms.

"See?" Reyann says, turning back to me with a smile on her face.

"That is good to hear," I say.

It's now or never.

"We got the results back. Unfortunately, they aren't what we had been hoping for. Your white blood cell count is in critical range. Your liver function test reveals significant functional damage. And your-"

"Just spit it out, Doc," Jeff says bitingly.

"Jeff!" Reyann scolds him.

"I'm sorry, Reyann. The chemotherapy didn't work. The cancer has spread to your lymph nodes and other distant organs." This time when I speak, I look directly at Reyann. She nods at me silently, a tight smile still on her face. We are staring at one another in silence and only I can see the pain on her face and the tears starting to form in her eyes.

"What are the other options?" Tom says. "Surgery? Another round of chemotherapy? Some sort of trial program in Spain or something?" The desperation in Tom's voice continues to escalate with each word.

"Tom, dear," Reyann says quietly.

"No. There has to be something. I've been reading about new drugs and treatments. Aren't you guys coming up with new things every day?" Tom says to me. He releases his wife's hand and takes some steps towards me.

"Tom," Reyann says again but he continues to ignore her.

"Do you know of alternative treatment places in Mexico? A guy I work with took his father there and he was cured. Maybe-"

"Tom! Enough! There isn't anything else she can do," Jeff yells from his corner.

I move my gaze back to him and I see he has his hands in his back pockets. He did that every time he became upset because he wanted to ensure he didn't do something he would regret with his hands. I'd seen him do this multiple times over the last few months. Usually, it was in response to his mother's health.

"No, Jeff, we can't just give up. Mom, we will figure something out. This hospital may not be able to do anything more but maybe another doctor can," Tom says as he kneels down before his mother.

Reyann smiles tentatively at her son. She is still silently crying but she reaches out to provide comfort for her younger child. She grabs a hold of his hand.

"I'm dying Sweetie."

"No. There is still time. Tell her there is still time," Tom turns to me and pleads.

This entire scene is destroying me, but I can't afford to let that show. I have no choice but to remain stoic and professional. Quickly, I look over to my right at Brad. He remained seated and silent this entire time. I'm not sure what I expect him to do but he does nothing. He just continues to sit there in silence.

"How long does she have?" Jeff again.

Moving my gaze away from Brad I look at Jeff. He is still staring at me as if I have betrayed him. This time I don't look away from him as I answer his question.

"Two months. Maybe less," I say.

"What? No," this time it is Tom's wife who protests. Tom immediately stands and goes to his wife. He takes her in his arms, and she starts to sob into his chest.

"Chastity will provide you hospice options if that is something you wish to pursue. If you would prefer to remain at home to receive palliative care, there are some private at-home nursing services that Chastity can set you up with. Whatever you decide we will help you make sure it is set up," I say to Reyann.

"I understand. Thank you, Stacey," Reyann says.

I nod, quickly glance around at the sad faces in the room and land on the one angry face in the room. Jeff just continues to glare at me. I take a few steps back and in my haste to escape his stare I stumble a little.

"I'll send Chastity back in right away," I say and reach behind me for the handle on the door. I don't wait for anyone to respond, and I leave the room quickly.

Moving through the halls I quickly return to my office and shut the door behind me. I lean against the door and throw Reyann's chart across my office. It lands on the sofa, and I slowly drop down to the floor. My breathing starts to quicken, and I recognize the early signs of a panic attack. Frantically, I glance around my office for something to distract me. The last time I had a panic attack in this room it was Jeff's hands on my ass that pulled me out of it. If his glare was any indication than I knew he wouldn't be coming to my aid any time soon.

I am thumping the back of my head against my office door trying to snap out of my downward spiral that it takes me a moment to realize someone is knocking on the door. Quickly I stand and open it. Brad is on the other side. He doesn't say anything as he enters and closes the door behind him. He doesn't have to. All it takes is one look from him and I collapse into him. Brad holds me as I sob.

"I'm sorry, Stacey," he says into my hair.

"What are you sorry for?" I hiccup.

"That you had to experience that. I know how hard that was for you. None of them blame you for what happened," Brad says, and I pull out of his arms.

Wiping away my tears I look at him cynically.

"One of them does," I say.

"No, he doesn't. He's just in shock right now. He knew this day was coming but he still held out hope that some miracle would happen."

"Yeah, and I just crushed that hope like a tiny bug. I'm a terrible doctor," I say and go sit on the sofa. I pick up Reyann's chart and straighten out the papers inside it.

"You're a great doctor. Sometimes people are just too sick. You can't save them all," Brad says with a shrug.

"Why the hell not? Why can't I save them? Or at least one more? Why not her?" I say and point at the office door in frustration.

"I don't know. I don't pretend to understand the workings of the universe," he says and sits next to me.

"Are you now going to feed me some line about how everything happens for a reason? Because, don't bother."

"No. I'm not sure everything has a reason. I still struggle with finding the reason in some things," Brad says and sits back against the cushions.

I know he is talking about his brother. Many years ago, Brad's older brother had committed suicide after years of attempting. Brad had taken it pretty hard, and that tragedy is what sparked his substance abuse issues. In his devastation he had used drugs and alcohol to mask his pain. The two of us are actually quite similar. Both of us had turned to destructive behavior in the wake of our personal tragedies.

"How do you manage to keep from falling apart?" I ask him the one question I never had the balls to ask him.

"I don't know. I take it one day at a time I suppose. Your sister helps. I want to be the man she deserves so I do whatever I can to keep the promises I made to her. How do you do it?"

"Oh, that's easy. I don't. I fall apart on a regular basis. I'm just really good at faking it," I admit and earn a slight chuckle from Brad.

"You might not be as good as you think. You know Jeff asked me some things about you over the years. I never thought much about it at the time but now that I know how he feels about you it all makes sense."

"What are you talking about? What things?" I turn to look at Brad.

"At first it was just things like what you did for a living and

191

whether or not you liked the holidays. You know, typical things people usually ask about others. But then one day he asked me if you were happy. I told him you were. He said he didn't think you were. I used to think his questions were strange back then," Brad admits.

"They were. He never spoke to me. I mean, not really. He probably won't want to speak to me again after today, so I guess none of this even matters," I say and stand. Putting some distance between me and Brad I go to my computer and start examining the rest of my schedule.

"If you believe that than you don't really know Jeff."

"Okay. Fine. What are you trying to tell me, Brad?" I say impatiently and click through my schedule.

"I'm saying I understand you've got your own issues going on right now and I get you're hurting. But please don't hurt my friend."

Immediately I turn to look at him, my body half bent before my desk as I take in what he just said.

"Jeff isn't the type to give up easily and he is loyal to a fault. I think he may have been waiting for you Stacey and I know how the heavy things scare you. You're like me. We are runners. If you run from my friend, if you hurt him, you'll regret it." Brad stands and starts to walk to my office door.

"Are you threatening me?" I ask, stunned by Brad's words.

"No. Not at all. Consider this a friendly warning from someone who knows a little about regret," Brad says as he turns the handle of the door. Before he exits, he pauses and turns back to me. "Please call Kelly. She needs her sister."

With that last request Brad leaves and I am left alone to ponder what he said. All these years Jeff has been stealthily inquiring about my well-being. He had told me that he had cared about me for years, but he had downplayed it. What Brad just described to me was much more than what Jeff had admitted to. In all honesty, it was much more than I was prepared to have in my life.

Brad was right. I was a runner. Every cell in my body was

192

screaming at me to run as fast I could from the heaviness of the relationship I had with Jeff. I could no longer tell myself that I was only in this for the fun of it. I was knee deep in the heavy stuff now and I was scared shitless.

-23-

Reality

It didn't take Jeff long to come to me. While I thought he would remain as far away from as me possible it seemed Brad's assessment was more accurate. The same night I had revealed that his mother had less than two months to live Jeff came to my apartment. It was nearly midnight, and I had been sitting awake trying to distract my wandering thoughts as sleep evaded me.

Of course, prior to that I had spent some time alone in the bathroom with my old friend. It seemed I couldn't shake the habit of reaching for that slim sharpened metal when I felt like I was losing control. I had been examining the fresh marks when I heard the knock on my door. I opened my door to find a tearful Jeff on the other side. Neither of us said anything as I stepped aside and let him in.

After I closed the door, he came to me and pressed me against it. No words were exchanged as we used one another's bodies to quell our pain. With tears in his eyes, he kissed the side of my neck as he removed the thin straps of my night shirt off my shoulders. It was loose fitting, and it slid down my body as his hands wandered down. He paused his journey when he reached my stomach, and I felt his body shake with sobs. I moved my fingers into his hair and grasped a hold. The movement gave him the focus he needed, and he reached up to pull my shorts off of me. In less than a minute I was standing

194

against my door, naked and waiting.

He stepped away from me and stripped off his own clothes. Silently, he came back to me and without hesitation lifted me up and entered me in one swift motion. I wrapped my arms and legs around him and just held on. There were no more lingering kisses or caresses. He used my body to chase away the hurt and I clung to him, willing his pain into me so I could take it away. This was not an act of passion but one of mercy. When he was able to find his sexual release, he slumped against me. I still had my legs and arms wrapped around him as he buried his face into my neck and cried.

As he cried, I moved my fingers against his back, trying to provide any comfort I could. After many minutes had passed he finally lifted his head from my neck and looked at me. There was so much pain in his expression and I couldn't help but move my hands to his face. I used my thumb to smooth out his eyebrow and he closed his eyes at my touch. He kissed me on the lips then for the first time since I let him in. It was brief and gentle. Cradling me in his arms he pulled out of me and carried me to my bedroom. We made love once again, still saying nothing.

Sometimes words weren't enough to express what one was feeling. He didn't need to speak to me for me to know how much he was hurting. Every kiss, every touch was laden with his pain and all I wanted to do was take it from him and make it my own.

"Stacey, you need to wake up. Stacey, wake up," I heard the voice drifting into my slumber, invading my dreams.

I groaned when something started to shake my sleeping form and tried to push the invader away, but it refused to let me be.

"Wake up," Jeff said again, with more force.

"What is going on?" I asked with a yawn and tried to sit up in my bed. I rubbed my eyes and blinked them closed swiftly when Jeff turned on my bedside light, effectively blinding me in the process.

"Why did you do it?" he asked.

"Do what? Turn off the light," I said, using my arm to shield my eyes.

"I didn't know. I should have known but like an idiot I thought you were done with it." He continued to ramble on, but he wasn't making any sense.

"What are you talking about?" I asked as I let my eyes adjust to the new lighting.

Jeff was sitting beside me in the bed, shirtless. After our love making, we had both fallen asleep from exhaustion, emotionally drained from the day's events. My alarm clock displayed 2:34 a.m. and I wondered what could possibly be so bothersome that he would wake me at this hour.

"Why would you do it? Why wouldn't you talk to me first?" Jeff asked another question that only had me looking at him in further confusion.

"You aren't making any sense. Go back to bed. You're exhausted," I said and tried to pull him back down into the bed with me.

"No. This isn't something you can just keep avoiding and pretending like it doesn't matter. It matters to me Stacey. You matter," Jeff said and pulled his arm from my grasp.

"Okay," I said and held up my hands. "You matter to me too."

"Do I? I'm not so sure I do because if I did you would know how much you hurt me when you do it."

"Do what? What are you talking about?" My voice is raised because he keeps talking in circles but we aren't actually getting anywhere.

Suddenly, Jeff leaps from my bed and rushes out of the room.

Concerned, I throw the covers off of me and follow him down the hall and into my bathroom. The light is already on, and I am not prepared for what greets me when I turn the corner.

Jeff stands in my bathroom before the sink and vanity mirror, a small blade in his hand, my dried blood still on the tip. I stare at the blade and hold my breath. Then I see what he holds in his other hand – my wedding ring. I had finally removed it after my latest visit with my old friend. I had thought I was finally ready to take it off for good and I had set it down beside the razor I had used earlier. Why I hadn't disposed of the blade was not something I could answer.

"Did I cause this? Am I making you do this to yourself?" Jeff asks, his voice cracking. I rush to him and try to take the items from his fingers, but he steps back and pulls his hands away from me.

"No. I don't know why I felt like I needed to do it. It just all became too much and I needed to find control again. I only did it once and then I stopped. It won't happen again," I promise.

I can tell he doesn't believe me, and I don't blame him. I don't even believe me.

"Do you want to go back to Josh?" he asks, stunning me with the question.

"What? No. I took the ring off because I'm done with that part of my life. I don't want anyone but you," I say and try to reach for the ring again. Jeff doesn't let me take it.

"And this?" He says, holding up the blade. "Is this what you want?"

"I don't understand," my voice is panicked, and I squeak a little.

"This is more than just trying to remember your father. This is fear. Every cut you make doesn't just make you bleed. It isn't you that hurts alone." Jeff turns the blade over in his fingers.

"Jeff, just put it down. I won't do it again."

He looks away from the blade and at me. There is so much hurt in his eyes but there is also so much more brewing beyond his iris' that I am not prepared for what happens next. As we are staring into one another's eyes he turns the blade onto his own chest. I watch as he presses the sharpened edge to his pectoral.

With a cry I move forward again and try to take the razor from him, but he steps to the side and uses his free arm to block me.

"Every time you cut into your skin you might as well be slicing into mine too. What will it take, Stacey, to get you to stop? How much blood has to be spilled before it's enough? Before you are able to look at yourself and not want to make another scar? How many?" he asks and makes a small slice in his own chest.

I'm crying and sobbing and begging him to stop. My attempts to take the blade from him are thwarted and I watch as a thin red line forms on his perfect, unblemished skin.

"Stop!" I cry as he starts to make a second cut.

"Why? If you bleed, I bleed. If you hurt, I hurt. I can't make you stop but I won't let you suffer alone," he says and makes a third cut.

I watch as the blood from the three lines merge together and make a trail down his stomach. I watch as another person cuts into their skin and my heart breaks apart. It is unbearable to watch, and I close my eyes when he goes to make a fourth cut.

"No! No more. Please, no more," I plead with him.

I am met with silence, and it is the silence that allows my pounding heart to slow. My breath regains its normal rhythm and once I feel I have myself under control again I open my eyes.

Jeff is standing there, watching me as the blood continues to drip down his chest. Neither of us says anything as I step forward and hold out my hands. Silently, Jeff brings his hands to mine and deposits the blade in one and the ring in the other. I place the ring on the sink and throw the blade in the trash. Then I turn and open my medicine cabinet. I remove my first aid kit and take out the necessary items.

It strikes me now how frightened Josh must have been when he found me hurting myself all those years ago. The strength he had to remain calm is astounding to me. I am barely holding myself together as I tend to Jeff's wounds. In fact, I am still crying and I jump slightly when Jeff's finger touches my cheek to wipe away a tear.

"What can I do to convince you that you don't need to do this anymore?" Jeff asks.

I am still holding a gauze covered in anti-septic to his chest, my gaze cast down in shame. Never once in all the years that I had been creating scars on my canvas had it occurred to me that with every cut I was hurting more than just my own skin. I had never thought of the pain I was inflicting on others. It wasn't until I saw that blade pressed against Jeff's skin that I knew a different kind of fear.

"I-I don't know if you can. I don't know if anyone can."

"Help me understand why. Is it the stress?"

"Yes. And no. Stress can be a trigger, but I think it's more about the control and the reminder that I'm still here. That I'm still me," I say.

I use the gauze to wipe at his wounds and he gently closes his hand over my wrist and removes my hand from his chest. He takes the gauze out of my hand and throws it in the sink. Then he takes my hands in his, leans forward and places his forehead against mine. We stay like that and just breathe together.

"You are more than those scars but if they are something you need than I will match you, scar for scar," he says.

"No. I don't want you to hurt yourself," I reply and lift my head away from his.

He just stares back at me, and I realize that he fully intends to keep his word. If I cut myself again, he will do the same. Some might say he was trying to manipulate me into stopping my behavior, but I knew that wasn't his intention. He didn't want me to hurt myself any more than I wanted him to hurt himself, but he knew he couldn't make me stop; just like I couldn't stop him from hurting alongside me. The only way either of us would stop hurting is if we did it together.

Maybe what happened next was completely crazy, or perhaps everything that had transpired before was the crazy part. Either way, I didn't think before I reached out and traced the fresh marks on his chest. I didn't think before I leaned forward and kissed them just as he had kissed my scars. And I certainly didn't think about how seeing those marks on his chest awakened something inside me that I was only ever able to get by cutting my own skin.

I can't imagine many thoughts were running through Jeff's head when he suddenly lunged forward, picked me up and wrapped my legs around his waist. He stumbles his way out of the bathroom, down the hall and back into my bedroom where he deposits me on the bed. I look up at him and see our movements have made his wounds open up and begin to bleed again. He doesn't seem concerned about it as he leans over me on the bed and he doesn't shy away from me when I lick his wounds and taste his blood.

No. He doesn't push me away. He doesn't leave the room and make me feel shame. Instead, he watches me and when I am done, he hungrily kisses my lips and removes my clothing. We claw at one another, and we take our frustration out in the only way we can. I know there will be marks on both our skins but for the first time the marks won't be made out of fear, or a desire to regain control, they will be made out of passion and I am finally able to find the feeling I have been chasing for so many years.

I find me and I'm not sure I like her.

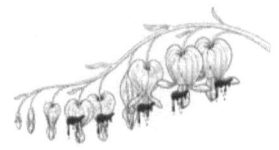

"She isn't going to make it to Christmas, is she?" Jeff asks me later as we lay tangled together in my bed after another round of love

making. Our hands are joined, and his fingers are moving along my palm.

"I don't know. She might. Anything is possible," I say softly.

"Anything except a cure," he whispers.

I stiffen. He didn't mean it as a jab against me, but I can't help feeling like it is a reminder of my own failure. Despite knowing from the very beginning how this was going to turn out I, like him, had foolishly hoped for a miracle.

"Are you hungry?" I ask and try to move out of his embrace. He simply holds on to me tighter and pulls me back into his body.

"I already ate," he says and reaches a hand down between my legs to caress the very part of me he had "eaten" earlier.

"That isn't what I meant."

"I know. I'm fine. I don't need anything other than what we are doing right now. Just stay here with me," he says and holds me a little tighter.

It seems he is trying to hold on to me and I'm just trying to get a little breathing room. What the two of us need at this moment is in direct conflict and I don't know how to ensure we both get what we need.

"Tom and Nina are staying until…until it happens," Jeff says as he places his chin on my shoulder. My back is to him, and his body is pressed into mine.

"What about his work?" I ask.

"He owns the firm. The boss can take off whenever he wants, I guess," Jeff shrugs.

"That's good. I'm sure your mother will like having them around."

"Yeah. What about you? Will you be around?"

His question stuns me, and I turn my head so I can look at him.

"What do you mean?" I ask.

Jeff sighs and his hold on me loosens. "I can feel you pulling away already. I know I wasn't exactly my best yesterday and I'm

201

sorry for how I treated you. Hearing my mother is dying kind of shook me and I took it out on you. I'm sorry for that. I don't want us to end because I couldn't handle my temper," he says.

Turning away from him, I look at the wall of my bedroom and try to wrap my mind around what he is saying. He thinks my desire to run is because he was a little brass with me after I told him his mother was dying. Jeff has no idea that my ability to run from reality ran much deeper than our history.

"Tell me what you are thinking," Jeff says against my shoulder. He is so close, his voice vibrates against me.

"I'm no good for you," I admit.

"What? Of course you are," he says and sits back. He turns my body, so I am facing him.

"No, Jeff. I'm not. I'm messed up. When I found out about your mother the only thing I could think about was how it was affecting me. I'm selfish and cruel. I'm only going to end up hurting you," I say and place my hand on his chest, above the wounds he had just inflicted upon himself a couple hours before. He puts his hand over mine and grasps my fingers.

"You aren't any of those things. I wish you could see you the way I see you. You are kind and brave. You are strong and stubborn but also timid and affectionate. You aren't selfish. You have made sacrifices your whole life for others. I love how you take care of everyone around you even if it is hard for you. You are amazing and I love you," Jeff says as he clings to my hand.

"Don't say that," I beg.

"Why not? It's true. Stacey, I've been in love with you for years."

"What?" I'm truly stunned by his revelation. How could he possibly believe that? He didn't even know me until recently.

"Frankly I'm surprised that you never knew," Jeff says and smiles at me.

"Of course I didn't know. Jeff, we barely even spoke to each other over the years."

"That isn't true. We've had many conversations. You just don't remember them, but I do. I remember them all."

This couldn't be happening. I thought I was the one that lived in fantasy land but here was Jeff talking about imaginary conversations that had never occurred. Why did I choose men that refused to live in reality?

"Jeff, I don't know what you are talking about," I say and try to pull my hand out from his grasp so I could get some distance between us. Jeff doesn't loosen his grip, however.

"The first time I met you was at Brad's twenty-second birthday party. Kelly had rented the back room at that Italian restaurant and your entire family was there. You came late because you were in medical school and lost track of time studying. You still had your books with you and when you walked in the door your kids went running to you and you dropped those books so fast so you could hug your kids. You picked them up in each arm and walked over to us and left your books on the floor. I remember how you were smiling when Kelly introduced us. I know the smile wasn't for me but, God, Stacey I thought how I would give anything for that smile to be directed at me. I also remember how jealous I was when Josh came up to you and kissed your cheek. I wanted to pummel him right there."

Jeff finishes his story and while he's distracted by his memory I disengage from his embrace and move to the end of my bed. I'm bending down trying to locate my clothes when I feel him move and come up behind me. He places his hands on my shoulders, and I move out from under his touch. Moving off the bed I go to my dresser and pull out the first pair of shorts and shirt I can find. I pull them on quickly and turn back to my bed. Jeff is kneeling on the mattress, staring at me. He is still naked but all I can focus on is the hurt I see in his eyes.

"So, you are trying to tell me that you've had a crush on me all

203

these years? I don't buy it Jeff. Sure, I can understand maybe thinking I'm attractive but love? You didn't even know me!" I say and cross my arms over my chest.

"But I did know you, Stacey. I spent years getting to know you. You just didn't notice," he says and stands up from the bed. He moves over to me, and I step away.

"Please put some clothes on," I say and hold up my hand to stop him from coming to me.

Jeff does as I ask and puts his pants back on. The break is too short and he is once again moving towards me. I put my hand back up in warning. I don't think I could handle him touching me right now.

"The Christmas before you graduated medical school you started to question whether or not you should make oncology your focus. You weren't sure you could handle it, and you almost switched your focus to obstetrics," Jeff says.

"What? How do you know about that?" I ask, once again surprised by his knowledge of my personal business.

"Because you told me," he says.

"No, I didn't."

"You did."

"I think I would remember telling you that. I didn't tell anyone about that. Not even Josh," I protest.

"You were in your parent's kitchen washing the dinner dishes. You never volunteered to wash dishes before but this night, you did. I could tell something was bothering you and that you needed a break from all the festivities. I came into the kitchen and offered to dry while you washed. You asked me a question after a few minutes," he says and tries to take a step towards me again. I take a step back.

"No. I would remember this," I say shaking my head.

"You asked me what I thought about babies and if I could spend day after day watching women push out babies."

204

As he continues to tell me the details of this encounter the memory slowly starts to come back to me.

"Do you remember what my answer was?" he asks.

"You said it depended on the woman," I reply.

"That's right," he smiles at me. "I asked you why you were concerned about women having babies and you said-"

"Babies were easier than cancer," I finish. My eyes grow wide as the rest of the memory plays out before me. Jeff had paused drying the dishes and he had given me his full attention. He had told me that babies may be easier, but they were boring. I had laughed at that because it was a ridiculous thing to say. Who would choose cancer over babies?

I did.

"The year after Jenny died and her kids and husband came to visit-"

"Stop!" I say and turn to leave the bedroom. I go to the living room and just spin in a circle. Damn this stupid apartment. I didn't have anywhere to run to.

"That was the first time you considered leaving Josh," Jeff says from behind me.

I spin around and see him standing just out of the hallway to the bedrooms. He doesn't try to reach for me, but he doesn't stop talking either.

"You knew then that you weren't happy, and you didn't want to keep living a lie. Jenny's death reminded you how short life was and seeing how devastated Evan was by Jenny's death you saw what love can be. Love is pain," Jeff says to me.

"What did you just say?" I ask him, my body stiffening from the words.

"Love is pain. You believe this."

"I know that but how do you know that." The desire to run is strong and I'm frightened that Jeff, of all people, knows the very thing I say to myself when I'm hurting.

205

"You said it to me. The kids were playing in the living room, and we were the only ones left in the room with them. Evan and Brad's sister were in the kitchen. Brad and Kelly had gone upstairs, and Josh went to the bathroom. I came to sit next to you on the couch, and I said something about how the kids were having fun. You said it was good that they had come to visit because family was important. I saw you look towards where Josh had gone and then look at your own kids. You then asked me how it was to grow up without one of my parents. I told you it was hard. I regretted saying that to you for so long. Maybe if I had said something different you would have found the courage to do what you wanted to do then."

Once again, as he retells the events of my life I am able to recall the details. What I had always viewed as offhand remarks or trivial comments Jeff had viewed these moments with far more significance than I ever did.

"That still doesn't explain how you know I think love is pain," I say trying to recall the rest of this event.

"Later that night when everyone was saying goodbye you and I were by the door. Becca was hugging Jenny's daughter goodbye, and you whispered it."

"You heard that?"

"Yes. Why do you think I replied that love was groovy?" he asked with a laugh.

"I thought you were high or something. Who says groovy?"

"Stacey, I've never been high a day in my life."

"Okay. So, we've apparently had a few more conversations over the years than I originally thought. But none of these things you are telling me can possibly explain how you have had feelings for me all these years and just kept it to yourself. Suppose I believe that you have harbored some attraction to me that still doesn't explain why you never acted on it. You expect me to believe you just kept coming around and never once said anything?"

"Oh, I definitely said something. You just never took me

seriously. Usually, you would just roll your eyes or tell Brad his friend was creepy."

"Are you talking about the times you would say things like I had electric moves?"

Once again Jeff laughs. "Yeah. Something like that."

"But you were high!"

"No. I wasn't. I dug you and wanted you to know it."

"Then why didn't you just come out and say it? Why say the things you did?"

"Because you were married. You were my best friend's sister-in-law. I couldn't exactly go up to you and say, hey, let's make out," he explains like I should already know his options were limited.

I shake my head and start to pace in my living room. None of this was making any sense. Ten years. He was trying to tell me he has had feelings for me for ten years.

"Have you just been waiting all these years for the perfect time to swoop in? Was this your plan all along?" I ask, horrified by the possibility that everything that has transpired between us in the last few months was completely manufactured by him. That last night was nothing more than a manipulation on his part.

"Are you seriously asking me that question? I never had a plan. How could I possibly plan any of this? I haven't been a monk all these years. I wasn't waiting to do any sort of swooping. I dated. I just never dated anyone that stuck."

"But you were engaged!"

"Yeah, I was. It didn't stick," he says, almost with humor.

"I just can't accept this. I can't. This is crazy. You're crazy," I say and shake a finger at him and resume my pacing.

"I love you, Stacey. If that's crazy, then so be it," he says and starts to walk towards me again.

"No. No you don't. You just think you do because you are going through an emotional time and you think you need to cling to something. I just happen to be here and so you've projected feelings

207

onto me. You don't love me, Jeff. It isn't real," I explain away his confession. He is just confusing his pain with a desire to be loved. My patients did this all the time. Grief caused people to do funny things sometimes.

"I'm not projecting anything on to you. Things would be much easier if I didn't love you. I could just walk out that door and go on with my life, but I can't do that. You have seeped into my very being and you can try to explain this away, but you won't be able to because I do love you. And you love me too," he says and finishes his advance to me.

"No, I don't," I protest.

Jeff smirks at me and tries to pull me into his arms. I jerk away and he quickly reaches out and pulls me into him. His arms encircle me, but I keep mine firmly crossed in front of me.

"Like I said before, I'm a patient man. I can wait for you to figure it out. Now, can we get back to bed?"

"I want my painting back," I say against his bare chest. Jeff chuckles and holds me tighter to him.

"You'll get it back. Once the ransom has been paid in full," he says and kisses the top of my head.

Love was surely pain but love was also confusing the hell out of me.

-24-

Sisters

Jeff's confession of his ten-year unrequited love for me was simply too much for me to handle. After his confession we went back to bed and when he left the next morning, he told me not to "be weird" and over think what he had said. He said we had more things to discuss but that they could wait. He then invited me over to dinner at his mother's house. I declined. He then told me he would be picking me up on Monday night for dinner at his mother's house, kissed my cheek and left my apartment.

I'm not sure how long I stood at my door just staring blindly into space before I regained my senses and closed the open door. I knew what would happen next. I would spend the next few hours trying to avoid thinking about the events of the previous day and fail miserably. I also knew that if I remained in my apartment and didn't find some distraction that I would most likely engage in behavior I would regret. So, I did the next best logical thing.

I went to my sister's house.

In order to get my painting back and make the world right again in some infinitesimal way, I had to make up with Kelly. I may not be able to save Reyann's life, but I could get my painting back on my wall where it belonged, dammit!

Brad answered their door, surprised but glad to see me. He embraced me when I walked through and this time, I actually returned the affectionate gesture. I knew Reyann was like a mother to him and that he was also hurting by the news I had delivered yesterday. He was the closest thing I had to a brother, and I loved him. I had never wanted to bring him harm.

"She's in the kitchen. Gearing up for Thanksgiving," Brad tells me as he takes my coat and other winter gear. The holiday was less than two weeks away and my sister always hosted since Christmas had been moved back to our parents' house. I had never hosted a holiday at my own home, despite it being the bigger location. The thought had never even occurred to me over the years.

"And Jenny Lynn?" I really didn't want my niece to witness what was bound to be another blow out between me and her mother.

"At a friend's house."

"Good. That's good," I say and glance nervously at the now closed front door.

"It's just a conversation, Stacey. That's all," Brad says in response to my obvious desire to bolt.

"You are the last person who can lecture me about avoiding a conversation. You dodged my sister for years and made her friend and family promise to keep things hidden from her," I point out and Brad smirks.

"Yeah. I really was a jerk. So, take the lesson I've learned, and don't avoid this any longer. Everything will be fine."

I give my brother-in-law one last doubtful look before I make my way to their kitchen and the sister I had intended to avoid for much longer than a few days.

Kelly is at the stove, her nose in a cookbook, an apron tied around her waist and a mess scattered around her. Every year she tried to outdo her previous meal. I never understood her desire to compete with herself. We would have eaten sloppy joes every year and never complained. Well, maybe the others would have been fine. I most definitely would have said something to her about the meal from a can.

"Brad, love, can you run to the store and get me some more butter. I'm nearly out," Kelly says when she hears my steps approaching.

"Love? That's cute. Almost as decadent as butter," I say.

Kelly stops stirring whatever she is stirring and turns to see me standing beside their four-chair kitchen table. Her lips tighten and she remains silent.

"Not Brad. Just the bitch sister with her tail between her legs," I begin. Hopefully humor will soften her mood.

"I need more butter," Kelly says, still staring at me.

"Okay. Do you want me to go get it?" I ask and shuffle my feet a little from nerves.

"Don't be ridiculous. Brad! Can you get me some more butter?" She calls out to her husband.

"Salted or unsalted?" his voice responds from some nether region in the house.

"Unsalted please. And you might as well get some more condensed milk. Oh, and-"

"Make a list!" Brad's voice interrupts his wife and she immediately drops the spoon to go to the refrigerator.

As Kelly is writing out the list of items she needs on a magnetic note pad I take in the little scene of domestic bliss I had just witnessed. All the years of my marriage I had never had such an interaction with my husband. Even the times that may have seemed like teasing to outside onlookers were really resentment filled jabs. Despite Kelly's belief that I had been the one to get pregnant on purpose, I had always harbored resentment towards my husband for putting me in such a position. I used to think if anyone was to blame for Becca's conception it was Josh. He should have known better after all. He was the oldest between us and I was still technically in high school when I met him.

Of course, I never shared those thoughts with anyone because as soon as I felt them I immediately felt guilt. How could I be angry with the father of my children? How could I resent the man that had willingly entered into my shit storm and did everything he could to make me better? What kind of person would I be? A truly terrible one.

"List ready?" Brad asks as he comes walking into the kitchen.

"Yep. Thanks, Sweetie," Kelly says as she hands Brad the list. He takes it, kisses her quickly on the lips and whispers something to her before leaving.

Once we are alone again the tension between us returns to the room and Kelly continues to stare at me. Not sure how to get the conversation going, I rely on old tricks.

"Your food might burn if you let it sit too long," I say and point at the contents on the stove.

"I turned it off," Kelly says, her arms crossing over her chest. I glance around her and see that she had indeed turned off the stove. Great. That meant she would be entirely focused on me.

"That's good. Wouldn't want to ruin our next Thanksgiving meal. What are you making this year?"

"I don't want to talk about food," Kelly says.

"Okay. How about them Packers?"

She just glares at me, her arms crossed, and her entire body language screams she is not having any of this.

"You aren't going to make this easy, are you?"

"No," she says, and I swear her lips curl into a quick smirk.

"Alright, can I at least have a glass of wine or something?"

Kelly sighs, tilts her head slightly and glares at me.

"Right. I forgot, dry house," I say and take a step to the chair nearest me.

"Of course you did," she sneers.

It is the sound of her voice that makes me snap. It is dripping with disgust and this time, maybe for once, I don't deserve it.

"Despite what you may think of me, Kelly, I don't always say things to be hurtful. I really didn't think about how you don't keep alcohol in the house. Honestly, I forgot."

"Just like you forgot last Thanksgiving?"

"What are you talking about? I brought my own. I always bring my own," I say and turn back to her. For years I had always been the one to bring the liquid spirits to family gatherings because I was a terrible cook. Kelly knew this. My entire family knew this. The only thing I could cook well was breakfast food and packaged pasta; hence my contribution in the form of bottled libations.

"Yes. And you made a big display about how it was a good thing that you had stopped to get those two bottles because you 'forgot' we didn't have any wine," Kelly replies.

"Oh, God, Kelly. Do you just hate me? Why does everything I say offend you? Yes, I said that. But I wasn't being malicious. I like wine! I like wine with my turkey and stuffing. And I did forget! I forget all the time because unlike you I'm not constantly looking at Brad like he is some recovering addict that needs to be coddled. I am fully aware that that is your reality, and you are doing what you believe is best but the rest of us aren't living your life. Don't get pissy with me because you aren't entirely satisfied with the circumstances," I defend my actions over the years.

I'm expecting a repeat performance of what happened at Jenny Lynn's birthday party, but to my amazement, Kelly doesn't respond with anger. In fact, she doesn't respond at all. She just continues to blink back at me while I awkwardly stand there in her kitchen, not sure what to do.

"Stop staring at me like that. It's creeping me out," I finally say and shiver from the creepy vibes emanating off of her.

"Sorry. It's just. Well, you're right."

"Wait, what? I think I just had a transient ischemic attack because I think I heard you say I was right."

"Don't be condescending. Just say stroke and you are, on occasion, known to be right. This just happens to be one of those times," Kelly says and grins at me.

"Now who's being condescending," I say and grin back.

"Stay right there," Kelly replies and walks out of the kitchen. Stunned, I watch her leave and eventually sit down at the table to wait for her return from the abrupt exit.

"Here. It's not chilled but you will just have to accept that. Beggars and all," Kelly says when she returns.

In her hands is an unopened bottle of wine. To say I am flabbergasted does not do my feelings justice. Where did she get that so quickly?

"Um, Kelly, where did that come from?"

"The laundry room." She struggles to work the corkscrew, and it only reminds me just how many few times I've ever seen my sister with a bottle of wine her hand.

"Explain please."

My sister takes a deep breath as she is pouring wine into two glasses before she begins her explanation of the magically appearing wine bottle.

"I keep a bottle in the laundry room behind the detergent and other cleaning supplies," she says as if that explains everything.

"Why? How long have you been holding out on me? Does Brad know you are keeping this massive secret from him?"

"Stop, it isn't that massive," Kelly says, laughing, as she walks over to the table. She hands me a glass, and I take a sip. It's white, warm and dripping with sisterly bonding so I take another sip and hide how I wish it was red.

"It's pretty big for you two. I mean, I never would have guessed you two had any secrets from each other. You're always going on about honesty and how important it is."

"It is. And I honestly believe Brad knows about my hidden stash," she says as she sits next to me.

"So why not just keep it in the pantry? And why doesn't he say something about it?"

"Because I'm the one that needs to keep it hidden."

"I don't understand? Are you an alcoholic too?"

"No," she rolls her eyes at me. "But I enjoy the occasional glass of wine, and I feel guilty about it. So, I keep it hidden because for some reason that makes me believe I'm not rubbing my husband's face in it or something like that."

I must have given Kelly a look of disbelief or something because she responds by shaking her head and saying, " I know it sounds ridiculous but that is what I need. So, Brad pretends not to know, and I pretend that he doesn't know."

"Marriage. The art of pretending," I snicker. Kelly picks up on the bitterness in my voice.

"No, not like that. I love my husband, and I trust him. I never have to pretend that. We have rough patches, but we always make them work," she says.

"How? How do you make them work?"

"I don't know. We just-do."

"Really? That is your great words of marital wisdom? You 'just do'? That doesn't exactly help me."

"I wasn't aware that you needed marital help. I thought your marriage was very much over," Kelly says and takes her first drink from her wine glass. She winces at the taste, and I laugh at her.

"It is over. But I'm a scholar. I'd like to learn from my mistakes. So, if, you know, in the future I am ever in a similar situation I can, well, make better choices," I stumble my way through my explanation.

"Did you ever love Josh?"

Her question shocks me to my core. Did the rest of my family have this doubt? Did my own children? Did Josh?

"Yes, of course I did. Do. I still love him. I care for him very deeply but I, just…I don't…what I mean is…" I trail off.

"You aren't *in* love with him," Kelly attempts to fill in the blanks.

"No. It's more than that. I will always love him for what he did for me. But I also resent him for what I was unable to do for myself."

"Now, I'm the one who doesn't understand," Kelly says.

"I'm a cutter," I blurt out.

"A what?"

It never occurred to me that Kelly wouldn't know about my little secret. I thought for sure Tasha would have told her or that Josh had shared the information with others besides my mother. But Kelly's reaction tells me that she was unaware of my little bathroom habit during our teen years.

"I cut myself sometimes. It started after my dad died. The only one who knew about it was Josh. Well, I thought he was the only who knew. But apparently, he told Mom about it. I assume she told Paul too. Josh got me to stop doing it. I hadn't done it in years but then I did it again a few months ago. I told myself I did it because I needed to feel something I was lacking in my marriage, but I think I really did it out of revenge or something." I wasn't sure if I believed what I was telling Kelly. In all honesty, I wasn't sure why I had cut myself again. I only knew that the desire had emerged and so I did it. And then I left my husband. Maybe the two events were connected. Maybe they weren't. I just didn't know for sure.

"Oh, Stacey, I had no idea," Kelly says and reaches out to touch my arm.

"It's alright. I didn't want you to know," I shrug.

"No. It's not alright. I was a horribly selfish teenager that never paid enough attention to those around me. I'm sorry I wasn't there for you. More than you will ever know, I'm so sorry. I don't want us to be distant. I want us to be true sisters. You can always come to me. I'll always be there for you and I'm sorry, too, for the fight. I said terrible things that I didn't even mean. Please forgive me," Kelly says and before I know it, we are both tearing up.

"What a pair we make? Can I tell you something now without you getting upset with me?" I ask.

"Of course, anything."

"This wine is absolutely disgusting," I say and Kelly snorts.

"Yeah. It really is. I think it has gone bad," she laughs and holds up the glass, inspecting the contents.

"What? How long has it been in the laundry room?" I ask and take a horrified look at the bottle.

"I don't know. It's been a while," Kelly admits.

"You won't be offended if I dump it?"

"None at all. I was only drinking it because I thought the bad taste was just me not appreciating the wine or something. Let's toss it," Kelly says, and we both gladly dispose of the awful elixir.

For the next few hours we continue to tell one another all the things we were too afraid to say when we were kids. I tell her about my marriage to Josh and how my feelings had evolved. She comforts me and assures me I am making the right decision about ending my marriage. She says both Josh and I deserve a shot at being happy. She tells me the kids will be fine and that Becca will accept things in her own time. She tells me she loves me.

I tell her I am sorry for all the mean things I have said over the years and I promise to do better. I tell her how impressed I am with her strength. She has always been the example to follow and I reveal that I have been jealous of her. Of course she doesn't believe me, but it is true nonetheless. I tell her I envy her relationship with Brad and she asks me about Jeff. This is where I clam up. She assures me Jeff is a great guy and that she is thrilled to see us together. I don't share my misgivings about Jeff with her, but I do share my regret about Reyann's condition with her. Kelly demands I go to dinner with Jeff and his family on Monday, just as Jeff had done.

Eventually, I leave before Brad has returned from the store with the baking goods. It never occurs to us to wonder where he has gone to. For the first time, Kelly and I truly talk like we are sisters, and I don't hate it at all. The encounter makes me hopeful. This is not a feeling I am accustomed to and despite the surface being filled with hope the parts underneath are swimming with dread of the unknown that is yet to come.

-25-

Dinner

True to his word Jeff picks me up at my apartment for the scheduled family dinner. I had spent the weekend trying to weasel my way out of it, but Jeff told me he wouldn't give me Rockin' Jesus back unless I personally picked it up – Monday night after having dinner with his family.

The things I did for Jesus and guitars.

I barely say three words to him on the ride over to his mother's house. I know his brother, Tom, will be there with his family and I can't help but feel like I am going to be outnumbered by an enemy I don't want to face. I know Tom and his family aren't truly my enemies, but I am the evil queen that had essentially forced a poison apple on all of them. I would forever be that woman who told them their beloved mother and grandmother was going to die. There was no way to erase this image from anyone's mind. I knew this. I had lived this and even now, years later, I could still recall the face of the man that had told my mother and I that my father was as good as dead. He had said it with more tact, but I knew what his words truly meant.

"Hey, turn off the counterproductive thoughts," Jeff says to me, and he grabs a hold of my hand.

I chuckle. What a ridiculous thing to say to me right now.

"They are quite productive. All my thoughts are," I say and

stiffen my jaw to prove I'm right.

This time Jeff chuckles.

"I'm sure they are. But they aren't always necessary. Mom adores you. She always has," he reassures me.

"It isn't Reyann I'm concerned with. It hasn't even been a week since I told the rest of your family that there was no more hope and Reyann is going to die. I'm sure they all hate me right now."

"They don't hate you. They were just in shock. We all were. Their reaction had nothing to do with you."

"Just like how yours had nothing to do with me?" I keep my head straight but look at him out of the corner of my eye, trying to glimpse his reaction.

He is silent for a stretch before he responds, and his words are measured, carefully chosen.

"My reaction was...unfortunate and not at all how I would have liked to have handled that scenario. I think in that moment I needed to distance you the doctor from the woman I fell in love with. In that moment I couldn't have you be the same person, so I reacted poorly. I'm sorry," he says and glances at me.

Every time this man apologizes to me, I am baffled at how easy the words come to him. Unlike me he does not have a physical reaction to the loss of pride, of strength. In fact, I almost believe he finds strength out of his humility. Where I was cold steel, he was a warm blanket. I was the bitter cold, and he was the sun. I couldn't possibly see how any of those items could coexist in any environment.

We arrive at Reyann's house with those thoughts, the counterproductive ones, playing through my head. Even though I enter the house with Jeff at my side I don't feel the usual comfort his presence gives me. I am too focused on what is to come.

What comes at me are two little girls, laughing with sticky fingers stretched out in front of them. They run right up to Jeff, giggling and calling out his name. I watch as Jeff kneels down, growls at his nieces and scoops them up in each arm. He twirls them around as they place their fingers, covered in what appears to be some sort of dough, all over his face. It is a one-of-a-kind family scene, and it brings back memories of my own children doing similar things with their father when they were little. I hate how my thoughts drift back to Josh in this moment. It feels wrong to be here with Jeff but reminiscing inwardly about my past with my husband.

Husband.

Josh is still officially my spouse. Even though the papers had been filled out the divorce isn't final yet. There is still one signature that is required.

"Gracie Ann and Robyn Marie you two get your butts back here and clean up this mess," a woman's stern voice comes from around a corner.

I tear my gaze from Jeff and the two little girls to see Nina, Tom's wife, approaching around a corner to what I assume leads to the kitchen. Nina is wiping her hands on a dish towel, and I see remnants of the same dough substance that is now all over Jeff's face.

"Oh, dear. They got you too?" Nina asks Jeff.

"Sure did. I was ambushed," Jeff laughs as he puts the girls down so they can turn to their mother.

"He's all sticky," Robyn says with a giant grin.

"Shticky," Gracie says and holds out her fingers, half bent, towards her mother.

"Yeah. I see that. And so is the kitchen counter that you two attacked. Get your butts back in there and help your father clean up before dinner. Go on now, scamper off," Nina says as she pats each of her daughters gently on their butts with the towel to get them moving. The two girls squeal as they run back towards the kitchen.

"Please forgive my little devil children. They got over stimulated with helping me make biscuits. To be perfectly honest, they weren't much help and made a terrible mess but at least they were entertained," Nina says, directing her comments to me.

I just smile at her.

"I'm Nina. We weren't properly introduced the other day," she says, wiping her hands one last time and offers me one of her hands to shake.

I take the hand out of courtesy and ignore the remaining sticky parts on Nina's fingers. The fastidious doctor in me wants to immediately wash my hands and rid myself of the stickiness, but I resist the urge.

"It's understandable, considering the circumstances," I finally say. Nina's eyes flash briefly, and I realize I said the wrong thing, again.

"Yes, well, it is nice to meet you, officially. Reyann is in her bedroom, resting. Would you mind seeing if she is ready to join us, Jeff?"

"No problem. Be back soon," Jeff says to me before he walks down a hall to our left and disappears in the darkness. My gaze lingers on his retreating frame, wishing I could go with him too.

"We are all in the kitchen," Nina says and gestures with her hand for me to follow.

Silently, I trail behind Nina as she guides me to the kitchen. I'm expecting to see Tom and the two girls cleaning up a mess, but I walk into a game of chase as Tom stalks his daughters around a table and island. The girls are laughing, and he keeps saying he is going to catch them.

"This doesn't look like cleaning," Nina immediately scolds all three of them. They all stop instantly and turn to the clear authoritarian of the family.

"Ahh, Mom!" Robyn whines.

"Yeah, Mom!" Tom mimics his daughter and is greeted with a stern stare from his wife. He swallows, straightens up and turns to his daughters. "Your mother is right. Games later. Clean now," he says and the three of them get back to their assigned task.

"If I didn't love him, I swear I'd leave him," Nina says to me, and I just smile back at her. I can tell she is expecting more from me, but I simply don't have it in me.

Impatiently, I look back down the way we had come, hoping for Jeff's presence. The doorbell rings and I quickly announce I will get it. Grateful for the distraction and the escape I returned to the front door. Brad and Kelly are on the other side, and I have never been so thankful to see them before in my life. So thankful in fact that I lunge for them both and throw my arms around them.

Laughing, Kelly juggles the dish she holds so she doesn't drop it. "That bad already?" she asks.

"You have no idea. Not that I'm not grateful but why are you two here?" I ask as I pull away from the hug I forced on them.

"I invited them," Reyann says from out of the darkness, and I see Jeff wheeling his mother into the foyer. She has her usual colored scarf covering her head to hide her baldness, but the scarf can't hide the sallow appearance of her face. Though she is smiling at us it cannot be ignored that she is very sick, and very tired.

"Brad and Kelly are family. Nina will be happy to see you, Kelly. Is Jenny Lynn joining us?" Reyann asks.

"Not tonight. She is staying at my parents' house tonight," Kelly answers.

"Oh, how nice. I'm sure they love living so close to their grandbabies. Jeff, let's join the others."

"Yes ma'am," Jeff says to his mother, and he winks at me as he passes me.

Brad takes Kelly's and his coats while I pull Kelly into an alcove for a moment of privacy.

"Nina hates me," I whisper.

"No, she doesn't. She just doesn't know you," Kelly dismisses my comment.

"Nope. Pretty sure she hates me," I insist, looking around her to make sure Nina is not around the corner, listening in. Kelly waves me off and I have no choice but to follow her into the kitchen, my feet shuffling in procrastination.

"Kelly!" Nina exclaims when she sees my sister and she quickly rushes over to embrace Kelly in a giant hug. Over Nina's shoulder I give Kelly a widened look to emphasize my previous comment but she rolls her eyes at me dismissively.

"Hey, Doctor Stacey," Tom says, and he is suddenly at my side. I startle slightly from his sudden appearance. "Skittish?" he asks.

Once again, I just smile back, awkwardly.

"Did you want something to drink?" he asks me.

"No, thanks. Actually, maybe just some water." I needed to keep my wits about me tonight. Being in enemy territory and all. Tom nods and sets about getting my requested water.

Reyann is now by her grandchildren, and they are regaling her with stories about how they made the biscuits. After Tom brings me my water, he drifts over to his wife who is talking animatedly to Kelly and Brad. I remain standing off in the distance.

Jeff comes up behind me and whispers in my ear. "You look frightened."

"Just uncomfortable," I admit.

"Give them a chance. They might surprise you. Except Tom. He's pretty much an asshole," he says as he steps out from behind me, a grin on his kissable lips.

I smirk slightly at his comment but do not engage further. Once again, I can tell this is the wrong response because Jeff's shoulder's sag slightly.

"You're important to me. And so are they. I want the people I love to be able to be together. It's no different than you are with your family," he says.

"Are you kidding me? You've seen me at my family events. I'm terrible at them!" I reply, horrified.

"No, you aren't. You just think you are." Jeff smiles at me encouragingly and takes my hand. He pulls me further into the kitchen and I groan as I let him take me towards his brother.

"I can't believe how big the girls have gotten," Kelly says as we approach.

"I know. I wish I could slow time down. They are growing up too fast," Nina says and looks lovingly at her daughters.

"Before you know it, they will be asking to go to their first sleepover," Brad laughs and the others join in on the laughter.

"And then you'll find used condoms in their rooms," I chime in. *Oops. Wrong thing to say.*

All eyes are now on me, and no one is laughing, let alone smiling.

"Maybe that only happens with boys," I try to recover. This time I do earn a laugh, from Jeff.

"Pretty sure Mom came across a few of those in our rooms," Jeff elbows his brother in the side.

"I don't even want to think about the day I have to chase away some sex crazed boy from my daughters," Tom shakes his head as if he can clear the images of the future from his mind.

"It isn't so bad. I think my kids were more uncomfortable with the sex talk than I was," I try again.

"But you're a doctor. You are probably used to having *those* kinds of talks," Nina says.

Something about the way she says it makes my skin prickle. I look over at Kelly and see that even she noticed the variation in Nina's voice.

See, I'm not as crazy as you think I am. I manage to convey using only my eyes and micro movements around my brows.

"Mom! We hungy," Gracie says, leaving out the r in the word, and everyone begins moving about to get the meal set and started.

I watch as my sister moves freely around the kitchen and opens up the right cabinets and drawers to set the dining room table. I knew Brad had been involved with this family for many years, but I had never quite realized just how involved he and Kelly had been. I try not to be jealous of my sister but her ease in this place that is so foreign to me brings those feelings forth.

Once everything has been situated and places assigned, we all sit down to eat the meal that Nina prepared. Gracie and Robyn proudly pass out the misshapen biscuits and I thank them as they give me two. Jeff is seated next to me, and Tom and Nina are across from us. Kelly sits on my other side with Brad next to her. Gracie and Robyn are situated on either side of their parents with Reyann taking up the head of the table. There is one solitary chair that remains empty and I glance over to it. I can't help but feel like I am that empty chair at this dinner table among people that I suspect don't want me here.

"Let's say grace. Stacey, would you like to start?" Reyann asks.

"That's my name!" Gracie proudly announces.

"Yes Dear, it is. Stacey?" Reyann turns her gaze towards me, a smile upon her face.

"I'm sorry. What?" With wild eyes I look at Reyann and then to Jeff.

"To thank the Lord for our meal," Reyann says and gestures to the food before us.

"Oh, um, I'm not sure I'd do it right."

Reyann smiles back at me. "There is never a wrong way to say thank you," she says with such affection that I can feel myself relaxing. She nods at me, encouraging me to try. The members of the family have joined hands, and they are waiting for me to get started. I look over at Jeff's hand, turned out and up for me to take and I swallow down my fear. I take Jeff's hand.

"Ok. I'll give it a shot. God. It's been a long time." I pause because it really had been a long time since I had addressed the metaphysical being of our creation. I had lost any faith I had years ago. Watching people die on a near daily basis tends to have that effect on a person.

Clearing my throat, I close my eyes because I think it would be easier to continue if I didn't have to actually look at anybody.

226

"Anyway, we thank you for the food we are about to devour, and you know, all the other stuff in our lives," I finish. Slowly I open my eyes, and I'm greeted with a scowling glare from Nina, a slightly amused one from Tom and an affectionate one from Reyann.

"Very good," Reyann says. "Amen."

There is a chorus of Amens around the table and then everyone starts to eat their meal. I realize my hand is still firmly holding on to Jeff's. He is the only one not eating, besides me, because he is looking at me with concern. Quickly, I untangle our hands and pick up my fork. Jeff's gaze lingers for another few moments before he too turns his attention towards his plate.

The chatter around the table strays to typical family conversation involving work, the children's school events, rising taxes and other things typical American families discuss over the dinner table. Every now and then Kelly tries to throw me a lifeline and engage me in the conversation but either Nina or Tom seems to steer it in a different direction after I contribute. It becomes clear to me that I am definitely the outsider here and I decide to just make it through the dinner.

Reyann is completely pleasant to me and often speaks to me through dinner. She seems oblivious to the tension between me and her daughter-in-law as well as her youngest son. It is clear she is enjoying having her family around and I make a comment about how she is glowing with their presence.

"I'm really fortunate that Tom and Nina are able to stay for so long this time. I've missed my girls," Reyann says.

"I bet. It is always hard when people are far away. I can't say I enjoyed sending my kids off to college but what could I do? Go back to college with them?"

"Knowing you, you probably would do something like that," Kelly jokes and I silently thank Reyann for inviting my sister tonight.

"You may be grateful they are here, Mom, but if I find any more

227

of Tom's hairs in my sink there just might be a scuffle," Jeff continues the lighthearted joking mood.

"What is wrong with you?" Tom says to his brother.

I recognize the tone in his voice before Jeff does. Perhaps it is because I have more experience with being on the receiving end of someone's anger, or maybe Jeff is simply too close to the situation to read it accurately.

"What? It's been over twenty years since we shared a bathroom and you are just as disgusting as you were then," Jeff responds with humor.

"We aren't here for a *visit!*" Tom shouts.

Gracie and Robyn look over at their father, their eyes wide at his sudden outburst. Nina quickly reacts and she instructs the girls that they are going to have their dessert in their room tonight. The girls cheer, thinking it is a treat when it is really a tactic by their mother to distance them from the rest of their father's outrage.

Once the kids are out of the kitchen Jeff responds. And I brace for the hurricane that is bound to follow.

"You need to take a moment and calm down," he tells his younger brother.

"No. You need to take a moment and stop pretending like everything is okay. Nothing is okay, Jeff. Nothing! Mom is dying and you want to have a nice family dinner to introduce your girlfriend like she isn't the one that gave up on our mom!" Tom uses his hand to gesture at me, and he looks at me for the first time since dinner started. It isn't a friendly glance.

"Now hold on. You can say what you want to about me, but you won't talk about Stacey like that. She-"

"She's useless! The great Doctor Stacey!" Tom shouts just as Nina returns to the table. She stands behind Tom and places her hands on his shoulders. To anyone else it would appear to be a calming touch but I know she is actually giving him support. She shares Tom's opinion of me.

"You have no right-" Jeff is once again cut off by his younger brother.

"I have every right. She's my mother, too!"

"And you weren't here! Neither of you were here!" Jeff is now shouting, and he has pushed his chair back so he can stand. The fork that was resting on his plate clatters to the table, sending food bits on the wooden table. I stare at the bits of food.

I feel Kelly take my hand and I let her hold it, but I don't respond. I just continue to stare at those food bits as the chaos ensues around me.

"I have a family. Obligations. You know I couldn't get away," Tom defends himself as he stands to match his brother stare for stare.

"We are your family too. A fact you often forget because of your *obligations*," Jeff retorts.

"Just because you chose to stay in this nowhere town doesn't mean I wanted to. You've always hated me for wanting a life outside of Farley & Sons. I never wanted to be a *gardener*." Tom says gardener with such disgust one would think he had said murderer instead.

"A gardener? You think all I do is cut some grass and trim some trees? You've always looked down on me and Mom, but you forget it was *gardening* that put clothes on your back, food in your belly, and a roof over your ungrateful head!"

"You pompous ass-"

"Enough!" Reyann manages to shout and slam her fist down on the table as best she can given her condition. Her tiny, cancer-ridden body shakes with the effort and energy she exerts.

I can tell the exertion is a lot for her and I immediately get out of my chair to go to her. *Useless Doctor Stacey* is in her doctor mode. I take her wrist and check her pulse, take note of her clammy skin and the slight wheeze in her chest.

"Reyann, you shouldn't stress your body any further," I say

229

softly, and she smiles at me.

Jeff and Tom have now come around the table to be closer to their mother, both concerned for her.

"You two will not talk to one another like that. I'm dying but I'm not dead yet. No sons of mine will say such hurtful things," Reyann scolds them.

"Yes ma'am," they say in unison.

"And you," Reyann addresses Tom, "you will show Stacey the respect she deserves and has earned. Cancer is killing me. Not Stacey. This is still my house, and she is my guest. *My guest.* Do you understand me? *I* wanted this dinner. *I* wanted my family together because I don't know how many more times I will be able to see you all together like this. And even if Jeff had been the one to invite her here you should still be kind to her. This is the woman he loves, and you should respect that too. Just as he respects your choice in a life partner," Reyann scolds, and she sags a little from the lack of breath.

"Reyann, you need to rest," I say.

"No. There will be plenty of time for me to rest soon enough. Family is all that matters now. Now, boys, apologize," she orders her sons.

Both Tom and Jeff begrudgingly apologize to one another.

"Now, Tom and Nina, apologize to Stacey for being so rude to her."

"Mom, Nina didn't-" This time Tom is the one interrupted.

"Oh yes, she did. Nina, I love you like a daughter, but you and Tom think too much alike sometimes. Stacey didn't have to remain my doctor. In fact, she tried to tell me to get a different doctor, but I refused. I wanted her because I trust her. She is family. Family is all that matters," Reyann repeats.

"I'm sorry, Stacey. There is no excuse for my behavior. We aren't normally so, well, awful, but we are scared. We love Reyann so much. We don't want to lose her," Nina says as tears start to fall from her eyes.

Another stage of grief I recognize.

"I understand," I reply.

"I'm sorry too," Tom offers. I nod my head in acceptance.

"Well, I don't know about the rest of you, but I could really use a drink," Brad blurts out and all of us turn to look at him.

Tom has a horrified expression on his face, Nina is confused, Kelly pats her husband's arm sympathetically and Reyann looks concerned. Jeff and I, however, are grinning like complete idiots.

"You and me both, Brother," Jeff says.

Brad grins back at Jeff and I can't help but burst out into laughter. Before I know it, I'm crying and now all eyes are on me. I'm a hysterical mess of laughter and tears.

"What just happened?" Tom asks.

"I think we broke Stacey," Nina answers her husband.

I just keep laughing, crying and holding on to Reyann's arm like if I let her go, I just might fall over. She lovingly pats my hand and looks at me with concern. Jeff comes up behind me and puts his hand on my shoulder.

"Stacey?" Kelly asks, concerned for me.

"It's just so funny. They hate me," I say and point my splayed hand at Nina and Tom.

"No, we don't-" Nina starts.

"Oh no. You absolutely hate me. It's okay. I would hate me too if I was you," I say and start to stand from my kneeling position beside Reyann. I shake off Jeff's hand from my shoulder and turn to Brad.

"And my life drama is causing you to break the tension with jokes about your sobriety. My sister must really love me right now." I'm laughing like a maniac, but I can't help it.

"I do love you," Kelly interjects. I can tell she is wary about where I am headed with my little scene, but I ignore her pleading gaze and forge ahead.

"And you," I turn to Jeff.

231

"You love me. It seems you love me enough that your dying mother had me over for dinner before she dies so your girlfriend, which I'm assuming you told her I was, could *meet the family*", I use air quotations around the last part.

"Stacey," Jeff tries to reach for me. He knows me well enough by now that he knows what is coming around the corner.

"No," I say and step out of his reach, holding my hands up.

Glancing around at all the confused faces I do my best to keep my raging emotions in check. I have something I need to say but I do not want to cause this family any further pain. They have a hard enough road ahead as it is. My gaze finally lands on the kind face of Reyann, still displaying her concern for me.

"I'm truly sorry I couldn't do more for you. You will never know how much I wanted to save you. I tried. I know that isn't enough, but I did try," I say, all laughter out of my voice as I glance quickly at Tom and Nina.

By now my tears are flowing freely, and are spilling out more often, clouding the painful expressions on Tom and Nina's faces.

"Thank you for inviting me over. I know this wasn't exactly the dinner you had planned. I suppose that is my fault too."

"No, honey, it isn't at all. You have done nothing wrong," Reyann says with such compassion that I nearly break apart.

"Maybe that's true too. You see, all my life, I've broken things. I won't go into detail. Kelly can tell you all about it later." I gesture with my hand to Kelly but don't look at her. I can't look at her now.

"I know you were hoping I could come in and fix everything," I turn to Jeff. He is looking at me with pained eyes. I shrug my shoulders slowly and shake my head slightly.

"I'm not a miracle worker. And I'm not the person you need me to be. Frankly, I'm not even sure who I really am. Am I doctor? A sister? A mother? A wife? A girlfriend? I only understand one of those roles and it isn't the one you want from me. You should have someone at your side who can sit down at a dinner like this and not have their skin crawl. All I could think about since the moment I walked through that door was how much I wanted to get out of here. It's not because of you," I say and look over at Tom and Nina.

"Well, actually, it's slightly because of you," I clarify and take another step back. "And some of it's because of you," I look at Jeff. "None of it is because of you," I look at Reyann.

Taking another step back I turn once again to Jeff.

"But mostly, it's because of me. I don't love you. I don't think I ever could, and I won't drag this out any longer. It wouldn't be fair to you. Reyann, if you need anything please call Chastity and we will make sure you get the help you need. Tom, Nina, you won't ever have to see me again. Chastity is more than qualified to handle everything from this point forward. Brad, Kelly, I'll call you…some other time," I say, my voice breaking.

I'm more than halfway out of the kitchen and Jeff is still standing in the spot I left him. His body is turned to follow my movements, but he doesn't attempt to advance towards me. Maybe it's because I have one hand up in front of me as a warning for him to stay at bay.

"Don't call me. Don't follow me. Please, forget these last few months ever happened. Forget me. I'm sorry," I say and turn quickly on my heels.

I run.

I run from that dinner.

I run from that house.

I run from him.

But mostly I am just running from everything in that house that reminded me of my younger self. I am still very much trapped inside a fifteen-year-old girl's mind and sitting beside that family while they were soaking in whatever time they had left with their dying loved one only brought forth the reminder that I had rejected those last few moments with my own father. It is overwhelming.

And I feel the control slipping through my fingers.

So, I run.

-26-

Daughters

I have never pretended that I was a good person. In fact, I was pretty honest about my truly antagonistic nature. I wasn't the soother or the kind-hearted person one would turn to for a sympathetic shoulder. Some women are described as born nurturers. Not me. I was more the, get back up and take it kind of person. I had no sympathy for quitters.

And yet, that seemed to be a habit of mine.

Quitting.

I quit on my father.

I quit therapy.

I quit my marriage.

And now, I had quit on Jeff.

Kelly had said she admired my drive and fortitude, but I wasn't so sure I was worthy of that admiration. It seemed I was only driven to complete the things that were important to me. As for the things that were important to others – well, those could be sacrificed. I could not be bothered.

It has been one week since I walked out of that dinner. As requested, Jeff did not follow me. He did not call me. He stayed away. Just like I wanted. You'd think I would be satisfied with that, but I couldn't tell what I was feeling. Probably because I was deliberately avoiding feeling anything.

Almost.

It took me less than twenty-four hours to pick up that razor again. I justified my running away from Jeff by telling myself at least he wasn't here to see the cuts and make ones of his own.

Just like before there was the initial intake of breath, the sting of pain followed by a hollowness that was draining. Then I would repeat the process. I did this every night, and I still hadn't been able to find any answers in the streaks of blood that once held all the answers.

I hadn't lied to Jeff. I don't love him. How could I possibly love someone right now when I didn't even love myself? I didn't even know who I was anymore. Actually, I wasn't sure I had ever really known who I was. Even all those years ago when I turned away from my father. I didn't recognize that person because I would have sworn, I would have never done such a terrible thing. But I did it.

And I just kept doing terrible things to the ones I was supposed to love.

Kelly.

My mother.

Josh.

Becca.

Jeff.

I had hurt all of them at one point or another and instead of making it right I just pretended like it never happened. Just as I had pretended that I hadn't told my father to go ahead and die.

Amidst all this internal confusion I had decided that I couldn't even focus on the one thing in my life I was sure of. I took a leave of absence from the hospital and left my patients in the care of another oncologist. I was still available if absolutely necessary, but I had told my colleague to reserve that contact for extreme cases only.

That meant I wouldn't be contacted regarding Reyann's further care. Her case was no longer considered emergent because it was beyond anything the medical community could do for her now. Aside from the day-to-day care to prepare her for her last days there was no need for additional medical intervention. Chastity had tried to give me a report on the services being provided for Reyann, but I had cut her off. She received the message and never brought up Reyann again.

This was how I wanted it. I needed to cleanse myself of all that was creating doubt in my life. I needed to focus on me.

But I wasn't really focusing on anything.

I was just…numb.

Except when I was cutting.

Even though I was only able to feel something for a fraction of a minute I chased that fraction because it was the only part of my life that made any sense to me right now. I was struggling with the reality that truly existed – my career, my beautiful children, my privileged life and my caring family – with the warped existence inside my own head. I could only see the streaks of blood clouded by the last image I had of my father and the girl I once was. That girl had big dreams and in every one of those dreams her father was right there, cheering her on. That was the reality I wanted. That was the girl and the life I had failed to mourn all these years. Or, perhaps, I had been stuck in mourning this entire time and had never truly moved beyond my darkest hour.

I was unworthy after all.

A person that had done what I did didn't deserve to be happy in any existence. Despite my attempts at atonement by entering a profession that would save the lives of others, like the one I had turned away from, I was still very much unworthy of forgiveness.

And that was the truth of it all.

The one person that I sought forgiveness from was incapable of giving it to me because he had died. And I had let him. No, I had encouraged it.

Sitting inside my darkened apartment I stare at the empty space on my living room wall where a whimsical painting once hung. I am not sure what possessed me to purchase the silly long haired, robed man playing the guitar while words of scripture were written in the background. I had never been a religious person. Neither of my parents were particularly religious in nature and I continued this non-tradition. Why this particular painting, this particular scripture called to me was a mystery to me. And though the painting is still in the possession of Jeff I am staring at the wall as if it is still hanging there, judging me.

For He has rescued us from the dominion of darkness and brought us into the kingdom of the Son He loves, in whom we have redemption, the forgiveness of sins.

Why someone had transposed an image of Jesus playing a guitar as if he was in a rock band to this particular scripture was not something I understood. I didn't even understand why I was sitting in the dark, staring at an empty space where the scripture used to be as if it held all the answers. I don't know why I had memorized the words, or why they kept repeating in my head. It was just a painting that made no sense to me.

Here I sit in the darkness, seeking forgiveness from an absent painting and an absent presence. Why would God concern himself with me when I had no concern for him? I sought redemption but it was a redemption that was undeserved.

"You left me," I begin, speaking to that empty space on a wall, but also the empty space inside me.

"I told you to go, but you didn't have to listen to me. What did I know? I was just a child, a stupid, silly girl. It hurt so bad," I suck in a breath and close my eyes, feeling the tears pooling in my eyes. Trying to get a grip, I harden myself and square my shoulders back, then open my eyes.

The empty space greets me, taunting me, and that angers me. I jump up to my feet and point an accusatory finger at the wall, where a mockery of what should be sacred used to hang, just like my own heart inside my chest.

"I needed you! I cried out for you, for help, and you just left me! Was it what I said? Am I so bad that there was no hope for me? I was a child! I didn't know it was the last time he'd be there. I didn't mean it! I didn't meant it! Why don't you love me?" I cry out and fall to my knees, looking up at that empty space, feel it consuming me from the inside.

On my knees, crying out for my own father, to God, I realize why I bought that painting, why I held on to it for so many years. I wanted to believe that I wasn't the problem. It wasn't me; it was God. After all, he was just a silly man playing a guitar, plucking the strings without a care to those who heard his twisted tune. I only ever focused on the picture, but I had still memorized that scripture.

For He has rescued us from the dominion of darkness and brought us into the kingdom of the Son He loves, in whom we have redemption, the forgiveness of sins.

It had never been about the man playing the guitar. It had always been the words that drew me back. Because I wanted so desperately to believe that I was worthy of forgiveness. That my past sins could be washed away and I could be better, but that day never came.

Because I was unworthy.

My body deflates and I fall to the floor, curl up into myself, and cry for the little girl who lost her father and her faith.

"Mom! Mom, open up. I know you are in there," a voice calls to me from beyond the walls of my apartment.

This apartment was once my sanctuary but I created a prison out of the place I believed to be my safe harbor. A prison of self-flagellation.

"Stacey, Dear, open the door," another voice calls to me.

"I brought wine," a third voice.

I can hear them all calling to me, imploring me to let them in, but the empty space calls to me more. The answers have to be here.

"Mom, if you don't open this door right now, I am going to

238

break your window. You don't want that do you? For me to commit a felony? Breaking and entering is a crime and I could go to prison all because my Mother refused to open her door."

Mom.

Me. That's me. And that is my daughter begging me to open the door. The daughter I had hurt. The daughter I love so much.

Unknowingly, my body responds, and I pull myself off the floor, wipe the tears from face, and open the door to my pleading daughter. She is flanked by my own mother and sister. They all look at me with concern and it is the look of complete helplessness in all their expressions that has me snapping back to abject despair. I fall to my knees and the tears come flooding out again.

"I'm so sorry. I didn't mean it, Mom, I promise. I was just so angry, and I didn't know what to do. But I never meant for that to happen. I never wanted that. Why does it still hurt so much? Why can't I just forget him?" I beg my mother for the answers.

Looking up at her from my knees, the position of forgiveness, I wait for the one person in the world that is supposed to have all the answers. Mother. So many times, we turn to this force to provide comfort and right the wrongs we have experienced. I had rejected her for many years because I foolishly believed her to be weak. But she wasn't the weak one. I was. I was the one that had fallen apart amidst tragedy. She had forged on. She had thrived while I had merely faked it for years, playing the part.

"Oh, Stacey, what is going on with you?" she asks as she falls down to her knees with me and pulls me into her arms.

I cling to her just as I had once clung to Rachel. Unlike my time with Rachel, however, I do not pull away. I hold on to my mother even when she tells me to stand and she guides me to my hideously outrageous couch. She sits beside me and continues to hold onto me as she strokes my hair, just as she did when I was a child.

I can see my daughter and sister walk into the room as well and take seats on the other sofa. Kelly places a bottle of wine down beside her feet and she looks at me with a concern that sisters seem to reserve only for one another. Becca is frightened as she looks upon my crazed state. She has never seen me cry. I have never allowed my children to see me in a moment of weakness. I never wanted them to know that part of me I keep hidden from the world, and sometimes even myself.

"Tell me what happened," my mother says softly beside me.

"I can't. It's just too terrible to say," I shake my head and try to hide my shame.

"Stacey, there is nothing you can do that will ever stop me from loving you. You are my flesh and blood, my daughter, and I would move the earth to take away your pain. Tell me what happened."

I hesitate and start to shake from the shame.

"Mom?" Becca calls to me.

I turn to her, and she smiles slightly at me, trying to comfort me.

"We all love you. We just want to help you. I'm sorry that I've been avoiding you. And I'm sorry for the terrible things I said to you. I was just angry, and I didn't understand what was really going on between you and Dad. I didn't know. I'm sorry for hurting you. Please let us help you. Please," she begs.

I'm not sure why but I look over to the other person in the room. The only person who hasn't spoken yet. She was another I had sought forgiveness from, and she had freely given it to me. Without hesitation Kelly had extended a branch to me when I hadn't deserved it. How she was able to set aside all the pain I had caused her to help me heal was another thing I didn't understand. So many things I just didn't understand.

"Some things just need to be released. Holding on to them only causes destruction. I learned this many years ago when Brad lost his brother. There is no shame in asking for help; only in rejecting it. Don't reject us Stacey, please," Kelly begs.

Calling upon the strength of my sister I force down the fear and allow the words to flow forth.

240

"When Daddy was sick, I told him to go ahead and die. I told him we would be better off without him. I refused to listen to him when he was saying goodbye and then he killed himself. I killed him. I didn't mean to, but I killed him," I reveal and turn away from my mother. I can't look at her in the moment of my confession. How could I? I had stolen someone very important from her.

The room is silent but my shame screams at me loudly.

"Sweet girl, have you thought this all these years?" my mother asks me.

I nod.

"You were the only one of us that was truly innocent during all of that. You didn't cause your father's death." She has moved us so her hands are on the sides of my face, and we are staring at one another. She moved on of her hands and brushes it through my hair, like a mother does when her daughter is sad.

"Don't make excuses for me, Mom. I was old enough to know that my words had power. Old enough to recognize that he was hurting and I just hurt him further. He begged me to go back to him, but I ignored him. *He begged me, Mother*." More tears and shakes.

"No. I won't allow you to take this burden on. You didn't kill him. Cancer killed him. You know this to be true Stacey. Your work proves this to you every day. Cancer was the killer. Not you and not your father. We were all helpless in such a state of loss and confusion. You were hurting too, and you said something you regret but you did not cause any of the events that followed."

She keeps trying to convince me that I am blameless, but I know in my heart that I'm not. This is how cause and effect worked. There is the initial catalyst followed by an effective event. I was the cause and my father's suicide was the effect. This was what all my training taught me. First there was the foreign agent and then there was the disease. I had acted like a virus and caused Armageddon.

Shaking my head I remove myself from my mother's embrace. She tries to reach out for me, but I move further away.

"No. We would have had more time with him if I hadn't told him to die. I told him cancer wasn't the problem. I told him he was the problem and that we would be better off without him. He listened to me, Mom. I caused it all."

"Mom," Becca moves quickly off her sofa and kneels before me. She takes my hands in hers and catches my gaze with her own.

We stare at each other silently for a few moments. She smiles tentatively at me, and I return the soft smile. She squeezes my hands.

"Was I to blame when Cooper broke his arm falling off the swing?"

She is referring to a time when Cooper was seven and she was four. He had been on a swing at the park, and she had absentmindedly walked in front of the swing and her brother had thrown himself off the swing in an attempt to avoid hitting her. Cooper had broken two bones in his arm when he landed on the ground.

"Of course not, Baby. You were just a child. You didn't know any better," I say.

"Exactly."

I know what my daughter is trying to do but there is no comparison between what my fifteen-year-old self did and a simple action of a four year old not being aware of her surroundings.

"Oh, Becca, I was older and I knew better."

"Ok. So that means Cooper is to blame for killing my pet guinea pig."

"What? No it doesn't."

"He was sixteen. A year older than you were when Grandpa died. He took Wiggles out of the cage and outside. He wasn't watching him and that stray cat killed Wiggles. He was old enough to know better."

"Becca. A guinea pig isn't a person. And you had asked Cooper to let Wiggles outside while you were on that school trip. It wasn't his fault," I say. I love my daughter for trying but nothing compares to what I did.

242

"No. A guinea pig isn't a person, but I had loved that little guy and at thirteen I was so upset. I blamed Cooper. I blamed him for so long, but you were the one that told me people make mistakes and sometimes bad things happen. You said it isn't anybody's fault. It wasn't your fault, Mom. Sometimes bad things just happen," Becca says and squeezes my fingers again.

I smile at her but I'm not buying into her theory.

"I read the note Kevin left for Brad after he killed himself," Kelly suddenly says.

We all turn to her. She isn't looking at any of us but off in the distance. My gaze travels her path to the empty space on my wall. It is like she can see the painting that used to hang there, and the words it held.

For He has rescued us from the dominion of darkness and brought us into the kingdom of the Son He loves, in whom we have redemption, the forgiveness of sins.

"It wasn't what I had expected at all. I thought he would apologize for what he was about to do. I thought he would tell the brother that had loved him so much that he didn't really want to leave him behind but that wasn't in the letter. The letter justified what he was about to do. He explained how he was nothing but a burden and that everyone would be better off if they just forgot about him. One moment he's telling Brad he loves him and the next moment he's talking about how his suicide is for the best of all of them.

"Brad was destroyed by this, and he disappeared into the pain and the failure he felt. He believed he had failed to save his brother and that was the cause of Kevin's death. He was wrong. And you are wrong too," Kelly turns to me.

"Kevin made his own choice. He said he did it because it was best for everyone, but it was only about what he wanted. Brad and Lily didn't want their brother to die. And you didn't want your father to die. You said something in a moment of hurt because

243

someone you loved was also in pain. Brad spent years blaming himself for all the harsh words he had uttered in moments of anger caused by a pain he didn't understand. Becca is right. You aren't to blame for the choice your father made. But, I'm not so sure anyone is to blame.

"Kevin mentioned forgiveness in his letter, but he also said he didn't think Brad would offer that forgiveness. He knew what he was doing was going to hurt someone who loved him. But he did it anyway. I'll never understand that. And I'll never be able to understand how Brad was able to finally feel that forgiveness for not only Kevin but for himself. It took him a while to come to terms with what Kevin had done. I don't think it was ever about the choice Kevin made. The only thing that mattered was the love two brothers had for each other. That love doesn't go away when one of them dies. You still love your father, and it is because of that love you are unable to forgive yourself. You couldn't save him, Stacey, but nobody could have."

Once again, we are plunged into silence. Silently, we exchange glances with one another, speaking without words. Three generations of women finding comfort and strength from the other. Mothers and daughters, bound together by more than blood. I had spent so much time pushing them away when I should have let them in. My isolation was my own doing and it was causing my own destruction.

"I've been cutting again," I confess and turn to my mother.

"I know. I've always known, Stacey. I am sorry I wasn't strong enough to shoulder that burden for you. I shouldn't have allowed Josh to carry that. It should have been me who helped you through your pain. I will bear that cross for the rest of my life. I failed you and I'm truly sorry," she laments.

"Oh, Mom. You had your own issues to deal with. I don't blame you for that. It was something I chose to do, and I could have told you a million times, but I thought I was protecting you. The last thing I ever wanted to do was hurt you too. I thought I could handle it. I thought I could handle everything on my own. I was wrong," I admit and turn to my daughter.

"Your father is the best man I have ever known and I didn't deserve him. I will always be grateful to him for giving me you and your brother and I'm sorry I let you down," I say and stroke the side of her face.

"You did deserve him. He loves you and I think you love him too. I know you guys aren't going to stay married and I get that. Dad kind of talked to me about some things and I understand more now. I'm sorry I was so mean to you. I didn't know about all the things you were going through. Do you forgive me?" she asks, still on her knees before me.

"Of course I do, muffin. I love you and you were right about me. I am selfish."

"No, Mom. You are the best. You were always doing things for us. In fact, I never realized before just how much you do. You are amazing and I won't let you forget that. You're my hero," my daughter says.

"Mine too," Kelly echoes.

"And mine," my mother agrees.

I chuckle slightly at them.

"I think you guys need to expand your horizons."

"Nope. It's always been you. You are the glue that holds this family together. You take on every burden and you do it without complaint because you are selfless," Kelly says.

"I'm not so sure I am. Look at what I've done to Josh, and Jeff."

"Mom, you need to go talk to Dad. He isn't as broken as you think he is," Becca says as she stands.

"As for Jeff, well, that one might not be so easy," Kelly says.

"Why not? He loves her, doesn't he?" Becca asks as she takes her seat beside Kelly.

"Well, yes, but-"

245

"I was a complete bitch to him and his family," I answer.

"Oh, I don't believe that for a minute," my mother says.

"Believe it. It was like I was a swamp monster at that dinner. I insulted his family and told him I could never love him."

"You didn't," Becca says appalled.

"Oh, I did. And then I told him to never call me again and ran out of the house."

"Okay, so you reacted rashly. What woman hasn't? If he truly loves you, he will forgive you. Go to him," my mom encourages.

"I'm not sure I'm ready for that."

"Then you get ready. No more sitting in the dark, Mom. You always told me we had to be the ones to make things happen. That we couldn't just sit back and expect things to come to us. So, get up, get moving and get your man," Becca instructs me.

I gaze at her and start to laugh. This was my daughter? Giving me life and love advice?

"Get my man?"

"Yeah. I mean, isn't he your man?" Becca looks at her aunt for backup.

"Oh. That man is most certainly hers. She may not know it yet but everyone else does," Kelly confirms.

"Alright, first we get you in a place where you don't feel so defeated. Then, when you're ready, we get your man," my mother echoes. "Kelly, open up that bottle and let's strategize."

Divorce

For the first time in my adult life I leaned on my family. I took the help that was offered from my mother, sister, and daughter. Our family had certainly been blessed, but we were no strangers to heartache. My mother lost her first husband at a young age and was thrust into single motherhood all while struggling to manage her own loss. Kelly had been abandoned by her mother and left to eternally wonder what became of her. She fought hard for her relationship with Brad and stood by him during his struggles with his own personal demons. All of us had endured the tragic death of our friend Jen and had rallied around her husband and two young children. All of us, in some fashion, had tragedy befall us. It took me nearly twenty years to realize that I wasn't alone and that my family understood all too well what I had been struggling with all these years.

The women in my family remained with me through out that day and into the night. We had an adult sleepover, and I learned more about my mother, sister, and daughter that evening than I had known my entire life. That one night had given me what nearly ten years of therapy could never provide – a sense of belonging. Ever since the death of my father I had believed there was no place where I belonged completely. The two of us had been so in sync that when he had died, I hadn't just lost him. I had lost a part of me that I had fought to find. I never expected to find the missing piece of me in those that remained.

It was true that my mother and I were very different, but we found commonality that night in our hopes and fears of motherhood. She shared with me all of the doubts she had as a young wife and mother, just as I once held. She revealed how hard it had been for her those first two years after my father had passed away. She too had been angry at him for what he had chosen to do but she told me that she was able to forgive him after finding refuge in a support group of others that had lost loved ones. I had never known she had sought such assistance and knowing that she had helped remove some of the shame I felt for seeking out therapy.

Kelly shared with us the details of what had transpired all those years ago, between her and Brad. Once again, I was confronted with just how little I knew about the ones I loved. She had never before let on just how bad things had been with Brad and his struggle with addiction. I hadn't known about all the times he had rejected her and, in the process, hurt her. Kelly even shared how she felt guilt for choosing Brad over her college boyfriend; a man that had loved her and treated her with kindness. Even now, eighteen years after she had graduated college, she still thought about him and hoped he was happy in his life.

And Becca, my beautiful daughter, told me she had been dating someone for six months. In fact, she admitted that he was the reason she chose to go to college in Vegas. They had met on a school trip she had taken with her junior class and had been talking long distance ever since. They had both decided that the University of Nevada was a college they both agreed on and they'd been a couple ever since their reunion in August. She told me she kept it hidden because she hadn't wanted me to be disappointed in her choice of college because of a boy. This admission broke my heart because I had never wanted my daughter to feel like she had to hide things

248

from me. I knew I had a tendency to allow my opinions to over-power conversations and it saddened me that I had inadvertently forced my daughter to keep her happiness hidden.

Becca showed us all a photo of Brandon, her boyfriend, and told us about him. He was the same age as her and they had met during a Future Business Leaders of America conference in D.C. He was from Montana and lived in a small town with one stop light. He grew up on a farm and wanted to own his own restaurant one day. He was pursuing a degree in culinary arts and had even saved up money from his youth to one day apply to his dream. Based on her descript-tion he was responsible, caring, and everything I had hoped for in a match for my daughter.

After we had shared our pasts and dreams for the future, I had gotten my divorce papers from the kitchen table and signed them while they all looked on. I admitted that a part of me had doubted my decision because I was terrified that without Josh, I would cease to be me. Or, at the very least, the me I thought I was. With the strength I had borrowed from my mother, sister, and daughter I signed those papers and promised I would stop hiding from the things I needed to do.

The very next day I kept my promise and went to see Josh. He agreed to meet me at the house we once shared and I was nervous about the meeting. Despite the assurances from my daughter that my soon to be ex-husband was stronger than I thought I still feared the hurt I would cause him.

When I arrived, he opened the door with a friendly greeting and told me he was glad I had called him.

"I should have done it sooner," I admitted as I stepped through the door. The familiar feeling of being in the home rushed back to me and I started glancing around with jerking movements. Josh saw my reaction.

"It's weird, isn't it, walking back in here? I get that feeling every time. I think it's time we put the house on the market," he says so nonchalantly that I am shocked out of my own thoughts.

"Really? You don't want to keep the house?"

"Stacey, I only moved here because I thought it was what you wanted," he reveals as we both take a seat at the kitchen table.

"I'm going to say something, and I don't want to hurt you but I feel I need to say it," I say.

"Do what you have to."

"I hated that about you. I hated that you did things only because you thought it was something I wanted. I wanted so desperately for you to just tell me what you wanted but you never did. I felt like I could never relax around you because I could never tell what you were thinking. I doubted everything I did or said because I could never tell if you liked it."

Josh stares at me for a minute before his lips tick slightly in the left corner of his mouth and he sighs. He brings his hands up and rests them on the table.

"I never have been good about sharing my feelings, have I?"

"No, you haven't," I agree.

We both share a timid smile with one another, and I take this moment to place the divorce papers on the table. He looks at the papers between us before speaking again.

"I did love you. I never kept that from you. I thought I was making you happy. That was all I ever wanted," he says.

"I know. I've never doubted your love. It was my love that I doubted. I was so messed up that I couldn't identify if what I felt for you was the kind of love you deserved or if it was just extreme gratitude. And I was so young. I clung to you because I was terrified of losing someone again. It wasn't fair to you and I'm sorry for that."

"I knew you weren't happy. I'd known for years but it was me that was afraid of losing someone. I didn't talk to you about it because I was afraid it would only push you further away. I thought if only I could make you happy things would fix themselves. So, I

250

just gave you whatever you wanted. It never occurred to me that you saw my acquiesce as a form of detachment. I should have talked to you, Stacey. I should have gone to therapy with you. Hell, I should have done a lot of things. We are both at fault here," he says and reaches out to take my hand.

I laugh and squeeze his hand quickly.

"This has got to be the most amicable divorce in the history of divorces. You and I have never been conventional. I suppose it is only fitting our divorce follows that path," I say with another laugh.

"I've never had any ill feelings towards you. Even when things went bad and you told me you had cheated on me. You are my best friend and the mother of my children. I will always love you, but I know we can't pretend our future is with each other. I would still very much like to be your friend, Stacey. You are an important part of my life, and I can't imagine my life without you in it in some way."

I'm crying now because who wouldn't want this man to be their husband? I was a terrible wife to him and all he wants is to still be my friend. I truly didn't deserve his gentle spirit.

"I never deserved you," I whisper and wipe away a tear.

"That isn't true. I think we were exactly what we needed at that time in our lives. You did deserve me and I needed you. You've given me so much, Stacey. I couldn't ask for a happier twenty years. I'm not going to say that all the moments were good, but I wouldn't trade the ones that were for anything. Cooper and Becca are my everything and you gave them to me. All the rest, this house and the things inside it never meant anything to me. You shared your family with me, which was something I never really had before. We had a good life," he says and holds onto my hand a little bit tighter.

"What do we do now?" I ask.

"Well, I think the first thing we need to do is give these papers to the lawyers. Then we need to meet with a realtor. With that hideous fountain gone I think we could probably move this house pretty quickly," Josh jokes.

"I knew you hated that thing! I can't believe you let me buy that monstrosity." The laughter comes to me easier.

"I thought you wanted it," Josh shrugs.

"No one in their right mind would want that mess."

We share a laugh together, exchange a loving look and release our joined hands.

"Did you know Becca has a boyfriend?" I ask.

"What? Who? Since when?" Josh fires the questions at me and deep down a part of me is glad that she kept this information from the both of us, and not just me.

"His name is Brandon, and they met over a year ago when she took that school trip to D.C. He is the reason for the Vegas college venture."

"Oh. Well. That explains a lot of things actually. The hushed phone calls and the strange packages she would get every now and then. Montana?" Josh asks me.

"Yes."

"She told me they were amazon purchases. Our daughter isn't the greatest liar."

After a shared smile, we fall into a calm silence. Our thoughts have strayed to the same topic because Josh's next statement has me looking at him with a stunned expression.

"Jeff is a good man."

"What? I mean, I know he is but what does he have to do with anything?" I ask.

"Stacey, I know you have been seeing him lately. I can't say I'm surprised," he says and stands from the table. I watch his movements as he begins to assemble the items for a pot of coffee. My ex-husband lived on coffee.

"What do you mean by that?"

"Jeff, like our daughter, isn't very good at hiding his feelings. I've known for years he hasn't exactly thought of you as 'family'."

"Why does everyone keep saying things like that? We barely even spoke to each other, and it was only at family events. There was no secret harboring of feelings."

"Maybe not on your part but as for Jeff, he definitely had me worried for some years," Josh admits as he sets the coffee machine to brew.

"Really? But why? Nothing ever happened."

"I know. I always trusted you."

I wince at that statement because I had betrayed our marriage once.

"It's in the past Stacey. I've moved on from it and you should too."

"Okay," I say slowly because I know if the situation had been reversed there was no way I would have been as forgiving as Josh.

"Jeff never spoke to me about his feelings for you directly. But I had overheard enough conversations between him and Brad to put the pieces together."

"Well, I doubt there is anything more to any of that. I pretty much sabotaged any chance of continuing that relationship," I say and turn back around in my seat.

"Is that what you want?"

"Ha," I laugh.

"I'm being serious, Stacey," Josh returns to his seat at the table and turns me in my chair so I'm facing him.

"What do you want?"

Such a loaded question.

What do I want?

"I'm not sure."

"You know, after twenty years I've become pretty good at picking up on your tells. I think you know exactly what you want but you are afraid."

"Don't be ridiculous. What do I have to be afraid of?" I ask, invoking bravado into my words.

Josh just smiles at me as the coffee pot announces the completion of the brewing cycle.

"Of feeling," Josh says and stands to retrieve his coffee.

"What is this? Twenty years and you say nothing but suddenly you have all this insight and advice? I don't get it. What's changed?" I follow his movements as he prepares his coffee.

"Everything has changed. We may be ending our marriage, but I still want to see you happy and healthy. If you think you are able to find those things with Jeff then I hope you take the chance before it passes you by."

We may be ex-husband and wife, but he is perfectly right. I am afraid of feeling things for Jeff that I wasn't prepared for. I am afraid of the feeling of failure when I am sure to destroy whatever foundation we could build. But mostly I am afraid of the feeling of loss. I am not sure how it happened, or when it happened, but I had fallen in love with that man, and I am absolutely terrified of that love ending. It is easier to pretend it had never existed and turn from it because I had known loss before. And I had barely survived before and ran this time because I was sure I couldn't survive another loss. All I had managed to do this time, however, was repeat past mistakes and it only took two words from Josh to reveal what my true fear had been along.

-28-

Celebration

How do you fix something you broke when you didn't have all the pieces? There wasn't enough tape in the world to patch up the mess I had made with Jeff. Even though I felt like I was making giant leaps forward in my journey to heal the void inside me there was still enough of the fear I once clung to that prevented me from just going to Jeff and relying on his mercy.

As I did with Josh I thought about how I would have reacted if the situations were reversed. I wouldn't be so quick to forget all that had happened and I allowed my own misgivings to keep me away. I couldn't hide forever because despite my history with Jeff there was a longer standing history between Brad and him.

Thanksgiving was here and Kelly was hosting. This meant that the Farley's; Reyann, Tom and his family, and Jeff would be at the holiday gathering. There was no more avoiding him or Reyann. During the adult sleepover with my family my Mother had identified this opportunity as the perfect time to make amends. After all, it was the holiday of giving thanks and coming together.

To say I was panicking was an understatement.

I was in full on nightmare mode.

"Mom, calm down, everything is going to be fine," Becca says to me as she helps assemble the table scape Kelly had prepared for the festivities.

"Yeah Stacey, it's all gonna work out," Brandon, Becca's boyfriend says beside her.

I met him for the first time about an hour ago and for some reason he had been addressing me by my first name. I am not exactly thrilled by it.

"Becca, thanks for the encouragement but just let me have this moment of panic. Brandon, Dear, if you call me Stacey one more time, I swear I am going to put a turkey leg in a place that will be very uncomfortable for you. To you, my name is Ms. Cooper or Dr. Cooper," I tell the young man.

Brandon looks nervously at Becca and my daughter bursts out laughing. It is then I realize that my dear little girl had set her boyfriend up.

"You fiend. You told him to call me by my first name," I say and put my daughter in a headlock. She continues to giggle as she pushes against me.

"Oh, come on, Mom. It was funny. Besides, I didn't know what you wanted to be called now that I know you are dumping our last name," she says and successfully manages to free herself.

"Oh, Becca, it isn't like that. I just feel like I need to go back to my father's last name," I say and reach for her. I'm concerned I've hurt her.

"It's okay, Mom. I get it. I'm just messing with you. It is going to be weird calling you Ms. Cooper though when Cooper is around," she says and goes over to her boyfriend to kiss him on the cheek; her apology for playing a prank on him.

"Ain't that the truth," Cooper says as he enters the room with his father. They are holding various items Kelly had demanded be on the table; a cornucopia and a plush turkey among them.

"I think it's a fitting ending and a nice tribute to your father," Josh says. He places the items he is carrying on the table, gives me a polite smile and quietly exits the room.

"Ugghh, why can't you two just be like normal divorced parents and hate each other already," Becca feigns annoyance.

I chuckle at my daughter's sense of humor. She may look like her father, but she had inherited my dark sense of humor, and I loved her more for that.

"I don't know if I'll ever get used to this," Brandon says.

"You will," Cooper's girlfriend says from the opposite side of the gigantic table. She had been put in charge of folding the napkins into some sort of turkey shape. I didn't think they looked like a turkey, but Kelly had inspected the first two and gave Sherry the thumbs up of approval.

"Sherry's been in the thick of this chaos for two years now. If anyone is an expert at wadding through our family drama it is her," Cooper says and he shares a sweet smile with his girlfriend.

"She even has the perfect name to prove it," Becca says as she sidesteps a chair to get to the other side of the table.

"What does that mean?" Cooper asks.

"Sherry. Sher-*eee*. You can't tell me you haven't noticed there seems to be a trend with our family and names. Stacey," Becca says and points to me, "Aunt Kelly. Aunt Jenny. Aunt Lily. Hell, even Uncle Brad's and Greg's names have the same sound when you say their full name – Bradley, Gregory. Then there's me, Becky," my daughter concludes.

"Wait. You had me with all the other names, but you don't go by Becky. You've always gone by Becca," Cooper declares triumphantly.

"Not true. Mom and Aunt Kelly used to call me Becky until I demanded they call me Becca."

"Actually, you cried and threw a fit where you stated *I'm not Becky, I'm Becca,*" I point out.

Sherry snorts quickly with laughter and Becca throws her an evil glare.

"Careful there almost sister-in-law, you are on my good side now, but things can change like that," Becca says and snaps her

257

fingers for emphasis on 'that'.

"I hear a lot of chatter, but we are still miles away from being ready," Kelly announces as she comes into the dining area. Her daughter, Jenny Lynn, is right behind her.

"Hurry up everyone. They will be here soon," Jenny Lynn says as she skips around the table.

"Come here monster," Becca calls to her cousin and they engage in a game of tickles and giggles.

"I think you are more nervous than I am, Kelly." I say to my sister.

"Of course I am. I want this night to be perfect. This might be Reyann's last holiday celebration before...," she stops speaking and we all exchange pained expressions because we know the ending to that sentence.

"That is why we must make it perfect," Sherry announces and holds up her latest folded napkin.

Becca bursts out laughing. "It looks like the turkey is giving us the middle finger," Becca chortles.

"Really?" Sherry asks and turns the napkin around to inspect it. "Oh my gosh, you are right. What should I do?"

"Nothing," I say.

All eyes turn to me.

"Reyann will love it. Leave it exactly how it is and make sure it is on Tom's plate setting," I say.

"Stacey, no. I know things didn't exactly go well at the last dinner, but do you really want to chance another blow out?" Kelly asks me.

"Trust me, Sis."

"Okay," Kelly sighs and places the offending napkin on the plate before Tom's name card.

Yep, my sister went all out. She learned calligraphy so she could write everyone's names on a place card. She rented a table to fit all eighteen of us. She had a ginormous meal planned. In fact, my mother, Kelly, myself, and Becca had been in that kitchen for the past two days. Currently, Brad, my stepfather, Paul, and brother Gregory were watching the football game in the living room while the rest of us set things up before the arrival of our last guests. They had somehow managed to escape the last-minute detailing Kelly required.

"Brandon you really can join my husband and the others. You don't have to stay here with us. Cooper, why don't you go with him?"

"Oh, no, Mrs. Klauzek, I'm fine here," Brandon says.

"Don't fight it, Brandon. That's Aunt Kelly's way of telling us to disappear," Cooper says as he kisses his girlfriend quickly on the lips and starts to head out of the room.

"No. That isn't what I meant at all," Kelly tries to recover.

"It's cool, Aunt Kel. Commence with your girl talk. Us men folk will beat our chests and shout at the idiot box," Cooper says as he steers Brandon out of the room.

"When did he learn how to read me so well?" Kelly asks as she moves some items on the table to fit her high standards. I imagined her attention to detail stemmed from the early upbringing she had from her all too concerned about appearances mother. Sometimes I just wanted to grab her, shake her, and tell her she wasn't her mother but that would only make her feel bad and I was trying to be a better person.

"When he was nine. You are very easy to read," I answer.

"It's true Aunt Kelly. But that is a good thing. It means you are earnest," Becca says.

"Thanks Dear. Now, the reason I wanted it to just be us girls is because I have a surprise for Reyann and it involves all of us. Here, take these," she says and hands each of us a card.

"Are you sure you want me here for this? I'm not family," Sherry says.

"Don't be stupid. Of course you are," Becca says and pushes the card Sherry holds up towards her face so she can read it.

I look down at my own card and see my sister's handwriting. My card reads, *"For she is the strength we call upon when all we feel is fear. She is the love we will remember and honor for all that she has given to us"*.

"Kelly, what is this?" I ask.

"I know you all have encountered Reyann in some way and I wanted her to know how much she has meant to us over these years. I tried to get your cards to read what she has done for you personally. I hope I was able to capture things accurately," Kelly says.

"You got mine spot on. *For all the laughs, the tears and the cheesecake we shared throughout the years.*" Tasha, my mother, says. She is starting to cry slightly, and I wrap my arm around her.

"Mine too. *Grandmother is felt in the heart and from a gentle touch filled with love.*" Becca reads.

I hadn't realized my daughter viewed Reyann in such a manner. The usual shame I felt when I realized how blind I had been all these years starts to seep through, but I glance over to my mother and she smiles at me. Just as quickly as it came on the shame dissipates and I return to the moment.

"I can't believe you knew about this," Sherry says and she looks over at Kelly.

"I sort of eavesdropped. Sorry," Kelly says apologetically.

"Sorrow is meant to be shared and through a kind soul loss can turn into a connection that lasts beyond death," Sherry reads her card aloud.

"Oh my gosh. What happened?" Becca asks.

"Remember when my cousin died? Well, Reyann found me crying that Christmas and I spilled everything to her. She was so kind to me. She reminded me that death isn't the end and she made me feel better," Sherry reveals.

"Family is more than a word. It is a spark that illuminates the darkest of moments and provides comfort for those left behind,"

Kelly reads her card.

"What do you want us to do with these?" Tasha asks.

"After dinner I'll announce we have something special for Reyann. Jenny Lynn has a script she is going to read. When she is finished we will go in this order; Tasha, Becca, Me, Sherry and then Stacey. After that Brad has something planned for her too," Kelly explains.

"Are you sure about this? What about Tom? Will he be alright with this?" I ask.

"Frankly, Tom can kiss my ass. He's always been a bit of a drag. Brad can handle him," Kelly says surprising me with her candor.

"Okay. I'm all in," Becca says with delight.

Before I have a moment to process the doorbell rings out and Jenny Lynn happily announces she will get the door.

I'm still staring at my card and the words written upon it. *Fear. Strength. Honor.* Words I am all too familiar with and yet still struggling to live with. How could I possibly get up in front of everyone and say this to a woman I believe I have failed? And in front of a man I have disappointed.

"They're here! They're here!" Jenny Lynn proudly announces and all of us standing in the great room turned dining room for the evening turn our heads towards the direction of the front door.

Slowly, my family starts to depart the room to greet our guests of honor. Kelly and Tasha each stop beside me, flanking me. I glance at each one of them and smile. It feels right to have them here, by my side, because I can't help but feel like they had been present for all of my major life events. Granted, Kelly hadn't arrived in my life until I was in my teens, but she had become a constant presence ever since. We were three women, with three equally impactful pasts but somehow, we had managed to arrive at this point, together.

Reaching out I take one of their hands in mine and take a deep breath.

"Everything will work out. You'll see," my mother says to me.

261

"Yes. All you need is a little faith," Kelly seconds.

"I think I really need you guys. My family."

We share one last smile, release hands and walk together as a group to the front of the house. The scene is a crowded mess of people, coats, limbs, and laughter. Jenny Lynn is bouncing around Tom's kids and excitedly talking about things in her room. Brad and Tom are just completing an embrace as we enter the foyer. Tom's wife, Nina, is talking to my stepfather and brother as Reyann listens on. To my surprise, I see Cooper and Josh laughing in the back corner with Jeff. I'm not ashamed to admit that my eyes searched for him first.

Well, maybe I am just a smidgen ashamed that I didn't seek out Reyann first. She seems to be in the same physical condition I last saw her in. She is still in the wheelchair and quite pale but other than that I am unable to notice any drastic changes in her outward appearance. That is a comforting sign.

"Come in everyone. The house has more rooms. No need to remain in the doorway. Let's give them some space people," Kelly declares and starts to herd our family out of the entry way.

My eyes stay firmly fixed on Jeff as he moves to take the handles on his mother's wheelchair. I step back and wait for the procession of people to pass me.

"Stacey," Tom greets me and nods his head slightly in my direction as he passes.

"Tom," I say, sans nod.

Nina says nothing. She does smile at me nervously, however, so that is something. The kids ignore me of course because I am just another inconsequential giant to them. When Reyann and Jeff approach it is Reyann who speaks first. Reluctantly, I move my gaze away from Jeff to give Reyann the respect and attention she deserves.

"It is so good to see you again Stacey. We've missed you," she says and reaches out to take my hand.

I allow the gesture because I really do care for this woman. I knew my recent actions may have alluded otherwise, but I have always admired Reyann. I wish I had been able to do more for her. Actually, I wanted to save her, but I wasn't entirely sure I desired that solely for her benefit or for some selfish reasons as well. Either way, I did not want to see this woman depart this world.

"I've been a terrible person. I should have come to see you sooner. I'm sorry for all the trouble I've caused you," I tell Reyann and cover her hand with my free hand. Her hand is frail, bony, and cold. She gives me a reassuring smile.

"No need for apologies. But don't be a stranger any longer. We should talk again soon" she says.

My eyes quickly lift to Jeff's because, well, I am not so sure he is okay with me spending any more time with his mother. I am sure he is pretty upset with me for essentially abandoning her.

When I raise my head to look at him, I am sure he will be looking elsewhere, but our eyes meet instantly. He doesn't appear to be angry. But he also doesn't appear to be upset. In fact, his expression reminds me a lot of Josh's expressions when we would get into arguments. Jeff seemed to be – blank.

Emotionless.

No anger.

No joy.

Just – blank.

"Yes. You should stop by sometime and hang with Mom. You need to get your painting too," he says as if we are nothing more than causal acquaintances. Work friends who aren't really friends outside of the business place. The pity friend accept on Facebook.

He isn't being unpleasant. In fact, he's being very pleasant.

I hate it.

This is not the man I had come to know. He had always matched my fire with his own fire. The man standing before me now was Teflon. Nothing was sticking to him, and he wasn't going to let anything bother him.

Before I can respond, because I practically blank out, Kelly ushers everyone into the living room. The holiday festivities begin, and people split off into small groups. I watch Jeff sit on the couch with Paul, Brad, and Gregory to watch the rest of the game. I dare not go in there for fear of round two of *blank man*. So, I go back into the kitchen to aid in cooking details.

After about twenty minutes of sitting at the table doing nothing, because every time I started something Kelly would only come up behind me and finish it, I venture back into the great room where we would be eating.

Sherry is just finishing up the napkin folding as I enter.

"Need any help?" I ask.

"No, I'm finished. Just placing the last one now. Did Kelly banish you like she did me the last time?" Sherry asks.

"No. But I also didn't accidently turn off the oven," I say and use air quotes on accidently.

"It was an accident. I thought it was the timer button," Sherry says.

"Don't worry. You're secret is safe with me," I say and demonstrate a cross over my heart.

"This family," Sherry says. She is shaking her head but smiling as she exits the room.

I'm still quietly laughing when I'm joined by another person. As soon as I see that person, however, my laughter fades. I had hoped I'd be able to speak to Jeff alone before I would have the discomfort of talking to his brother. Apparently, I will not have that luxury because Tom comes right for me the moment I am alone.

"I've been told I still owe you an apology for the other night at dinner," he says.

"Okay," I reply.

"I don't agree with that assessment, however."

"Okay," I reply again and shrug my shoulders because really,

264

what was the point of us even talking to one another?

"I know my mother doesn't blame you for anything, but I still do. You shouldn't have agreed to remain her doctor. Not when you were sleeping with her son," Tom glares at me.

"You're right," I agree.

It seems I have stumped Tom because for a brief moment his angry glare disappears and a shocked one replaces it. He recovers quickly, however, and is right back to glaring at me.

"It was unprofessional and irresponsible of you."

"Right again," I agree.

"Is this funny to you?"

"Of course it isn't." Now I'm the one upset. "Nothing you are saying to me now isn't anything I haven't already said to myself. I regret the decision to remain Reyann's doctor. Not because it compromised the care I gave her but because it has caused a rift in your family. That was not a consequence I had intended and for that alone I apologize."

Tom purses his lips. He furrows his brow. Then he sighs heavily.

"My brother and I don't always see eye to eye, but he was right to point out my lack of presence during all this. I wasn't here. And Mother has made it very clear she wanted you to be her doctor. She has also made it very clear that I am not to interfere with whatever is going on between you and Jeff."

"However?" I prompt when his pause is a bit too long for my comfort.

"However," he begins again, "he is my brother, and I don't like seeing him hurt and humiliated. You did both of those at dinner. Look, I'm pretty sure you and I will never get along and that is something I can set aside because I love my brother. But I will never stand by quietly if you continue to pull the shit you pulled that night. If you can't be with him completely, then stay away, for both your sakes," Tom concludes and starts to turn away from me.

I hated when people did that. Spoke their peace and just walked away without allowing the other person to respond. It was a cheap power play done by domineering people and I absolutely hated it. I could feel the tips of my fingers heating from the anger inside me.

"Oh no you don't. You don't get to walk in here and throw the gauntlet down and then walk away," I say, rather loudly.

Tom stops his exit to turn halfway back towards me. I had advanced on him and was very much in his personal space. Two could play his game.

"First, you're an overbearing ass. That is something I can set aside because I love your brother. But something I will never stand for is you talking to me like I am some petulant flea you need to flick off. What is happening between your brother and me will NEVER be about you and what you think. Second, you better get used to this parasite because if I have anything to do with it, I'm not going anywhere. So, best get that stick out of your ass and make an effort to hide your obvious contempt for me. Now it's my turn to walk away from you," I say and push my finger into the center of his chest before turning on my heels and dramatically leaving the room.

I quite possibly sabotage any hope of reconciling with Jeff after this little stunt but that isn't what I am thinking about when I leave Tom standing in that room. The grin on my face isn't for any possible future with Jeff, but because in that moment when I stood up to Tom I felt like me again. It had only taken me twenty-three years to find her, but my father's daughter had returned.

-29-

Thanksgiving

The evening commenced and both Tom and Jeff somehow managed to avoid encountering me again until it was time for dinner. My glorious sister had strategically placed me next to Reyann which meant I was sitting directly across from Jeff. He did not directly speak to me unless his mother prompted him to and I find myself preferring he ignored me over being forced to converse with me. Tom sits beside Jeff and every now and then his glare falls on me and I simply give him the stink eye in return. He narrows his eyes and looks away. Nina just flat out avoids me. Luckily, the children are sitting at their own table in the corner of the room and they are not close enough to witness the hostilities.

Seated next to me are my daughter and her boyfriend. Brandon is friendly and blissfully unaware of the tense undertones between me and Tom. He eagerly speaks to the Farley family members and at one time even praises how nice I have been to him. This, of course, earns a choking noise from Tom, which he skillfully covers up by making some comment about food getting stuck in his throat.

Jerk.

Becca knew all the dirty details, and unlike her boyfriend, she seems to be trying to goad Tom and Nina into a response. When she is only met with silent, strained smiles she reverses course and tries to get a reaction out of Jeff.

"So, my parents are now officially divorced. The Big D. I am now an orphaned child," Becca says as she stabs at her pie. Brandon pats her hand sympathetically in mock concern. "Thanks babe," Becca says.

"You are not orphaned. Stop over exaggerating," Josh says a few chairs down.

"But I am Daddy. You are even selling our childhood home," she pouts.

"We didn't move into that house until you were ten. It's hardly our childhood home," Cooper says and earns a napkin to the face. He promptly throws it back at Becca.

"Kids, behave," Josh scolds them.

I remain silent during all of this. My gaze is fixed on Jeff, and I see his eyes twitch when my daughter mentions the divorce being finalized. He looks at me briefly but quickly averts his eyes. That simple shifting in his gaze gives me the encouragement I need to forge ahead with my plans.

"Ending a marriage is never an easy choice. It is fortunate that the two of you are able to remain so close," Reyann says to me.

"Yeah, as far as ex-husbands go, I hit the lottery," I remark and turn to Josh. He just rolls his eyes at me.

"This family is so weird," Brandon remarks.

"You have no idea," Cooper states and elbows Brandon.

My gaze wanders over to some movement further down the table and I see Jenny Lynn jumping excitedly next to her parents. Brad quietly leaves the table and when Kelly stands, I realize that the tribute she had planned for Reyann is about to commence. I had hoped for more time before I had to stand before the Farley family and speak such meaningful words about their loved one.

"Everyone, I'm sorry to interrupt but we all wanted to share something we planned for Reyann with all the people that love her," Kelly addresses the table.

Jenny Lynn is standing beside her mother holding a piece of

paper. Kelly gives her daughter a slight nudge and that is all the prompting Jenny Lynn needs. I turn to look at Reyann and see that she is smiling, her eyes twinkling with happiness.

"Hi everybody. I'm Jenny Lynn and Reyann is my other grandmother," she begins.

Her other-other grandmother, Tasha, laughs along with Reyann at Jenny Lynn's statement.

"Daddy didn't meet his Mommy until he was much older than me, but he told me she is the best Mommy ever. That's you," Jenny Lynn says and points at Reyann.

I see Jeff turn to his mother and smile at her. They exchange a look, and Reyann reaches out to take hold of Jeff's hand. Their hands remain clasped as Jenny Lynn continues.

"My Mommy says that family is more than blood. She says family is a feeling in your heart. My heart is so full of family and I am really happy. I am happy that we are all here, eating this yummy food," the room is filled with light laughter, "and just being together. Mom says we should be thankful today. I am thankful for family but mostly for my grandma because she loves me and I love her."

Jenny Lynn lowers her paper, and Reyann holds her arms out to her. Jenny Lynn runs eagerly over to her grandma and they embrace. Reyann kisses the top of her head and whispers her love to the little girl. Suddenly, Jenny Lynn lifts her head and looks at Tasha.

"I love you too other Grandma," she says and we all chuckle once more.

"We all love you so much Reyann and want you to know how much you mean to us," Kelly says and with a nod she gestures to those of us that she gave the cards to. We all stand on her cue.

I notice Jeff's eyes following me as I stand. I also can't help but notice Tom's pursed lips and Nina's disapproving look.

"For all the laughs, the tears and the cheesecake we shared throughout the years," my mother doesn't need to read her card. She memorized the words, and she stares directly at Reyann as she recites the phrase. Reyann holds her free hand over heart and mouths thank you to my mother.

"Grandmother is felt in the heart and from a gentle touch filled with love," Becca says. She is crying and she struggles to say the words, but she manages to complete it. I see she is holding on to Brandon's hand and I am glad he is there for her.

Reyann is starting to tear up, but she continues to move her gaze to the next person: Kelly.

"Family is more than a word. It is a spark that illuminates the darkest of moments and provides comfort for those left behind," Kelly says between tears. Brad has returned and he is now standing beside his wife, his arm wrapped around her as she pays tribute to the woman he calls mother.

"I love you," Reyann says to the two of them. All three of them are crying now. In fact, most of the adults are crying. Even crotchety Nina is tearing up.

Sherry waits for Kelly to urge her on before she reads her card.

"Sorrow is meant to be shared and through a kind soul loss can turn into a connection that lasts beyond death." Sherry doesn't stop at the card, however. "Thank you so much," a pause to catch her breath as she cries, "for everything you have done for me."

"It was my pleasure to know you and share your grief," Reyann says.

My turn.

All eyes turn to me. *All eyes.* Including a pair that is trying desperately to remain detached and another that is throwing daggers my way. They are sitting next to each other, and my gaze keeps shifting between them. This moment is supposed to be for Reyann but in some way the three of us are making it about me and the pressure is starting to build in my chest.

Finally, my gaze turns to Reyann. She is looking up at me, patiently waiting for me to speak but the words are stuck in my throat. I want nothing more than to honor her in a way she deserves.

Swallowing, I look down at the card in my hand and open my mouth to speak. Nothing comes out. I start again and again, nothing. Then I hear a snicker, and my head shoots up towards Tom. He is sneering at me and for some reason that sneer brings forth the same reaction our little encounter had earlier. I am reminded of the words my father once told me about never allowing anyone to stand in judgement of me. He told me there was only one power that could pass judgement on me, and until I met that higher power, to live my life free of regret and without reservation. Perhaps it was time I started living by his advice.

"I'm supposed to read the words on this card. And they are beautiful words, Kelly, they really are," I say and turn to my sister. She smiles at me sweetly and I continue on.

"I want to say them but there is something else I need to say first. I'm sorry," I say and turn back to Reyann. Her tears have slowed, and her expression is now one of confusion.

"I don't understand," she says.

"I'm sorry I couldn't save you. I wanted to. But mostly, I'm sorry that I turned away from you when you needed me most." My gaze slowly shifts to Jeff. He is watching me, his expression closed off. I turn back to Reyann.

"You are quite possibly the most amazing person I have ever met. Even when you were in pain you made sure I was alright. Even when I basically put a wrecking ball through your family you stood by me and I abandoned you. For the rest of my days, I will wish I could take that back. I know I have no right, but will you forgive me?" I ask.

"Are you serious right now? You are asking her for forgiveness?" Tom interjects.

Slowly, almost like glacier speed, I meet his gaze. Further down the table, my twenty-two-year-old brother speaks out.

"Let her talk," he states with more force than I have ever heard him say. Inside I am cheering out for the support my brother has thrown behind me, outward appearances, however, belie any cheering. In fact, I am sure my face epitomizes the phrase *if looks could kill.*

"Yes, *Tom,* I am asking her for forgiveness. Because I love her and I love him," I say and point to Jeff, "and I don't want another person I love leaving this earth believing I don't love them."

Quickly, I look down at the card in my hands and read the words written on it, "For she is the strength we call upon when all we feel is fear. She is the love we will remember and honor for all that she has given to us."

"Well, you aren't forgiven," Tom declares.

"Tom, my son, shut up," Reyann says, stunning all of us.

"Mother. You can't possibly believe anything she says. She'll say anything to get Jeff back," Tom explains to his mother. Nina nods along with her husband.

"If you two believe that than you don't know Stacey at all," Josh says.

With all the affection I have in my heart I look at my ex-husband, my best friend, and offer my silent thanks.

"Tom, you are hurting and I've made many excuses for you over the years, but my time is coming to an end and so is the time for excuses. I'm dying. There is no escaping this and you need to accept that. The both of you do," Reyann says as she addresses Tom and Nina.

"Reyann-" Nina starts.

"No, Nina. When I'm gone these people in this room will be what remain of your family. Family is everything. They mean everything to me. I love them all. Stacey, you have never needed my forgiveness but if that is something you seek than you have it. Every single one of you in this room has touched my heart in more ways than I can count. I will carry those moments with me. I have been truly blessed in this life. I have three beautiful sons," Reyann says and looks to Jeff, Tom, and then Brad.

"Two fantastic daughter-in-law's," she looks at Nina and Kelly.

"Amazing grandchildren and friends that have meant so much to me. This may be an ending, but it is a happy one and I thank you all for making my life worth living."

"We love you Reyann," my mother says.

"And I love you," Reyann says with a laugh.

"We have one last thing for you," Kelly says and steps aside so Brad can step forward.

Reaching behind him Brad picks up his guitar, places the strap over his head and settles it against his body.

"Words will never do justice to what you mean to me, but I wrote you a song," he says and begins to strum on his guitar.

Brad sings the lyrics, and everyone is focused on him but I'm looking at Jeff, and he is looking at me. He is no longer *blank man*. The man I knew has returned and I can see his emotions in his eyes. He doesn't have to say a word because I know without a moment's hesitation what he wants. He leans over to his mother, whispers in her ear and she nods slightly. With that, we both quietly get up from our chairs and leave the room together.

We don't say anything until we are both standing by the front door.

"Will you go somewhere with me? Somewhere we can talk privately?" Jeff asks.

"Yes," I say and we both put on our winter gear in silence.

I follow him to his car, but he pauses at the door.

"Tom will need my car to take them home," he says.

"I have mine."

Jeff nods and we both start to walk back towards my car. We get in and I start the engine. I'm not sure which direction I should go so I wait for Jeff to give me instructions.

"Turn left out of the neighborhood," he says and proceeds to give me directions until we are in the parking lot of the same hotel we used when we started this whole thing.

273

I place the car in park and wait for his cue. He is quiet for five minutes. It is a long five minutes, but I don't dare interrupt his reflecting.

"I don't think my brother likes you," he finally says.

I snort at his words and cover my mouth quickly. Turning red from embarrassment I look over to Jeff and find him grinning. My tension releases and I grin right along with him.

"No, I don't suppose he does. Nina might come around, though."

Jeff tilts his head in a gesture that clearly says he doubts my prediction.

"Okay. So maybe it won't be easy but I'm willing to stick it out. That is, if you want me to." I avert my gaze and look into my lap. There is still a strong possibility that he wants nothing more to do with me.

"I don't know. Leaving the way you did, walking away like that, I don't think I could go through that again," Jeff admits.

"You won't have to. I'm not going anywhere. I promise," I say and turn my body towards him. I need to convince him to not give up on me, on us.

"Why? Because you love me now?" He looks at me with such a pained expression that I recoil slightly. I deserve that look. I've earned it.

"Yes."

"Why now? Why not two weeks ago? Why not one month ago? What changed?"

He deserves answers and I want nothing more than to give them to him but I'm not even sure I have them. I am still trying to figure things out myself. My hesitation disappoints him, and he starts to open the car door to leave.

"No! Don't go," I say and reach out to grab his arm. His movements stop and he turns back to me.

"Why should I? You told me to stay away. You were the one that said you didn't love me."

"And you said you would be whatever I needed. You said you were a patient man," I counter.

"No one is that patient, Stacey. And I put up with a lot from you. I gave you everything I had, and it still wasn't enough," he says angrily.

"Don't you see, it was enough! It was everything and it scared the hell out of me. You were too real and all I wanted to do was live in a fantasy. My life was falling apart, and I was prepared for the fall but I wasn't prepared for you. You were just so sure and confident in me when all I felt was doubt. I couldn't be the person you thought I was and I ran. I don't want to run anymore," I say and cling to his arm. I need him to believe me.

He stares at my hand grasping his arm and sighs.

"How do I know you won't run again?"

"You don't. I don't even know that. All I can tell you is that I love you and I want to be whatever you need. I'm not the most patient person but I'll wait for you. If that is what you need then I will wait." Realizing I am out of my league, I utilize the strategy he had attempted to apply to me.

The car is once again plunged into silence, and I try to live up to my promise and patiently wait for him. However, as I had admitted, I wasn't the most patient person and the silence starts to allow doubt to creep in.

"What are you thinking?" I ask nervously.

"I'm thinking," he pauses and finally lifts his gaze to mine, "about how much I want to touch you."

It's like a dam breaks and a flood pours out because we are instantly reaching for the other and our lips crash together. We try to get our bodies as close as we can, but the gear shift is between us and we end up knocking knees against various car parts.

"Damn this car," he says against my lips. His hands are roaming freely over me and mine are clutching his arms.

"We are at a hotel," I say and he chuckles. "Was this your

intention all along?"

"What do you mean?" he asks coyly.

"Oh my God. You knew we would end up here, didn't you? You knew we would be having sex," I say and pull away from him to stare at him disbelief.

"Knew? No. Hoped? Yes. I did know it was only a matter of time before you realized you loved me and come crawling back to me," he says and I smack his shoulder in retaliation.

"You couldn't possibly know that."

"Babe, you aren't as sly as you think you are. I knew the exact moment you fell in love with me. You just needed time to catch up," he says and leans back in his seat.

"Oh, did you now. Please, enlighten me, when did I fall in love with you?" I expect him to give some bullshit answer but once again this man surprises me.

"It was the summer after Jen had passed away," he starts but I cut him off.

"What? That was nearly ten years ago, and we barely spoke then. How could I have possibly loved you then?"

"You came over to the house to drop off something for Kelly. I forget what it was but at some point, you made a comment about how pathetic it was for a grown man to still live with his Mommy."

"Oh, yeah, I do remember that, but I definitely wasn't feeling love for you. More like pity," I say.

"I told you I was recovering from a recent set back and you said grown-ups don't have setbacks only opportunities," he continues.

"That's right. You told me to fuck off," I remember and my eyes narrow. "Love was not an emotion I was feeling that day."

"Oh, you were. You thought you were upset with me but what you were really feeling was love. You loved that I didn't let you just roll over me. I challenged you and you loved me for it. All the rest that happened after was simply foreplay."

"Foreplay? For ten years?"

"What can I say? I'm a patient man," he shrugs.

"You are incorrigible."

"Yeah, but you love me," he says and leans towards me again. This time our kiss is slow and holds all the promises we have for one another.

"Are you ready to get out of this car?"

"Absolutely," I say.

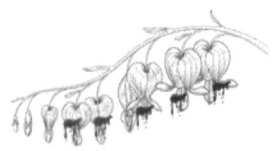

Later, we are tangled together in the sheets of the hotel bed, and he is softly caressing my back as I look at him, my head resting on my folded arms. We had just engaged in our most intense session of love making and our bodies are still glistening from the sweat. He is smiling softly at me, and the moment is just so perfect. I ignore the thought about it being too perfect and instead focus on the way his touch makes me feel.

"I can practically see the wheels turning in your head," he says, his voice dripping with concern.

"I'm just afraid I'm going to mess this up again," I admit.

His fingers pause their journey briefly before continuing on.

"You probably will," he says and I reach out quickly to smack his shoulder. He laughs at me and gives me a swift kiss on the lips.

"I'm sure between the two of us we will manage to screw things up plenty of times. I'm really looking forward to the make-up sex," he says. This time I'm the one laughing.

He has this amazing ability to pull me out of my spiraling thoughts and I loved him more for that.

"You know, that wasn't the moment I fell in love with you," I say.

"Are you sure? I think I'm right."

"Nope. The moment I feel in love with you was when you told that awful woman at the baseball game that the kid wasn't actually yours and then sped away from her. Between that and the beer you had painstakingly hid in root beer bottles I was hooked," I admit and shift over in the bed so I can drape an arm over his stomach and place my head on his chest. He pulls me closer to him and I feel his lips on the top of my head.

"So, you're telling me I could have won you over if I had just told that woman off sooner?"

"Uh huh."

"Well, damn. Eh, it worked out in my favor in the end. But if we ever go back to that park we are gonna have to go in disguise. I can wear my tutu, but we will have to get you a proper costume," he says and pulls me tighter to him as I giggle.

"I still can't believe you wore that thing."

"Hey, a bet is a bet."

"Yoder will never let you live that night down. He took photos you know?"

"Oh, I know. He has since hung them up in the bar and he points them out to everyone every time I go there. Thanks for that," he says and looks at me. I turn my head so I can meet his gaze.

"You shouldn't make bets you can't win."

"Is that so?"

"Yep."

"I bet I can rock your world three more times before this night is over. What do you have to say to that?"

I purse my lips and pretend to be mulling things over.

"I say prove it."

I'm giggling again as he lunges for me and while he may have lost our previous bet, he definitely wins this one.

Or rather, I win. Again. And again.

-30-

Forgiveness

We spend the day after Thanksgiving locked in that hotel room, worshiping one another and revealing things that the other may not have known. I learned that Jeff had been paying more attention to my life over the years than I had been to his life. When I expressed regret for this, he simply told me I was being foolish because I had my own life to focus on. I tried to tell him that wasn't the point, but he refused to let me believe I had somehow let him down. Besides, he said, we had plenty of time to make up for any years lost.

I told him I had cut myself the day after I had run out on him at that dinner. He took me into his arms and cried. No one had ever cried in front of me before because of the scars I had placed on my body.

"Don't you ever do that because of me. Promise that you will talk to me when you start feeling like doing that," he says to me.

"I don't think-"

"Promise," he demands.

"I promise," I reply and I truly mean it. I would never again do anything to hurt this man. He had believed in me when I hadn't believed in myself, and he never once gave up on me. I owed it to myself to do everything I could to keep that promise to him as well as to myself.

"I need you to know that I don't blame you for anything that is going on with my Mother," he tells me as I lay in his arms.

"I know. Tom does, though," I say sadly.

"Yeah, well, Tom isn't without his sins."

"Really? Do tell," I say and lift my body up so I can look at Jeff as he speaks. I know my face holds a joy that is probably inappropriate but the thought of having some dirt on the holier than thou Tom is very appealing to me.

"I don't think I should tell you," Jeff says with a hesitant look.

"Now you have to tell me. Please," I beg.

"I don't know."

"No secrets. This will never work between us if we keep secrets," I say. I am not at all ashamed that I use our relationship to convince him to tell me the dirt on Tom.

"Fine, but you can never use this against him. I forgave him long ago and I don't want old drama resurfacing."

"Promise," I say and only halfway mean it.

"Remember how I used to be engaged?"

"Yeah. She broke it off after cheating on you," I say and my eyes widen suddenly as realization dawns.

"He didn't!"

"He did," Jeff reveals.

"Woah. Your brother slept with your fiancé?"

"He has never really come out and admitted it but one year for Christmas he showed up with her and announced they were in love. This wasn't the first time he had brought home an ex of mine as his date. He had a terrible habit of seeking out the girls I had dated. I think he has always felt like he needed to compete with me or something. Anyway, he brought her home and was completely oblivious to how upset Mom and I were. He just couldn't understand why we weren't happy for him. He wanted to marry her," Jeff says.

"No! Not Nina?"

"Oh, gosh no. Tom ended up coming home a few months later,

heartbroken, because, surprise, surprise, she left him for her latest lover. Tom has never said he was sleeping with her while I was engaged to her, but I haven't actually asked him about it either."

"I understand. He's your little brother. You don't want to know if he betrayed you."

"Love is betrayal," Jeff says to me.

"Hey, not fair. You can't use those words. I wasn't exactly in the best of places when I said them."

"Maybe not but you are right. Love is pain and betrayal sometimes. But love is also this," he says and links our fingers together. "And this." He leans forward and kisses me passionately.

When I'm sufficiently breathless and wanting more, he pulls away. He is smiling at me and I'm just trying to catch my breath.

"How could you forgive him for what he did to you?" I finally ask.

Jeff takes a moment to think about his answer before he shares it with me.

"I love him. He may be a pompous ass, but he is still the same little brother I looked out for. He isn't perfect but no one is. I thought about how if the situation was reversed I hoped he would forgive me. It was never about him. I knew that in order for me to move forward I needed to forgive him," he says.

"I'm not sure I could have done that," I admit.

"You would have. You are stronger than you think are," Jeff says and kisses my hand.

"I hope you are right. I have a lot to atone for and could use some forgiveness of my own."

I tell him about my father and what I said to him in his final days. Jeff listens as I share the events of the last few days and how I admitted to my mother what I had done. I told him about all the lies I had told Rachel and my family throughout the years. I bare my soul to him, and he listens to every word. He holds me against him as I cry and set my shame before him. When I am done spilling my

281

secrets I hold tightly to him.

"Say something," I say when the silence becomes too much to bear.

"What do you want me to say?"

"I don't know. Anything."

"I love you."

"That's a good start," I say.

"Your father loved you and he forgives you," Jeff says and with those words my body begins to shake with fresh tears.

"You think so?"

"I know so. From everything you told me about him you were his whole world. He would never want you to keep hurting. It's time to let it go," Jeff says and he pulls me away from him so he can stare into my eyes.

"It's time," he repeats.

I smile tentatively at him and nod before letting out a long sigh. And with that sigh I do as Jeff instructs – I let it all go.

"Are you sure you want this back? He's gotten comfortable in this room," Jeff says as he hands me the rocking Jesus painting he stole from me.

We checked out of the hotel and drove straight to his house so I could reclaim what was mine. Now, I hold that painting to my chest and stare at Jeff in horror.

"Of course, I'm sure. Rockin' Jesus belongs to me," I say and pull the painting away from my body so I can look at the scripture.

For he has rescued us from the dominion of darkness and brought us into the kingdom of the Son he loves, in whom we have redemption, the forgiveness of sins.

"Ah, crap!" I say as I read the verse to myself.

"What?"

"Jesus is telling me I need to speak with your brother," I say and turn the traitorous painting around.

"What?" Jeff laughs.

"I need to forgive your brother too or it will fester and turn into a disease," I say and start to turn on my heels.

"Slow your roll there buddy. Are you sure about this? He is still the same guy that pretty much detests you," Jeff says as he holds on to both of my forearms.

"Yes. I need to do this. Rockin' Jesus says so." I turn the painting towards Jeff again and hold it up so he can see the scripture.

"Okay. Well, I'm not going to let you face him alone. Where you go, I go." Jeff grabs a hold of my hand, and I follow him out of his room and into the living room where Tom and Nina are.

They are sitting on the couch while their girls play on the floor at their feet. It is a domestic scene straight out of a home magazine. The quiet scene belies their hostile nature, but I walk into that room anyway.

"Tom, Nina, can I speak to you both?" I ask.

They raise their heads towards me and while their greeting isn't exactly friendly, they don't lash out in front of their girls. Nina tells the girls to play quietly, and we all walk into the kitchen.

"What do you have to say to us?" Tom asks as soon as we are all in the kitchen.

"Wow. Okay, so we are just gonna jump right in," I start because I honestly had no clue where to begin. Tom just shrugs at me.

"Well, I think it goes without saying that we aren't exactly fans of each other."

"That's for sure," Nina blurts.

Jeff sends a stern glare her way and she has the decency to look properly scolded.

"Anyway," I start again, "there is one thing we can all agree on. We all care very much for Jeff. I don't expect us all to be the best of friends but I would at the very least like us to tolerate one another. If not for his sake than for our own. It takes way too much energy to hate."

I stand there and wait for them to respond and as the seconds turn to minutes, I start to think that this was a lost cause. I look at Jeff in defeat and am resigned to walk away when Jeff speaks.

"It took me about a year to stomach being in the same room as you Nina," he says.

"What?" Nina asks, hurt and clearly confused by Jeff's revelation.

"I thought you were a mindless drone that agreed with everything Tom said. It made me sick to watch. The two of you were like the same brain. Despite how I felt I never once said anything negative about you to my brother because it was obvious he was madly in love with you. I never wanted to cause him hurt, so I took the time to get to know you. And now, I only get a little sick when you two agree," Jeff jokes. I laugh but Tom and Nina don't.

"You really hated me that much?" Nina asks.

"No, Nina. I never hated you. That's my point. I didn't know you and I made assumptions. I was wrong. Over time I got to know you and I saw how happy you made my brother. To me, that made up for all the things I was concerned about. It didn't matter what I thought as long as my brother was happy," Jeff explains.

"I understand," Tom says, surprising the hell out of me.

"I don't know if I'll ever be able to treat you like Brad does. Or anyone else in your family does for that matter. But, as long as you continue to make my brother happy then nothing else matters," Tom manages to get out.

I could tell it was difficult for him to swallow that down and normally I would have given him a hard time about it, but this isn't about me. It is about the man I love, the very same man he loves as his brother.

"Thank you," I say and take Jeff's hand in mine.

The road may have been long and full of plenty of curves, but I am glad I had taken the journey. I had embarked on this course many years ago when a young girl lost the first man she had loved. I had stumbled along the way to get to this point but just as my father had hoped for me, I had no regrets and I was no longer afraid of the unknown.

It took me twenty-three years, but I had found me again and I loved her; scars and all.

Not the Start, but not the End

Five months later

This office is stuffy. I had forgotten how stuffy it was. The walls were a pale white, and the furniture was slate grey. There was no personality in anything in this room, and it caused me to move my feet rapidly against the floor.

Tap. Tap. Tap.

Dr. Perkins just stares at me. It seems he recalls my ritual I used to conduct at the start of every appointment with him. I had once told him his office was just as drab as his personality and suggested a decorator. I could see he hadn't taken me up on my advice. I missed Rachel's poop chair. What I wouldn't give for some post flatulence swiveling.

"We can begin whenever you are ready Stacey," Dr. Perkins says.

"Right. I know that," I say defensively.

Doc Perkins just forges on like I hadn't just snapped at him.

"Dr. Cunningham filled me in on what has transpired since the last time we met. It seems there have been added stressors in your life," Dr. Perkins says.

"You could say that. Rachel has a tendency to over exaggerate though. What did she tell you?" I ask and pick at the arm of the sofa I'm sitting on.

"She said you recently lost a loved one."

"Yes. Reyann."

"You were close to her?" Dr. Perkins picks up his pen, ready and poised to take notes.

I remember now why I stopped seeing him. I hated how he took constant notes on everything I said like I was some subject to study. It annoyed me. Well, actually it made me nervous because he was a copious note taker and it made lying to him hard. He had written evidence of my contradictory stories. When Rachel insisted I return to Dr. Perkins I had resisted at first, but I knew he was the only one that could keep my old habit of lying from resurfacing and I had promised myself that I wouldn't drift away again. Therapy was part of keeping that promise.

"She is…was, my boyfriend's mother. She died three months ago, just right after the new year," I say and watch as Dr. Perkins scribbles on his pad.

"She had cancer."

Not a question but I answer, nonetheless.

"Yes. The same kind that my father had. Her case brought forth a lot of repressed feelings I had regarding my father's death," I admit. My therapist just nods as if my words are fact and not something that took me months to struggle through.

Pompous jerk.

"You are also recently divorced?" he continues on.

"That's right. But it's cool. Josh and I are cool. We even joined a bowling league," I say and earn a skeptical look from Dr. Perkins.

"No, really. We joined a bowling league with my boyfriend, Jeff, and my sister and her husband. We are a team of five and we bowl together every Thursday night. The only one of us that is any good is Jeff, but he is cool with our high handicap."

Why was I saying cool so much?

287

"It sounds like you and your ex-husband remain close. Does this cause a strain on your relationship with Jeff?"

"Not at all. Josh and Jeff are friends. Seems they have been for years. Josh is even dating someone too. She's some computer geek he met on one of his latest projects. She even speaks his language. As my daughter says, they are *sick-cute* together," I shift in my seat.

Dr. Perkins takes more notes. The pen scribbles across his notepad and I have to tell myself to look away from that constantly moving utensil.

"What else did Rachel tell you?" I ask, my eyes squinting slightly.

After Jeff and I reconciled I visited Rachel one last time at her office to come clean about everything that had transpired and what my plans were regarding my future. I personally brought her a bouget of flowers to make up for the birthday ones that had been 'misplaced' by her receptionist as a thank you for her continued patience and support. I even brought a nice box of chocolates for that temperamental receptionist, accompanied with a perfectly worded hallmark card addressed to Gwen. The ungrateful receptionist threw one of her chocolates at me as she called me a turd. I would say the visit was a success.

"That you had relapsed and cut yourself again," Dr. Perkins forges on, ever the professional.

"Ah, yes, that. I haven't done it for over five months now and I don't have any plans for a repeat performance. Ticket sales were disappointing," I add. Dr. Perkins purses his lips slightly.

"Even so, it is concerning that you have returned to destructive coping mechanisms."

"I know. I was very disturbed by it myself. So much in fact that I came running back to you," I try again to inject humor into this all too serious conversation.

"Stacey, Dr. Cunningham and I are very concerned that you aren't taking your therapy seriously," Dr. Perkins says.

288

Damn. He found me out.

"I think she is just still upset that I told her we slept together," I say and grin at the reaction I get.

"Wh-what?" he stutters.

"Relax, Doctor, I came clean and told her it was just a prank. Your reputation is safe."

"That isn't the point, Stacey. As a doctor yourself you know how important integrity is. If you continue to insist on such liable than I can't continue to treat you," he says and puts the cap back on his pen.

"Look, Dr. Perkins, I only said that to you now because I don't want to lie anymore. You need to know what I said and did if this has got any chance of working. I'm done with lying. I'm done with the games. I won't say I'm done being difficult because, well, a leopard can't change their stripes overnight, but I can promise you that I will try. Please, let me remain your patient."

It is the first time I have ever truly been honest with him. All the years he had been my therapist before I used to deliberately tell tall tales just to see if he had been paying attention. I used to believe he wasn't but based on his reaction just now it seemed he had been listening more closely than I thought he had been.

"Spots," he says, correcting my "mistake".

"Tomato, Potato," I reply.

"No more games," Dr. Perkins says and removes the cap from his pen, closing off any reaction he may have to my jokes.

We are back in business.

"In the spirit of full disclosure, I must admit that I will probably continue to be sarcastic and use humor to deflect the difficult questions. I know you probably look at this as some sort of character flaw that impedes my healing process or whatever new-age hippie therapist crap they are peddling at the conventions these days." I look briefly at Dr. Perkins to see how he was taking my latest addition of humor. The man actually smirks, but he quickly recovers and nods for me to continue.

"To be perfectly honest, I like that part of me. It took me a long time to accept that part of me as something that wasn't a bad thing. Is it for everyone? No. But it works for me and I'm trying this new thing where I accept me for who I am and not allow outside forces to shape the image I have of myself. A lot has happened since we last sat in these chairs and one of those things is that I realized I'm pretty awesome. Sure, I have asshole tendencies, but who doesn't. And perhaps my words hurt more than they are intended to, but I always feel badly afterwards and that is good right? Sympathy and stuff. Plus, I do save a lot of lives, so I think as far as the whole karmic balance thing goes, I'm sitting pretty."

Dr. Perkins scribbles in his pads, nods, and completely ignores the epiphany I shared with him. The least he could have done was give me an *"atta girl"*. Instead, I get rewarded with one of those deeply probing questions he was famous for.

"Tell me about your relationship with Jeff."

"Pass."

"Stacey," Dr. Perkins says sternly.

"I'm kidding. Just because I'm taking therapy seriously now doesn't mean I have to lose all sense of humor. Somebody has to liven up this office since you refuse to."

"Stacey." A warning.

"Jeff is everything I never thought I wanted. We rarely argue but when we do they are knock down shouting matches that usually end with us underneath the sheets, if you know what I mean." I wink at him.

Dr. Perkins knows what I mean but he doesn't look pleased.

"That doesn't seem like a healthy way to resolve your issues."

"But it is. After the sex part we actually talk it out like civilized adults. He says I'm fire and he's brimstone or gasoline and a match. We just go together like lighter fluid and a barbeque and when we ignite magic happens. He's a bit of a romantic."

"He knows about your past?"

"Every single bit of it. In fact, he knows more about me than you know about me, and I sat on this couch for three years straight. We don't have secrets. We tell each other everything. Reyann made us promise her that we would never go to bed angry and that we would always be honest. We keep our promises," I say with conviction.

Dr. Perkins nods and takes some more notes.

"Are there any other developments in your life?" he asks.

"I'm pregnant."

"Really?" He perks up and lifts his head from his notepad to stare at me in disbelief.

"No. I just couldn't resist. Now, don't lecture me. That was a good one."

"Do you want more children?" He continues on, choosing to ignore my latest deflection.

"No," I reply without hesitation.

Dr. Perkins doesn't miss a beat. He goes in for the kill.

"Does Jeff?"

"You'd think he would, right? I mean he is a man in his forties, and he doesn't have any of his own but we had that discussion. He said he's never really wanted kids and he's fine with just borrowing mine from time to time. He's almost too perfect to be real, right?"

"He sounds like a good man. Is he a satisfying partner?"

"Doctor Perkins. If you wanted all the scandalous details all you had to do was ask. The sex is mind blowing. He definitely satisfies. He does everything I ask him to do and more," I say in a slightly cheeky and seductive manner.

"I meant emotionally. Does he satisfy you emotionally as a partner?"

I can tell Dr. Perkins won't be taking any bait today because his tone remains flat. A part of me truly hoped this man had a lighter side to him that he let loose in his personal life. Another part of me

291

was glad he remained so focused and didn't allow me to distract him.

"He's the only man that ever has," I admit freely.

"Stacey, I have to admit that I'm struggling to understand why you returned to me. You stopped your appointments a year ago and from everything you've told me you seem to be in a much more stable place than you were last year. Why now? Why did you return?" Dr. Perkins puts his pen down and gives me his full attention.

I avoid his gaze for a bit and take in the rest of the grey room. It really is a bit depressing to look at. I miss Rachel's pastels and the lunches we used to share. Still, I knew I couldn't continue to take advantage of my friend's kindness and love for me, not if I wanted to maintain our friendship.

"I made a promise to the man I love that I would never hurt myself again. I want to keep that promise. And I think I still have a lot of work to do on forgiving myself for the things I've done. I know I can't do it alone. That's why I'm here," I explain.

For the next thirty minutes I lay down on that sofa and talk to Dr. Perkins about my father. I leave that office in tears, but they aren't from sadness. They are from reliving the happy moments I had shared with my dear father. I had avoided those memories believing they would only make me sad, but it was joyful to recall the man he had been and the happy child I had once been.

"Oh, no, did you bust a pipe?" Jeff says to me as I step out into the lobby.

"Ha. You've got jokes," I say and wipe my eyes.

"I also have chocolate," he says and holds up a chocolate bar before me. I go to take it, and he moves it out of my reach. Thus begins the struggle for the chocolate bar in my therapist's lobby as the receptionist and his next patient look on. I manage to get the chocolate bar by twisting some of Jeff's hair. He let it grow out because I asked him to. A request he was probably regretting complying with now, but he was extremely grateful for during our night time sessions.

I'm munching on the bar as we walk to his car. I offer him a piece as a truce and he accepts it by eating it straight from my fingers.

When we get to the car, he opens my door for me and I give him a sloppy chocolate filled kiss. He leans into me and presses me against the frame of the car as his tongue melds with mine. Chocolate kisses with Jeff were orgasmic. When he breaks away from me to go to the driver's side I groan with disappointment.

"We are on a time limit here. I've gotta get you back to the office so you can finish up and be done by six. We are meeting Josh and Gemma for dinner tonight," Jeff says as we both get seated inside the car.

"Ugg, why are you friends with my ex-husband and his new girlfriend?" I feign annoyance.

Jeff reaches out and takes hold of my hand. He smiles at me as we pull away from the parking lot. I loved this man so much more than I ever thought it was possible. He had thrown my world upside down and then turned it right side up again.

"Are you happy?" Jeff asks me suddenly.

"Of course, I am. Deliriously so," I say and squeeze his hand. "Are you happy?"

"More than I thought I could be. Thank you," he answers.

"For what? I didn't do anything."

"You let me in. You let me love you."

"Well, you didn't exactly give me a choice. I had to love you so I could get Rockin' Jesus back."

"Is that so?" Jeff asks, raising an eyebrow at me. He turns the car down the street that leads to my hospital.

"Yep. But don't worry. Rockin' Jesus forgives you for your transgressions. I, however, think you have much more penance to serve before you earn my forgiveness."

293

"Really? And how will I exactly accomplish this penance?" Jeff asks, turning to me after he puts the car in park in my assigned parking space.

"You can start by getting your sexy butt into that back seat and rocking my world," I say and point to the back seat.

"And what happens after that?"

"Whatever we want. I'm up for anything," I say and Jeff turns his hungry gaze over to me.

With a sharp intake of breath, we both make a mad dash to get into the back seat and as we crash together in a cacophony of limbs we eagerly tear at each other's clothing. Mixed into the dirty talk are words of love, threats of shaving off his hair, and a final sigh of knowing that we are both exactly where we belong.

And just as I think we are about to have a happy ending inside Jeff's car like a couple of teenagers the man I love, the man I gave my heart to says, "You only want me for the sex."

Without missing a beat, I disentangle from our joined mess and straighten my clothing and then my hair. I look at him solemnly and state with absolute steadiness, "It isn't that great."

With intent I open the car, get my bag from the front seat and start walking to the elevators. I hear Jeff exit the vehicle and come up behind me as I hit the button to go up to my office.

"Stacey, I was only kidding. I know what we have is real and I know you want me for more than just my body. I'm sorry, Babe," he says and takes hold of my hand.

"No, you got it right the first time. Your body is by far your greatest appeal. I've seen you try to complete crossword puzzles. I'm sorry to tell you but you aren't the brightest crayon; definitely not a goldenrod. At least you are cute," I say and pat his cheek in a patronizing way and give him a feigned smile of pity.

His eyes narrow and I can tell the moment when he realizes we are once again entering into one of our past time foreplay mock fights. Just as always, he rises to the challenge and meets me jab for jab.

"I can accept that. But what I cannot accept is that the sex *isn't that great*. Call me ugly. Call me stupid. Call me whatever you want just don't question my skills with the ladies," he teases.

"Ladies?" I give him a threatening look.

"Hey, you know it would be a crime to deny anyone the joy that comes from touching this work of art," he says and takes a step back from me so I can examine the work of art he is referring to.

"You're a pig."

"And you love rolling around in the mud with me. Don't forget, date night, pick you up in a few hours," he says and gives me a quick kiss on the lips before walking back towards the car.

"Hey, Jeff," I call to him as he reaches the vehicle. He turns and I step backwards into the elevator. "I've had better," I call to him and give him the one finger salute.

I'm grinning.

He's grinning.

The elevator doors start to close, and Jeff raises his own hand to return my gesture.

"I love you too," he says.

I'm still grinning when the doors close and it takes me a moment to realize that the man had done it again. He got the last word in. He was infuriating and wonderful and a jerk, but he was mine and I wouldn't have it any other way.

Author's Notes

What is there left to say that hasn't already been said by Stacey herself? I never actualized this would be the woman I would write about. I never could have imagined just how much I would adore this character and her spunk. She is flawed but is still a strong-willed, independent woman who realized she was losing herself and eventually found herself again.

Stacey isn't perfect by any means – but who is? She is haunted by demons that she believes are of her own making. While it is true that in her adult life, she was often the catalyst for her problems, they were all rooted in a pain she had no control over. Many times throughout the novel Stacey reveals that she identifies as the villain and sometimes she is. However, there are other moments when she is simply acting like a human being – hurting and desperately seeking an answer.

I understand if readers don't identify with her and keep her cast in the light of the villain but no matter how hard I tried I couldn't see her as the bad guy. In fact, I don't see any of the characters in this book as a bad guy. I just see them as everyday people struggling to figure this crazy thing called life out. Not everyone gets a happy ending and sometimes those that do have to travel a broken path before they get an ounce of happiness.

While Stacey struggles with her loss of faith and the pain she feels at believing God abandoned her, the scripture on the painting she keeps going back to her haunts her in a way. It is a reminder of what she lost, what she desperately wants to recover, and what she believes she does not deserve – a father's forgiveness. In my head, I believe Stacey receives the forgiveness she is searching for and that the anger she has with God is eventually healed.

For He has rescued us from the dominion of darkness and brought us into the kingdom of the Son He loves, in whom we have redemption, the forgiveness of sins.

One last comment regarding Stacey. Adult self-mutilation is more prevalent than people realize. Unfortunately, this practice is viewed as strictly a "teen" problem. It isn't. Stacey is a grown woman, engaging in harmful behavior that began during her teen years but that she returns to when she feels helpless. It isn't easy to just abandon a habit you engaged in for many years regardless of one's age. Dismissing someone that experiences this because they are "too old" is an injustice and only encourages secrecy.

And Jeff? Well, isn't he the man we would all hope to find if our lives took a complete left turn and we were left to wonder what happens next? I have heard the term "book boyfriend" many times and I think mine would have to be Jeff. He is patient, kind, funny, and passionate. Despite being a "kid in a man's body" he is the only one that saw things clearly.

So often we read books and once the happily-ever-after is revealed we don't get a look into what has transpired many years down the line. This book gave me the opportunity to explore that and show a different side. In the previous books it was alluded that Stacey had found her match in Josh, but life isn't always so clear cut, and I wanted to explore that area – when a person has to hit the reset button and figure things out again.

As always, it was nice to revisit the characters from the previous books in this series. It was even more thrilling to introduce a few new ones and get to know the next generation of characters that were spawned from my original four – Kelly, Jenny, Brad, and Stacey. The kids are grown in this one because it takes a significant time jump from the previous books. This book was supposed to be the last one in the series to bring the final tally to five. However, once I finished placing the last words down, I knew I couldn't say goodbye just yet.

Thus began the birth of a new endeavor. In my heart I know that my time with these characters is drawing to a close. I truly do hope

297

you have enjoyed reading about them as much as I have enjoyed writing about them.

Thank you for reading and please visit my Amazon page and leave a review. I love to hear from my readers and feel free to share my books with others you believe may enjoy them.

Much Appreciation – Angeline Larson

Some songs that provided me inspiration:

Wicked Games – Chris Isaak
Numb – Linkin Park
Sex on Fire – Kings of Leon
Whatever You Say – Martina McBride
I'm Not an Angel – Halestorm
Without You- Breaking Benjamin
Help – Papa Roach
When You're Young – 3 Doors Down
Away from the Sun – 3 Doors Down
Let's Hurt Tonight – One Republic
Bleeding Through – Papa Roach
The Real You – Three Days Grace

About the Author

Angeline Larson is a product of imagination and life. She is not perfect, but she tries. She is a human who loves dogs, likes watching chickens go about their daily tasks, reading, and even creating her own books. She is a mess, but she is a mess carefully crafted and that makes her unique in her own way.

More to Read by Angeline Larson

Contemporary Romance

Finding You
Back to You
Lost in You
Finding Hope
Saving Faith

Paranormal Romance

Destiny's Daughter

www.ingramcontent.com/pod-product-compliance
Lightning Source LLC
Chambersburg PA
CBHW050024120726
47903CB00006B/1904